Starting at the End

Starting at the End

JEREMY GRAY

T

Troubador Publishing Ltd
Unit E2 Airfield Business Park,
Harrison Road, Market Harborough,
Leicestershire LE16 7UL
Tel: 0116 279 2299
Email: books@troubador.co.uk
Web: www.troubador.co.uk

ISBN 978 1 83628 277 8

British Library Cataloguing in Publication Data.
A catalogue record for this book is available from the British Library.

The manufacturer's authorised representative in the EU for product
safety is Authorised Rep Compliance Ltd, 71 Lower Baggot Street,
Dublin D02 P593 Ireland (www.arccompliance.com).

Printed and bound in Great Britain by 4edge Limited
Typeset in 11pt Minion Pro by Troubador Publishing Ltd, Leicester, UK

For Sue

Chapter 1

Early June 2018

She was not as he had expected, and after her arrival nothing was. She'd barely said, when she'd rung the previous evening, why she wanted to see him except that it was about Jim. So, when he opened the door to her, he was surprised. She was younger than he'd presumed. Around forty, tall, with long blonde hair that came down below her shoulders, and a face that was well made-up but with wary, pale green eyes that said she knew very well what the world was like. She was dressed in a short leather jacket over a loose-fitting denim top adorned with a small gold brooch in the shape of a piano, jeans, and red shoes with low heels.

"You must be Scarlet," he said.

"And you're Robert?" she replied, offering him a hand to shake.

He beckoned her in. She declined a cup of tea or coffee, and they sat facing each other in the living room, the summer light shining on the polished floorboards, the well-worn chairs, the cluster of family pictures above the mantelpiece, each of them unsure how to begin, bearer and recipient, perhaps, of unknown and unwanted gifts.

"I didn't know," she suddenly rushed the words out, "if you'd want me to get in touch."

"You said you wanted to tell me something about Jim," he replied.

It felt strange to him to say the name. It had been over twenty years now, as he and Barbara had worked out. Stranger still to wonder if he wanted to know.

"Jim thinks he last saw you at Heathrow, when you and…" She looked away, embarrassed.

"Barbara."

"Yes, when you and Barbara and your two children came to see him off on what he calls his second American tour." She smiled slightly as she spoke.

She was an American, he thought, judging by the hint of a drawl, her voice rising at the end of almost every sentence.

"That's quite some time ago."

"He'd like to see you," she said.

He hadn't expected that. He and Barbara had presumed she was bringing a message, had guessed it could be bad news, but not that it might be an invitation. So he worried that his pause after she said those words sounded too much like a rejection.

"Where's Jim living now?" he asked.

"We're just outside Bath."

"I didn't know he was back in England."

"We've been there two years already."

Two years, Robert thought, without making the simple journey up to London, without even picking up a phone.

He waited, knowing she was trying to decide what to say and what to withhold.

"He's not well. He's really not well," she said.

Her eyes that didn't look at him directly, the hint of fear in her voice, the tense way she sat waiting for his answer, spoke more strongly than her words.

"Is Jim…" Robert began, and then it struck him that Jim mightn't know she was here. Perhaps she hadn't wanted – or maybe hadn't dared – to tell him she would be coming. For the first time a warmth suffused his reticence. "I'll talk to Barbara," he said.

She smiled and said no more about it. She offered no medical opinion, no reason for what she'd just said. She simply stood up and produced from her handbag a piece of card on which she'd written an address and her phone number in her big, loopy hand. She looked around the room. "The children must be grown up now," she said.

Robert stood up. "The twins are thirty," he replied with a rueful smile and a nod of the head.

"Jim doesn't really remember them, I'm afraid."

She squeezed Robert's hands in hers, said "Come soon," quietly, and then she was gone, in a hurry to get the tube and catch a train back to Bath.

"Twenty-*two* years, actually," said Barbara. "No Lauren. Just the twins."

"I didn't see him much in the thirty years before that, either," Robert replied.

They sat in the garden with their glasses of wine, the oranges and browns of the brick wall behind them, the dark green of the broad-leaved hostas brought out by the sun preparing to set behind the houses.

"They know you're a doctor, right?" she said. "You think that's got anything to do with it?"

"Probably," he replied.

"And you didn't ask what's supposed to be wrong with him?"

"I thought it had to come from her."

"But you'll go, I suppose?"

"He is my brother." He hesitated. "I can face him alone if you like," he said, knowing she wanted to come.

"And you don't know how long they've been together?"

He shook his head, used as he was to her telling him how he hid behind politeness as a way of never doing anything difficult. Together they walked round the garden, down to the end where a red oleander bush stood in its sheltered corner, a toxic mirror to the sun.

"You ready to meet the family?" he said, turning with a smile to look at her. "It could be the experience of a lifetime."

They rang, and learnt they could stay in Jim and Scarlet's house outside Bath, but only a little more about Jim's life. Robert, now semi-retired, had hospital work until Thursday, but then he would be ready, he said, to pack some clothes, a bottle of whisky, and drive across London and down the M4. Friday, Scarlet replied, would be a better day to come, and they were welcome to stay overnight. Barbara signalled she would have to go back in the evening, she had to see Lily on Saturday, but he could stay.

Hospital management had wanted a 'targeted case backlog reduction' and by Wednesday Robert had recorded that all his cases were 'progressed'. If that was the right word for Josie Peters, age about fifty-five, no fixed address according to her notes, with whom his sole business had been to confirm that morning that she had TB. To his surprise, she'd recognised him, and he'd recognised her, from the bridge by the local tube station. March had been brutally cold, he remembered.

The sample would be a formality: from her posture and her breathing, this was indeed TB, and entering in its final stages. She'd beckoned him forward, and whispered "Wilmer." Her dog, he presumed; he recalled that she'd had a brown mongrel on a string. "Mr. Universe's got him." She was exhausted and clutched at her next few breaths. "But he doesn't like dogs." The words floated out of her, with no breath to carry them.

Robert promised to check, next time he was there.

As he finished up in the evening, he thought about her again. She has a few weeks at most, he reckoned, while everybody here does what they can. He went back up from his basement room and along the green corridors. The painkillers she'd been prescribed were working, she seemed almost asleep, but she opened an eye as he approached, and he pulled up a chair and sat down beside her.

"I was the queen of the high wire once," she said. Her gaze drifted off to the ceiling, and didn't return. She beckoned him close. "You could pay to see me dance. You could pay."

"I would have liked that," he said.

5

Her breathing, shallow as it already was, became anxious. "You'll remember, won't you."

He nodded. After a time, she managed to say, "That's something, isn't it?"

He sat there for a while, until he began to feel useless. She didn't notice when he left.

Robert and Barbara looked at the house where Jim and Scarlet lived. It was early Victorian, down by the canal, and offered more conventional comfort than they had expected: the usual front of Cotswold stone, a short, tidy front garden, gated, with neat flower beds left and right, and a solid roof of dark tiles, all somewhere between mellow and in need of attention. Then Robert took a deep breath and got out, picking up the bag he'd brought with them from the back seat, while Barbara smoothed down her new dress, patted her freshly cut hair, hoping the new highlights were not too obvious, and let Robert push her gently towards the gate. But before they could reach it, Jim opened the front door and walked briskly down the path to greet them, transferring his cigarette from his right hand to his left so they could shake hands. Barbara smiled, but Robert felt a sudden chill despite the sunshine and stopped, unnerved. Jim's face was lined, and thinner than he remembered, his skin seemed parched, his dark hair had receded a little, but the eyes were quick, the smile still charming. He'd changed completely and he hadn't changed at all.

"You made it," said Jim.

"Pleasant journey, actually. I hope we're not too early."

"And you must be Barbara," said Jim, brushing away the remark. "Unchanged. How do you do it?"

"Yoga," she replied.

Jim turned and led them into the house, which had a pervasive smoky smell. "Let's have lunch," he said. "You can tell me all your news."

He took them into the kitchen, which looked out onto a warm, sunlit garden dominated by an old cherry tree, with an untidy circular flower bed fringed with begonias in the middle of a vigorous lawn. In the shade under the tree were two new wooden chairs, a table, and a deckchair. Jim found an extra chair and they all shuffled back and forth between the kitchen and the garden, putting bread, cheese, pâtés, salad and a jug of water on the table. Jim looked at it all, said, "Forgotten something," and went back in.

Robert watched him go, aware that patients always tell you a lot before they speak, by the way they walk into the room, the way they sit down, the way they fit themselves round whatever is wrong with them. By the way they smile when they first look at you, silently asking you to be their friend before you ask them questions they are afraid of, whose answers will haunt them like unwanted shadows.

"Well?" said Barbara.

"Medically, his face and eyes are a little yellow. His hair is thin, there's a hint of a stoop…"

"And his clothes are a little baggy. So?"

"It's indicative, but not conclusive. He's sixty-eight, after all."

And to himself he added, he's coping by trying to be in control. By a turn of his head, a choice of as little as a word, he's my brother again, watching the world, naturally

7

confident. Not a thoughtful person, but someone who sets up situations in advance, ones he can win. And I can feel myself trying to become the well-behaved guest, as instructed.

Jim came back with a bottle of Chablis and filled their glasses.

"Is Scarlet around?" Barbara asked.

Jim nodded. "She'll be back."

Robert leant forward, and trying to strike the right, neutral tone of voice, said, "And how are you?"

"Not too bad. I get tired in the afternoon sometimes, so I might have to lie down for a bit."

Robert stood up. "Before I forget, I brought you a present." He went back to his bag, fished out the whisky, and gave it to Jim. "Don't drink it all at once," he said.

"Not much chance of that anymore," Jim replied. He put it in front of him on the table, and waited until Robert sat down again. "Still, thanks for this," he said. "We'll have it with dinner."

They carried on talking quietly, Barbara asking polite questions and Jim pushing back with questions of his own until Barbara gave up, frustrated. Jim ate little, Robert noticed, and quite slowly, but he drank two glasses of wine. When he had finished, he offered them coffee, moved to the deckchair and lit another cigarette.

"Do you still get out and play?" Robert asked.

"Sure," Jim replied. "I've got a few songs left in me, if you like the husky, lived-in voice."

"I couldn't have done it. All that attention."

Jim smiled. "No, you were always the backroom boy. Well-prepared, top in all those tests."

"You had music."

"A fickle mistress, just like they say." He was quiet for a moment, and then he got up, took the whisky bottle, and started to walk indoors.

"Time to lie down, I think," he said. "Don't worry about dinner, Scarlet'll fix that."

When he had gone, Barbara said, "He's not dying yet, is he. Eating, drinking, smoking."

"Old habits die hard."

"So do their practitioners," she replied, sounding more sympathetic than her words. When he didn't respond, she said, "If it's OK with you, I'll go for a walk along the canal. I won't be long."

"I'll stay here."

"You sure?"

She gave him a kiss and walked back through the house, closing the front door quietly behind her.

Robert tried to let his thoughts settle, but they refused. He wanted to feel, in the slight breeze and the occasional sounds of birds and insects, the sense of belonging that such a very English place could offer. But this time it did not embrace him. Nor, he felt, could it embrace his brother. Not the runaway, who was here but did not belong. And who now disturbed his thoughts, so much so he couldn't say how.

He got up and looked around the house. It was the sort that gives an English feel to a town, and which tourists like in a general way before moving on to peer into the bigger and better ones. In the front room were a couple of battered armchairs and a baby grand Yamaha piano, polished and black, the varnish chipped in one corner. He leant forward and tapped a couple of notes at random; the sound was soft and incomplete. The two-seater piano stool concealed a disordered pile of scores. Over the mantelpiece were photographs of people whom Robert felt vaguely embarrassed not to be able to identify. A bespectacled black guy in an elegant white hat; another in a striped suit and a tie, with a white handkerchief poking out of a pocket; a third a small, melancholy, older man, his hands resting on a piano – pianists all of them, all their pictures autographed in the implausible manner of the photos that used to hang on the walls of old-style Italian restaurants. Off in an alcove was an engraving of a man walking alone down an abandoned street. The whole thing was barely sketched in with a thick black line that looked as if it was brushed on, but it had a permanent, basalt quality. All and only the essentials had been said, and now it was a question of what happened next. Not a comfortable question, and Robert moved to the living room, which he hadn't had a chance to examine before, and looked less lived-in than it surely was. A large television, some mundane pictures, a few old magazines scattered on a low table. No books.

He went back to the garden, sat in the sun, and tried again to collect his thoughts about a brother he hadn't missed, in whose house he now was, and with whom he had only managed to exchange pleasantries, but nothing more intimate. The one remaining connection to his childhood, as insubstantial and pervasive as smoke.

Robert heard a car draw up outside, a door slam, and someone walk through the house. It had to be Scarlet, and it was. She put down the shopping bags she was carrying, stretched out her right hand to him, and said, "Sorry I wasn't here when you arrived." She looked out to the garden. "Had a chance to talk to Jim?"

"We got here in time for lunch. Then he went and had a lie-down."

She smiled. "Put these things away, will you. If it doesn't go in the fridge, put it in the pantry. I'll go see how he is."

She was still upstairs when the doorbell rang and Barbara returned. Scarlet came down, gave Barbara a hug, complimented her on her dress, Barbara replied in kind, and in this way they made their way to the garden. Robert followed, carrying an extra chair. Jim came down to join them, but he was still tired and drifting into a half-sleep, so Barbara began asking Scarlet for stories about the music business.

"Did you ever meet anyone really famous, like the Beatles or the Rolling Stones?" she asked.

"No, never," Scarlet brusquely replied, and Barbara was stymied; rock'n'roll wasn't the music she listened to anymore.

Scarlet asked about children, and Barbara talked about the twins: Richard and Sarah, now both doing well, and Lauren, and Scarlet seemed more interested.

"What does Lauren do?" she asked.

"Bits of this and bits of that, really. I mean, she's not a problem, exactly. Not now. But she's still not eating enough, she's way too thin."

"Children can be a worry," said Scarlet.

"Do you have any?" Barbara asked, and Scarlet looked over at Jim and shook her head.

"And when did you meet Jim?" asked Barbara, aware that her question had somehow misfired.

Scarlet bent her head back, ran her hands through her hair, and smiled.

"Thinking about it," she said, "almost exactly twenty-one years ago. I was recording in Memphis, it was a hot, humid summer, and this huge fight blew up between the producer, the musicians and the pianist. Eventually the pianist stormed out, the producer disappeared to ring round the city and see if anyone was available…"

"At which point," said Jim, barely stirring in his chair, "they found me."

Scarlet crossed to join him, and brushed his cheek. She fussed around him, and then around Robert and Barbara, making more coffee, and when they were settled again Barbara looked at Jim and said, "When did you first go the States?"

"Seventy-three."

A grin crossed Jim's face and Scarlet looked over at Robert and Barbara. Robert guessed that she'd heard this answer to the unspoken question several times before – one of those moments when Jim liked to show he'd got something right.

"Over here Gary Glitter," said Jim. "The Osmonds, T Rex, Wings. Or you could have Dr John's 'Right Place, Wrong Time', Stevie Wonder, the Allman Brothers. Neil Young's 'Harvest' came out in seventy-two." He stopped abruptly and coughed, and coughed again. When he'd finished, he said hoarsely, "Look, if you like the blues, if you like rock'n'roll, you want to be in the country that made it. Everybody went. Eventually, I just stayed."

Then he pushed himself out of his chair, and, turning to Robert and Barbara, said, "I can play for you, if you like."

Scarlet took his arm, but he shook his head. She turned to Barbara, who said "Only if you want to."

"He won't ever say no," Scarlet said.

Once they were in the front room, Scarlet sat beside Jim at the piano and Barbara and Robert sat in the armchairs. Jim looked over his shoulder at them, smiled, said "I still play boogie woogie," and set his right hand going fast, his left hand beating out the bass. Robert glanced at Barbara, thinking how much the music was waking Jim up, and what that might say about him. "Albert Ammons's 'Stomp'," Jim said when he finished and turned to accept the compliments from Barbara and Robert.

Scarlet rested her hand on his shoulder and said "As if they didn't know. I think y'all deserve a drink after that."

"Always happy to accept," he replied. "But before the show is over…" and he began a slow, sad blues until Scarlet put her hand on his arm to stop him, then turned to look at Robert and Barbara, and said with a shake of her head, "He's incorrigible, really."

Barbara brought the conversation back to Memphis.

"Of course, they'd found Jim," said Scarlet. "He was in town working someplace else. He spent a few minutes listening to the tracks and to the producer play through what was wanted, and then he just sat down and did it. Just like that. I was so impressed."

"I could do that then," Jim said. "I'd been around long enough. It was harder getting them to pay me."

"And did you hook up then?" asked Barbara.

"Not then," said Scarlet. "Well, yes and no," and she glanced over at Jim, who looked back, happy at how things had gone, but wouldn't be drawn any further.

After dinner, Barbara made her excuses and Robert drove her to the station. As they left, Barbara said "We didn't learn much, did we?"

"It's early days," Robert replied, and they lapsed into an uneasy silence. After a time, Robert said "It's not like you to have nothing to say."

"You know what I'm thinking," Barbara replied.

"There has to be a conversation. That's all the letter's asking for."

"Let other people have it, not you."

"And the person who asks – begs – us to help?"

"I don't know, Robert, I don't."

"I'm not on the wards," he began, "but I know… "

"Robert, what makes it work is trust. And I trust you. I always have. I don't want you to come home with somebody's death on your conscience. Because you made it happen. It's not for you to say." And when Robert didn't reply, she said "I don't want you to have any part of it. For your sake. And for mine."

They drove the rest of the way in silence. At the station she reminded Robert she was seeing Lily on Saturday, politely kissed him goodbye, and made her way to the train. A bit too glad to get away, he thought. And the reminder about her sister a bit too obvious.

Scarlet was in the kitchen looking tired when he got back.

She offered him a drink, which he declined. She poured herself a glass of wine and sat down opposite him, with a watchful look that invited him to speak.

"How'd you get started?" he asked.

"You're at school and nothing makes much sense," she replied. "And then somehow music does. Oldies like Aretha Franklin, everybody." She tossed her hair back behind her shoulders. "I got into a band, a chick doing back-up, like they said, and then another, and we started to play every gig we could get. And learn lessons."

"Like?"

She saw a knife that had been left on the table and started spinning it round.

"You want to know the most depressing thing?" she said. "The most obvious, depressing thing? Turning up on time. And it ain't just the suits. It's the club owners. The punters. Even the other acts. Start on time, finish on time. If the next band can't find the door to the stage, keep their fans waiting an hour, that's their problem, but you don't do it for them."

"Don't tell me," he said, "I'm right not to have run away and joined the circus after all."

She stopped the knife with her hand. "The best bit's hanging out, playing with other guys, learning new stuff. But it doesn't pay the rent. So you go on tour." She gave a wry smile. "Do the gigs, do the covers, get the band to get up in the afternoon, stand in when someone's gone to Mars, and do it again."

Robert said nothing.

"D'you play?" she asked.

Robert gave a short laugh and sat forward. "We were

15

given a piano by an uncle when I was eleven, and Jim must've been fifteen. The embarrassing thing is, it was meant to be for me, the one who 'liked music', but any kind of an audience and I panicked."

"Playing's a special thing," she said, brushing her hair away from her face. "It's when you're most alive. Or you do something else."

"It would've been a disaster," Robert went on, "if Jim hadn't been able to sit down and play through the hits of the moment. With just a couple of lessons. It was weird. He'd never done anything more than he strictly had to and now he was practising nightly, learning routines from older boys at school, enjoying the attention, getting good at it."

"Were you proud of him? Big brother comes good 'n all?"

"I was eleven. I was probably jealous."

"Kids. How anyone ever learns to…" She let the sentence hang there, unfinished, like a door opening onto a room no one could enter. In the silence, Robert remembered that Jim had taken the piano with him when he'd left at sixteen and got a place of his own. It occurred to him at that moment that this afternoon was the first time he'd heard him play in more than thirty years.

Scarlet looked directly at Robert and said with gentle surprise, "You don't look very alike. I thought you'd look more…"

"Like brothers? Not really. Jim was the short, fit-looking one, who could run around all day and never sit still. He got his looks from our dad, if nothing else, and I was the tall, skinny, dreamy one, like our mother."

He turned his face fully towards her. She continued

to look at him across the table, as if noticing him fully for the first time. It wasn't intrusive, or particularly intimate. He felt as if she was examining links in a chain that bound him to Jim, links he believed had long since eroded away, but in her gaze were emerging, delicate but firm.

"Your hands," she said, "are much bigger. And somehow quieter."

Unsure how to reply, he looked at her and said hesitantly, "I don't really know why you asked me down here."

She finished the wine she was drinking, and said, "You're his brother."

"We haven't seen each other for twenty years. Longer, even."

"I don't know you," she said. A pause, and she added, "And you don't know him, either."

The accuracy of the remark caught him like a sudden stinging wind to his face.

"I've known him twenty years," she said. "We've worked together, sung together, been on tours together. I'm very fond of him – maybe I shouldn't be, but I am."

Robert heard the catch in her voice. He waited for a moment, pulling together the clues in what he had seen. "How ill is he, do you know?" he asked.

For a brief moment he thought she might refuse to speak, but then her shoulders dropped slightly, her eyes softened, and she said, "Yeah, we know."

"Known for long?"

"A couple years."

He waited. It had to come from her.

"Cancer," she said after a deep breath. "The bowel."

"Secondaries in the liver?"

"I knew you're a doctor. You can tell?"

"I can guess." He paused, and said, "I'm sorry." He waited again, but the usual comforting words that occurred to him would fall short, as they usually did, and he withheld them. "I really am." He waited, and said, "Got a good doctor?"

"McIntire? Yeah, he's OK."

"Jim trusts him? Asks all his questions?"

"I don't go in with him. He tells me it's OK. The medicine stuff's under control." She walked to the table, took their glasses to the sink, and stepped back.

"Was that really why you asked me to come? To stir my conscience?"

"Or his," she said, with a bleak smile. She looked at him, then down at the floor and back up. "None of us know what we're doing, do we?" she said. "The longer I live, the more I think nobody really knows what they're doing." She shrugged. "I could sit around every afternoon and get drunk. I'd like to. But if I do, I'll put on more weight, and in a year or two the gigs'll dry up. It'll just be TV ads, jingles, stupid stuff."

"Recordings? What about recordings?"

She stepped forward. "Robert, songs are like people. When you play them, they're alive. You can do new things with them. And then new people come along who've never heard of them, and don't care, and you never hear those songs again."

"You seem to be surviving."

She shook her head. "Angels don't even have names," she said.

I can't change things, he thought. I can't make Jim

better. You know that. But what do you really want from me? Do you even know? It's all right – the truth is, I'm afraid of what might start. And now you and I sit here not knowing what we want. Paralysed. A bond between us, of sorts.

Chapter 2

Early June 2018

On Sunday morning, Robert made his leisurely goodbyes.

"I'll come back soon," he said.

"Do that," Scarlet replied. "We're hoping to play a gig in a few weeks, if we can get the right guitarist. You and Barbara could come for that."

"That'd be nice," he said.

"Then you'll get to hear him play properly."

"Keep in touch," Robert said, shaking Scarlet's hand. "Keep in touch," he said to Jim, placing a firm hand on his shoulder.

"We're not going anywhere," Jim replied, and they shook hands.

Robert drove off. So he's dying, Robert thought, although not yet. Dying with pain that can be reduced but only for a time. Dying to his distress, and that of his close friends, and family. Who must have told him over the years, as he must have told himself, that drink, and cigarettes, and other drugs presumably, would either take your heart or give you cancer. Everyone knows that now, but there's no kindness in it, and kindness is needed. As for those friends, Robert assumed that there were some, but he knew only Scarlet; and Jim, Robert thought, had no family. Other than he himself.

He turned onto the M4, heading into London as the sun on his right cast slowly shortening shadows on the road, his mind filling up with an old, familiar memory. They were on a river somewhere in the Norfolk Broads. He was seven, Jim was eleven. Their parents had rented a motorboat, the holiday was supposed to be an adventure, but their father was spending too much time steering the boat, consulting the maps he'd bought for the trip, keeping his eyes open for currents and shallows and everyone else on the river, and their mother was always anxiously watching to make sure the boys didn't fall in. Robert had overheard them in the evenings talking in disappointed whispers about wanting the holiday to end early, if only it could without it being a defeat.

He wanted to read the books he'd brought with him, except that he'd finished most of them by then, and Jim wanted to run around, race Robert and the boat along the towpath, play football whenever the boat stopped, and eat sweets and ice creams all day; he pestered their parents every time they stopped. Their father had let Jim steer the boat occasionally, watching him carefully all the time, and rather less often he'd let Robert have a go, always with a hand on the steering wheel redirecting them when Robert got distracted by passing birds, the chance of seeing a big fish, or just his own thoughts.

Right now, the boat was moored by the bank. On either side were fields, the sun was hot, and the parents were resting. Jim charged off into the field with the football, dragging Robert reluctantly with him. It was a long field, separated from the water by a hedge with various gaps in it, one by the boat, and marked off on the other three sides by more hedges. Jim chose one of the narrower gaps as the goal and began to play against Robert. Jim would let him score, but made sure, as always, that he won. Robert's kicks would bounce along the rough grass and slip through the gap to the towpath, but Jim's would go higher, travel further, and have every chance of going into the water, so Robert would have to chase after the ball and catch it before it got there.

Jim then led them off on a tour round the hedges, looking for a way into the fields beyond, but the tangle of brambles and old fences underneath was impenetrable. The two of them pushed quite hard at some weak spots, but nothing gave way, and they began to trudge back up the field, idly kicking the ball ahead of them. When they drew near the goal, Jim gave the ball a mighty kick and it soared into the air, curving slightly towards the left.

"Run, or it'll go in the water and we've lost it," Jim yelled, and started to belt after it.

Robert followed, running as hard as he could. The ball landed well ahead of them, very near the gap in the hedge, and bounced up, still going fast. Jim was going fast, too, and Robert was running as hard as he could. The ball came down on the grass between the hedge and the towpath, and took off again with Jim now through the gap, and as it came down he hurled himself at the ball and caught it as it landed. He got up and gave a great cheer, and Robert cheered too, and Jim kicked the ball high in the air and back into the field.

They repeated their circuit of the hedges in a desultory way. They didn't say much. Jim talked about how the football season would be starting soon, and Robert asked him about what next year at school would be like, but Jim wasn't interested. "You'll find out," was all he said.

As they neared the goal, Jim nudged the ball a few yards ahead of him. "Your turn," he said, and gave it an enormous kick. It soared higher than before, curving like its predecessor slightly to the left, but this time he didn't run. He didn't even move. "Run!" he shouted. "Get it. Before it goes in the river and you've lost it."

Robert started to run. The ball hit the ground just before the hedge, landed on a tussock and bounced very high, into the gap and through it, and on towards the water. Robert ran as fast as he could, and he was getting close. The ball started to come down, he could see that it was going to land on the verge close to the towpath, and he just might be able to catch it if he ran as fast as he could. But he'd misjudged it, it was heading for the towpath itself. He got there at the same moment it did, and his feet skidded on the gravel. As he slipped the ball bounced in front of him, he reached out to grab it but it was too far away, and unable to stop himself he followed it into the canal. When he came up the ball was floating a few feet away from him, drifting slowly. He floundered to the side, but the bank was three or four feet high and there was nothing to hold onto so that he could pull himself out.

He couldn't swim, and he splashed around, desperately trying to grab anything and pull himself up, but his efforts forced his head under water, and every time he came up he shouted louder for help. Jim came running up and leant over to try to pull him out, but although their hands could touch he wasn't big enough to hold Robert securely nor strong enough to lift him out.

"Get Dad!" Robert shouted, "Get Dad!"

Jim ran the twenty yards back to the boat while Robert tried to find some way to keep enough of his head above water. Their father ran up with one of the long poles from the boat and Robert held on to it until he was lifted clear and was sitting on the towpath utterly wet and starting to shake. His father picked him up, carried him back to the boat, and put him on the deck at the back while his mother got him a big towel and some dry clothes.

"What happened?" their father asked.

Robert looked at Jim. "The ball went into the water," he said. "I thought I could get it."

"How did it get there?"

"I don't know. We were just kicking it about."

Their father looked at Jim, who looked back and said, "Yeah, we were just kicking it about."

"Who kicked it?"

"We were just having fun," Jim said.

"It sort of bounced funny," Robert said. "It wasn't meant to go in the water. Honest."

Their father looked at them. "You can't swim. Not you," he said, pointing at Robert, "And not you either, really," he said, pointing at Jim. "So you don't go in the water, and you don't get any nearer the water than you are now. Either of you. Any more nonsense like this and we're going home and the holiday's over."

That was all he said. Their mother confined them below stairs until dinner, and at some stage their father took the boat downstream to get the football, which he punctured and threw away. Jim didn't say anything either, but Robert had the feeling that Jim had won. That he'd let Jim win.

"Lauren's turned up," Barbara said as Robert walked in, in tones that struck him as a little forced.

"That's nice," he said, giving her a brief kiss.

"She's in the living room."

Lauren got up as Robert came in and waited for him to cross the room to give her a hug. She hadn't done much with her long brown hair, she wore a simple cream top, torn jeans, and oddly bulky black shoes.

"To what do we owe the pleasure?" he asked.

"She's out of money," said Barbara.

"What about the job?" Robert asked, sitting down.

"I gave it up."

"Why?" said Robert.

"It wasn't going anywhere. And the people were horrible. I mean, like, they just gave me all the shit stuff to do, and –"

"That's what it's like when you start a job," said Barbara.

"You don't get it, it's not like when you were young. It's all this crap, and nobody really cares. So I walked out."

"And now she needs money for her rent," said Barbara.

"Just for this month."

"That's what jobs are for, paying the bills," said Robert, not quite sure why he was pointing this out. "They don't have to be interesting, not at first anyway."

"You could always move back in," said Barbara.

"I'm not moving back in. I'd sooner sleep on somebody's sofa. And Jeff and Lisa said I could stay with them. Anyway, I'm doing some singing."

"Does it pay, this singing you do?" asked Barbara.

Lauren didn't bother to reply, but suddenly noticing Scarlet's card on the mantelpiece she picked it up.

"Who's this from?" she asked.

Robert quickly explained, and she said she'd heard them talk about Jim, but no, she'd never heard his music.

"Why would I want to? Jesus. But yeah, if he's dying, that isn't good." She carefully put the card back. "Have you been to see him?"

"Just got back, actually."

"What he was like when you got there?"

What does she want to know, Robert wondered. Surely not the full story, not all at once. But, he realised, seeing Jim walk down the path to greet him and Barbara had made it easier for him. Not dying that soon, after all. Not bedridden, not marked out, separated from all the rest of us scurrying about unaware we're alive until we're shocked by the cadaverous face, the torn voice, the cold bony hand so unlike our own. He walked and talked, and drank and smoked, and probably one or other was killing him. Just like we tell you it will kill you, he thought, looking at Lauren, (but not yet, at twenty you're still safe).

Barbara nudged his elbow and said, "She asked you a question."

He looked at Lauren. "A day and a half, all pleasant enough, catching up. As if I'd never been away."

"But in fact you'd never been to see him -- not in all the time I've been alive."

No, he thought, and nobody said that. Not me, not him, not even Scarlet, not right out. Twenty years. Twenty-two. A lifetime for you. Maybe you're the reason; you're a handful enough.

"Will you go again?" Lauren asked.

"Yes, I probably will," Robert replied, and Lauren looked thoughtful but said nothing except that she had to go. Barbara protested that they hardly ever saw her these days, but Lauren checked her bag and moved to the door.

"We do love you, you know, and worry about you," Barbara said. "Where are you going?"

"I know you do. I'm meeting someone. Just a friend – do you have to know everything? Just a friend."

A kiss, a brief hug and a kiss.

"And go for that other job, like you said," Barbara added.

"I will, I will. I said I will, all right?"

Barbara shook her head and sighed. "She fights with me rather than speaks," she said. "It's just demands, assertions, and promises you know she won't keep."

"You said the right things, she has to learn," Robert replied. "I sometimes think I'm saying nothing at all to her except platitudes, and at least you're trying."

When Barbara said nothing Robert went on, "She isn't doing anything that can't be put right."

"She could come and see Lily with me," Barbara said. "Lily would like that."

"Did you ask her?"

"She's very fond of Lauren, you know. She always asks after her."

"Did you see her yesterday? How was she?"

"Her sweet self. They're much nicer to her where she is now."

"I'm glad about that." He paused. "I'll come with you next Saturday."

"And you're OK?" Barbara asked. "It can't have been easy being there, even for you."

"Better than I expected, in a way."

"You're sure?"

"You saw. It was all about getting back in touch. The difficult stuff's still to come."

Barbara stepped closer to him, took his hands, and looked into his pale brown eyes. Your life's with us, she thought, with me, the children, the other doctors, your students. I just don't trust Jim, and I don't know why. "Be careful," she said. "That's all I ask."

Tuesday, as Barbara had just pointed out, was salsa evening. She stood by her open wardrobe, riffling through her dresses, while Robert watched her from the end of the bed.

"How does this look?" she said, pulling out a third dress, this one in red and orange, and holding it up against herself.

He tilted his head and gave a quick smile.

"It'll have to do," she said, slipping out of the top she was wearing and letting her trousers fall to the floor. "We're running late," and she pulled the dress over her head, smoothed it down, and started looking for a belt. With a sigh, she found one and pulled it round her waist.

"Why the sigh?"

"I'm not losing any weight."

"You don't need to."

"I know you don't mean it." She walked over to the long mirror. "Weight shows up on short people like me." She pulled on a pair of tights, selected some low heels, and crossed over to the dresser to run a brush through her dark hair, check her make-up, adjust her lipstick, and look for liver spots. Nothing new. She got up and spun round. "Can you face being seen out with me like this?"

"Sooner you than anyone else."

She took his hands and pulled him to his feet.

"You don't want one of those younger models – the ones that can really dance?"

"Well of course, but I don't think… " He stopped, and slipped his arms around her. "Hey, I'm yours, you know that." His hands slipped up to the back of her head, and they bent together and kissed. A slow, gentle kiss.

"Come on" he said, "salsa'll take your mind off whatever it is."

When they got to the class the music had already started. Barbara looked around, and stepped onto the dance floor, ready to give herself up to the music. Robert followed, not exactly reluctantly, but slowly, and together they began. It was fast and joyous, the horns brassy and exciting. When it stopped, the instructor demonstrated a couple of possible moves, and then another fast number followed, followed by a slower, more romantic one that brought out a spontaneous side in Robert that, Barbara felt, was hidden all too often. Sixty-four and he still didn't like making a fool of himself, which she'd long ago realised was the entry price for having simple fun. When it finished, she waved at Rhianne and Georgio who were dancing in the middle of the floor and said "I'm going to have a dance with our new friends."

She walked over to them and said to Rhianne "I'm going to cut in and take your husband, if you don't mind." Georgio smiled, Rhianne accepted gracefully, and the music began. Georgio could really dance, as if it was his normal state and walking a concession to daily life. Barbara let her body sway to the percussive rhythms, following his lead. This was the part she loved the most, when you got to dance with people. She looked over at Robert, who had been rescued by Rhianne, and after a couple of numbers she thanked Georgio and made her way back to Robert.

"What happens if I won't let him go?" Rhianne said.

"Then I'll just have to die of a broken heart," Barbara replied. "In Georgio's arms."

When the class ended after an hour and a half, things slowly segued back to how they'd been. Only when they were home did thoughts of Jim return, as if he had been looking after the house while they were away.

They sat down on the sofa, and Robert looked thoughtfully around the room, at the way the late evening sunlight diffused over the empty armchairs, the frames of the pictures on the walls, the spines of the books on the shelves, warming and deepening them.

"Would it surprise you," he said, "if I told you I thought I'd become an only child?"

"Yes," she said. "Yes, it would."

"Time for me to think again, then, isn't it."

Barbara waited, saying nothing. He looked at her, trying and failing to read the expression on her face.

"Don't worry," he said, "I meet lots of new people in life."

This one isn't new, she thought, but all she said was, "This one's still up and about."

"Do you think," he replied, raising an old family question, "I'm happier with the dead than the living?"

"I wouldn't go quite that far."

Robert took the point, and the truth it contained that enabled him to do his job to his colleagues' satisfaction, and do it every day. That had shaped his life with Barbara as subtly as the house they lived in, with the generous garden she liked and the equally generous kitchen where he cooked from his precise recipes. It's difficult for her, he reminded himself, as it had been for the children. When I come home from work she doesn't ask how I've dealt with the dead, or sometimes the dying. She's withdrawn from it – and who would spend a life with death? I can tell her about my colleagues, the people I'd met, the comedies and dramas on the days when I'd been in court, but not the body of interest. Was she right, is it, after all, easier for me?

"We brought up the children," he said. "That was quite a ride."

"I remember," Barbara said, "with Richard and Sarah, we all made a joke out of it. You're a doctor who never sees patients, at least not living, breathing ones. No one you can invite home." She gave a light laugh. "Richard used to enjoy you teasing him when you came home about whether there was "Anyone out in the car", and he'd eagerly rush out to see."

They stayed close together for a moment, and then Barbara said, "Now if you don't mind, I'll go upstairs and watch one of my guilty pleasures you can't abide."

But with Lauren it had been different. He remembered how, when Lauren was seven or eight, she'd come to his study, tense and fearful, the way she was when she was upset. Richard had been teasing her all afternoon as he did when he was tired of the way she always demanded and got her father's attention, and finally, he'd shouted, "You're just a spoilt little daddy's girl, and you know what your nice daddy does all day. He cuts up bodies."

So Robert had explained, as he had to Richard and Sarah, and Barbara many years before, that he didn't really cut up bodies. In the hospital he looked at little bits of bodies.

"Really little bits of bodies?" Lauren had asked – he could still hear her quavering voice, and his own attempt at a consoling one.

"Very, very small, smaller than a fingernail, down a big microscope, to see if they can tell me what's wrong with the person they've come from. Like when the doctor wiped your throat, remember, with some cotton wool on a stick?"

Lauren had nodded her head and chewed her thumb. "So why did Richard say you cut up bodies?" she'd asked.

And he'd tried to tell her that, well, people die, and sometimes it was his job to find out how. And Lauren had said nothing, and looked very solemn, and played on her own for the rest of the day until it seemed she'd forgotten it.

Robert went to his study. To other people he'd say

we pathologists are the opposite of midwives: they bring people into the world, almost always happily, and we count them out, quite often tragically. And yes, he was paid to live under the shadow of death, even though he would draw its pain if he could. He'd learnt not to say he was happy when there was a paper in it, and he could tell others what to look for sooner. "You write about it?" people would ask, as if that's more upsetting than anything else, as if it was morbid, and they would change the subject.

But it was true… he'd long since realised that dead people told him more than living ones. And Lauren, he knew, says he's never answered the question.

Chapter 3

Mid-June 2018

"Are you happy you invited him?"

Something about Jim's question and the sharpness in his voice, unsettled Scarlet. Without lifting her eyes from the magazine she was reading, she said, "Hey, he's a whole lot warmer than McIntire."

"Warmer, huh?" he said. "Standards are low."

She shrugged. "You want to stop seeing him?"

Jim said nothing for a while, then, in a quieter voice, he said, "What do you make of her?"

Nothing yet, she thought. It's too early to say. "He wanted somebody safe?"

"Safety's not much of a life."

She looked at him, then around the room. With the damp, it felt empty and cold, as if summer had failed to get started. Jim was sitting on the sofa, in a grey shirt and black trousers, staring at nothing, a folded blanket beside him. She crossed over to him and tousled his thinning hair.

"You've got me," she said.

"I have," he replied.

She looked around the room again, and at the rain battering a spider's web in a nearby rosebush, and sat down opposite him. In half an hour they'd talk start talking again, and talk about nothing, as they often did.

After lunch the rain stopped.

"Out of the kitchen while it's warming up," said Scarlet. "We're going for a walk."

"Who's this guy we're going to see?" Jim said, without moving.

"I told you," she said, "he's taken over the Goat's Head."

"The collapsing place we sang in a couple of times and then it shut?"

"That's the one."

Jim said nothing. He started to rub his hands, look at his palms, examine his nails – a sign, Scarlet knew, that he was still out of sorts. She waited.

"What do we know about him?" he said.

"He's moved out of London. Keen to revive the place as a music venue is what I hear."

Jim thought for a moment. "He's the guy's been doing up that big barn?"

She nodded. For the first time in the conversation he looked at her. "It could work," he said.

Scarlet smiled and reached out her hands to touch his. "Come on, we're going for a walk."

He protested, as he usually did, but she insisted that exercise was good for him, and, soon enough, she led him out of the house and up the hill towards the wood. As she usually did.

"Have we got a date for this guy?" he asked, as they walked up the narrow path that threaded through the beech and oak trees in varieties of green that shaded them from what sun there was.

She frowned. "Thursday. You going to be ready?"

He turned to her, out of breath, and said, "Fighting fit."

They climbed over a stile and followed the path until a view opened out before them of well-kept fields marked off by dry stone walls, darker woods beyond them, and in the distance low, purple hills.

"Vaughan Williams," he said. "Misty, ancestral England."

"Is it calling you home?"

He shivered, walked a few yards further along the path, and stood there with his hands in his pockets.

She walked up to him and tugged his hands out of his pockets. "Still think we should've moved to Bristol?" she said.

"It's a cool city. There's lots of music."

"It's an expensive city. We can't afford it."

He didn't reply. She didn't like that truth any more than he did, but they kept returning to it.

"Anyways," she said, "we have a nice place."

He looked slowly around him. "I never thought it'd be like this."

"You ask me," she said, "this whole country makes no sense." Some people barely say a word when you talk to them, she thought, and some call you 'love' right away, but you never know what they're thinking and no one seriously asks about you. Half of everything we've seen goes back five hundred years, and all of it's trying to look as if it hasn't changed in the last two hundred.

Jim let go of her hands.

"We're the strangers here," he said.

There was no way she could have turned back around, she knew that. She'd packed up, paid her last rent on her Memphis apartment, helped him sell their things, and gone with him not back to his roots, surely long since transplanted to Memphis, Chicago, St Louis, but back to a country that offered free medical care, praise the Lord, and lived, to hear everyone tell it, well in the past. Yes, the country of the Beatles and the Rolling Stones, but also of Churchill and beating the Germans, and beating the Germans before that, and beating the French. That had settled America, and lost America, and had had that empire they were so proud of and now seemed to want to shut out. The Brits she knew back home hadn't prepared her for this. If Jim didn't fit in, what the hell chance had she?

"But the cottage is a beauty," she said. She'd wanted it on sight. Not as a place to redecorate, because it would never be theirs. Not as a place for a fresh start, because she knew they could put down no roots. But it had gardens front and back for her to restore. Not big gardens. Just somewhere to sit out in if this goddamn country ever did summer. It had needed a piano, which had been installed almost as a living thing. They'd taken the place because it was a bargain, and because for both of them it was in deep ways utterly unfamiliar.

It was a way station.

She led them back down the path. "You real sorry we came?"

He lit a cigarette. "We'd no choice."

She knew it wasn't worth arguing. He'd told her enough times that she wasn't the one going through this, so he'd take the decisions, thank you the fuck very much, and she knew he meant the pain, the tiredness. But the sense of betrayal, did he mean that? When you had to call on it, modern medicine only promised, it seemed, to surrender one step at a time. And listening to the doctors, he said, was like learning a new language, so like English and yet so foreign, or a new instrument: easy to get started, but years of practice to master. Something was stage four, it had penetrated the muscle wall and spread to the lymph nodes, but quite how bad this was the doctors hadn't been able to say. In fact – and this was unsettling in its own right – the answers to all Jim's questions came clouded in uncertainty. "It's around forty per cent of people with what you have who will live for five years," one doctor had told him, in neutral, professional tones. Not making it to seventy is a shock, when you hear it like that.

So Jim had endured five months of chemo; a private, wasted time when most days the pain, nausea and disabling drugs had taken him over and he'd tell her the collapse of his liver felt like he was filling up with shit. The skin on his hands had turned red and he couldn't play the piano. And all this time, she'd tried to be someone he could hold on to. And then there came a time when the hospital docs had said the cancer had been pushed back, and there'd been three months of speculating, worrying, getting back to practising, and learning to believe what they were told, not just to hear it. And when they could just believe it, they were playing and singing again, meeting new musicians, getting out of the cottage, becoming alive once more. One year, and the next. She risked trips back to Memphis to see her family, went up to London for session work and some useful money. And they went to little clubs, places nearby, and did their favourite numbers for guys who really liked his piano and her voice, and hadn't heard that rock'n'roll was dead.

Until the day when the hospital confirmed the cancer had returned, and with it, disabling fear.

Thursday wasn't an audition. "You're far too good for that, far too well known," the guy on the phone had insisted. "I wouldn't be insulting you. Just come over, and we'll see where I can fit you in."

Scarlet drove them over, it wasn't very far, and there was Poker Martin, a wiry, balding man, surprisingly slim for someone who ran a pub, with two days of white stubble that passed for a beard, a small ring in his right ear, and penetrating blue eyes. "I've heard you more than a few times," he said. "And more than you might think. So it's an honour to have you here."

Then he turned his attention to Scarlet, and she started to relax, and talk, and let herself be shown round the Goat's Head, and marvel at how old it was.

"Built before America became independent, so it is. Parts of it, at least," Poker said.

She let herself be flattered that he knew she sang, and let herself be talked – it wasn't difficult – into singing something. So now they were on the new little stage the pub had, with lighting and sound gear stacked round the sides, and Jim at the piano already feeling at home. She glanced at him, he nodded and played the opening chords of '(You Make Me Feel Like) A Natural Woman'. When she finished singing Poker said nothing, but Jim could see Scarlet had got across. Time to skip down one of their regular set lists to one of his piano solos. He chose a Jimmy Yancey number, which they were pleased to see Poker obviously knew, and as soon as Jim finished he began 'Back In The USA', and as they sang Poker smiled as if the old beams in the ceiling had suddenly turned to gold. "I've just the guitarist for you for that," he said, "wonderful, wonderful man. You'll enjoy playing with him."

"I'm sure we will," Jim said. "Introduce us."

"When he's around. He's elusive, but he'll play with you, for sure."

So the visit was a success, which hadn't been in doubt on Poker's side, she thought, but Poker himself was a surprise. If he turned it on, the man had charm enough to stop a thunderstorm, but better there was a fan inside him, maybe even a musician. That was something to look forward to. Then, as Jim got up and took a couple of steps away from the piano, a pain in his stomach caught him. Scarlet noticed; she hoped that Poker hadn't. She stepped up at once to Poker, and said with a grin, "Do we get the gig? We're looking for a regular slot." Probably that did it. He was taken with her, and she'd sung really well; he wouldn't have seen the grimace come and go.

"I've maybe a surprise for you," Poker said. "Come this way."

They followed him out through the back door, across the puddled car park, towards a barn at the back, Scarlet doing the talking. When they reached the barn door Poker undid the big locks and slid it aside. He stepped into the barn and put on the lights, and rows of vinyl, tapes, CDs, videos and DVDs stretched before them. Jim and Scarlet stood for a moment, astonished at the sight. Jim managed to whisper, "Jesus, I've never seen so many, in one place."

"I've recording companies asking about them," Poker said, standing in the doorway with a smile on his face. "Copyright, all that stuff."

They ran in like children at a party, fingering the albums, calling out the names on them, imagining hearing this one, that one, and then this, and all of them, and time expanding like a bubble to allow them to listen to it all, and listen again.

"How'd you get so many?" Scarlet asked.

"Won some of it in a bet with an exec," Poker said. "Got some working for little companies as an agent, touting acts that didn't make it and one or two who did. And a lot are tapes of shows. And I mean a lot."

"It's like being a kid again," said Jim. "Going to the record store, trying to buy blues records."

"Who'd you buy?" said Poker.

"Every name I'd ever heard of. I didn't know anything, which was more than the kids behind the counter. They weren't more than two years older than me and they'd look completely blank and try to sell me Cliff Richard."

"Over there," said Poker, pointing to his right.

"God, why?" said Scarlet.

"I'm a collector," Poker replied. "I've got Acker Bilk, Lonnie Donegan…"

"Just promise me," she said, putting a hand on his shoulder, "you don't secretly come in here and play them."

"Hang me sooner," he said, turning to Jim and back to her, "Anything you really do want to hear?"

Jim and Scarlet moved slowly down the aisles, picking out items and putting them back, asking for things, sometimes telling stories about the greats they'd met, or only heard of, or even played with. When they'd picked out a few songs, Poker took them over to the array of speakers on the back wall, showed them to their seats, took the Jimmy Yancey recordings from Jim and some bootleg Joni Mitchell from Scarlet, and said, "Let the show begin."

They drove back talking about music, excited to look forward to playing again with somebody really good, talking about the times they'd had all the way until she parked the car outside their house.

"The Memphis party," she said. "That sealed it for me."

"What d'you remember?"

"You playing most of the time, any title anyone called out. Music spilling down the lawn, filling the warm Memphis evening. A woman with long brown hair, in a long silk dress of faded green and pink, crazy from the pills she was taking or the meds she wasn't, down at the end of the long garden, screaming about some man who'd left her."

She remembered the woman wandering towards the other guests, shouting at them, beseeching them, challenging them, and then walking away again, back to where she was hidden among the long, mossy branches of the southern oak trees that drooped down to the ground.

"You must've stood there waiting for her to see you," Scarlet went on. "And listened to her talking, and shouting, and crying, long enough for her to let you walk her up the garden, through the house, and into the ambulance that came to take her away."

"I even visited her the next day while the party rested."

A woman lost in a world of good and bad pills and good and bad men, Scarlet thought. And that evening Jim had gone back to the piano and rocked. And the next evening too. The joyous, never-ending Memphis party.

"When everyone had finally gone," she said, "we walked down through the trees where it was cold and fresh and still dark, and I felt exhausted but so alive, and I kissed you and knew even then, holding you next to me, that I wanted you there forever."

The Jim your brother's never seen.

It's a strange thing, she thought. Robert's never known what you were really like, not at your best. You're supposed to grow up together, share your lives. But you left for a strange land as soon as you could, and now you've come back old, with your stories and not much else. Robert hardly knew you then and he hardly knows you now. What can you two make of each other, when you're starting at the end? What can Robert really make of you when you're just stories to him?

"You suddenly looked lost," Jim said. "Come on in."

They walked back into the house, and into the kitchen. Jim poured them both drinks, and on an impulse put his arms around her. "You want to get a little drunk? Go upstairs and maybe fool around?"

"Maybe put some music on and dance," she replied, taking a drink and looking at him over the glass.

"I think, Miss Scarlet," he said, downing his drink in one, "I've known you long enough not to need… "

She kissed him. "Don't mean we need to rush." She finished her drink, ran her hands through his dark hair, and looked at his face, worn, yes, but with a smile she'd always found hard to resist. Then she kissed him again, more strongly this time, and he returned the kiss, moving his body to fit more closely to hers.

Upstairs, he quickly undressed and slipped into the unmade bed. She dropped her jeans and top to the floor and joined him, and gradually she let him move his hands over her body, remove her underwear, and start to touch her more intimately. She had always enjoyed making him wait, even when he was hard, and she did now, as they kissed and she drew her fingers slowly over his shoulders along his spine and down his back, then up again. He pushed her away and she looked at his face, at the signs of age, of his condition, at his deep brown eyes, and pulled him back towards her. Her hands went down to the top of his thighs, and grabbing him firmly she rolled over on top of him and he was inside her. They moved slowly at first, and then more quickly, their breaths gulping as if for life, and he came, and she came, and covered in sweat she rolled off him and they lay there, staring at the ceiling.

He reached over to his bedside table and took out a joint.

"Sustain the mood?" he said.

"Forever," she replied.

In time, took he went out to the garden and sat in a deckchair. She followed him, but, distracted for a moment by the mess in the kitchen, let herself follow a memory that ran through her life as intimate as blood.

You heard something in my voice. You heard it when I didn't, when I knew I was just one of a thousand girls with no more'n a bit of a voice, who'd run out of school and run out of what little talent I had. All gone, all used up. How many more years of being picked up and put down could I have taken? – Sing this louder, sing it higher. A little more Celine, a little more Whitney? You done cowboy numbers? You don't take it, I can get another chick easy, there's a hundred like you, you ain't no different, sooner you learn that the better. You better work nine to five, you think we've booked this studio for ever? These guys behind the screen, you see them, they've got homes to go to. So you hear what they say? You hear what you're singing? Step right up to the microphone. How many years before what? Before I got a job in a supermarket? Prettied up an office downtown? Got married?

She shook her head to try and free herself of it, and went out to sit on the grass beside him. She took one of his hands in hers. He didn't stir, and for a time neither did she in the breathless afternoon. Then he opened an eye.

"It *is* you," he said. "I was dreaming it was. What're you thinking?"

"That back in the day you'd have me over and play just to hear me sing. And you'd keep saying, the thing about ballads is they have to sound like you mean it or you've just turned a tap on. You're going to break your heart every night if you're any good. Break it, and bounce back."

He nodded. "You've got to let the song take you over, lose yourself. You've got to let go."

She stroked his hands gently. "And I told you, I'm just a chick in a band, nobody's going to be writing songs for me."

"You were what then? Twenty?" Jim said. "That's too young to run away from yourself. Like I told you – you could be a singer."

After a time it was uncomfortable. She stood up and smoothed down her jeans.

"I'm going in," she said. "You want a glass of water?"

He closed his eyes without speaking.

She went to the kitchen, poured herself a glass, took it to the living room and sat in a chair looking out to where Jim sat facing the sun with his back to her.

I knew what people would say, of course, before I ever heard anyone say it. I didn't need anyone to tell me I was moving in with my father, or maybe the father I'd never had. That falling for an older man is heartbreak, they're all born bachelors and they'll just move on. That's the reason he's bothering with you, and sure he likes you, but it ain't nothing more than that, anything else is just talk, and boy ain't they all practised talkers? You want to settle down, hang around the churches, find someone there, and even that won't do it. But this is music, honey, what *are* you thinking? You want an older man 'cause you never had a daddy? Well, one thing this one's got in common with your real daddy is he ain't going to stick around neither. And you'll get tired too, maybe even before he does, and that's how it is. Just look around.

And why I don't hate you I don't know. Why I don't despair, why I don't walk away. Because of Ryan. Because I knew you always said you weren't going to be involved, you'd live on your own sooner, because it was my choice, and I made it, knowing. Because I can't believe it, and one day you're going to change. When he was just a baby, and you moved to Chicago because you said that's where the music is, I was so hurt, and I wanted you so much, and Mom was telling me leave him, just leave him like he's left you, because he has, darling, and men like him do, they always do, and I knew I loved Ryan and I loved you, and I wanted so much to bring us all together. And I didn't know why you wouldn't love him, why you were set against him. And I still don't. And he's turned to hating you, won't hear your name even, and I'm two people, loving him and loving you.

Suddenly it seemed as if everything was motionless. She looked at the deckchair, weighed down by Jim's body, and a flicker of alarm possessed her, chilling her skin. It was impossible, she knew that, but she hurried back out.

He opened his eyes and said, "Did you bring me a glass of water?"

"No. No," she said, "I forgot."

"Doesn't matter."

She knelt down and took his hands.

"We've had good times," he said.

"Real good times," she replied. "Like the year we

started off in Baton Rouge and over to New Orleans, and chased the summer north, playing all sorts of clubs, cafés and bars, 'cause we didn't have much?"

He nodded.

"Up to Kentucky, across to California. Worked all the way up Route 1, to The Great Highway, and San Francisco. That was good. Good enough for both of us."

"We finished up in St Louis," he said. "A real blues city."

"I couldn't have done it without you." She squeezed his hands, and looked at him, uncertain what she should say. "And then we had one hell of a row," she said. "You stayed in St Louis; I left in this huge storm. We didn't speak for months. It hurt so much. I then saw you one evening, playing in a bar in Atlanta, and I went up and sang with you, and we were back together. Just like that. Didn't think twice. I couldn't've done different. You never learn what you don't want to, I guess."

Jim took the point, smiled even, and then grasped her hands and said, "I want one more gig. I want it more than any I've done. One last show."

"Don't think of it like that."

He shook his head, and briefly, she thought, he looked lost. Then he recovered himself.

"You know what I miss?" he said.

She waited.

"Being on a boat. We could do it, you know, in a month or two."

"Are you kidding me?"

"I don't mean I'd sail it. We'd get someone."

"I'm not spending a night on board with you. Not with you in your… "

"OK, we return to the harbour in the evening. One last holiday. We could do it."

Madness, she thought. Madness. OK, he'd sailed Lake Michigan many a time, but that was then.

"We could sail down the Bristol Channel."

She shook her head and stood up. Really, even if he just sat there, let someone else do the hard work, took all his meds with him… it was still crazy.

"And stay where?"

"There'll be somewhere. We'd book it all in advance."

She wasn't even going to say no. Just let it all blow over. A couple of bad nights and he'd forget it. Realise it wasn't on. But she couldn't wish for that, not now he was, praise be, happier than he'd been for weeks. It would be the last time, but that was no reason to stop it in its tracks.

Restless in bed that night he turned to her and said, "You were ill once."

"Sure. My mom must've called you, I was too sick. I remember you by my bedside, holding my hands for hours, telling me I was the one. The only one. You'd do the shopping, and sit down at my piano and play, while she chopped up onions and peppers and stewed the beans and the chicken, and you'd get Mom to sing along with you…"

"She had a sweet voice."

"And for the first time she started to like you. 'He's not so bad after all,' she'd say when you were out, 'this Englishman you let into your life. Maybe you weren't such a damn fool.' "

"I was starting to like her. Didn't mean she didn't keep

49

pointing out my faults the same way she kept pointing out yours."

"She didn't say she loved you, either, but she was starting to, because she likes to love people, and tell them what's wrong with them but how it's OK because we're all sinners and yet most of us going to heaven somehow."

She gave him a kiss.

"And when I was clearly on the mend," she said, "she'd let you play 'Wayfaring Stranger', which always made her cry, but now it was all right 'cause I wasn't going over Jordan after all."

And then I was better, she thought, and you were gone, and I had to learn that being at peace wasn't your thing. That you had to be moving and playing and could never be still. That you were on the road because you could never truly be at home. You weren't built for comfort, you did anger and sorrow, you were up or you were down, you were fun or you were lost, deep enough in yourself to drown, and when you were on the road I saw you checking in to those cheap hotels when you should be with me. For real, in front of me, in those cheap rooms straight out of the movies, with a TV and a bed and a bathroom, and a car park and a neon sign you could see a mile down the road. Checking in, and I wanted you with me so bad, and I knew you wanted to be with me but you couldn't stop. Always the next place, and the next.

And now you're really sick. And we're just talking about less and less, not saying what we should, just waiting it out. Hoping every day's the same, so that it won't be worse. Only half alive, when nothing changes. And I'm holding your hands, as well as I can.

At three in the morning Jim gave up hoping he would get to sleep. He got out of bed, grabbed some clothes, and made his way downstairs in the dark. It was cold, he blundered his way to one of the chairs in the living room and sat for a while looking at nothing. Gradually, he could see the outline of the garden revealed by the waning moon and the stars beyond. He went to the window to look at the view more fully, and returned to the chair. He pulled his legs up underneath himself and closed his arms around them. He could easily have poured himself a whisky, a bottle and a glass were before him, but he didn't. He looked around the room, which was barely lit, slowly coming to feel he was in the wrong place.

He'd been someone who'd played in this band, and would play in that one, always ready to slot into a session, always invited to join in whenever he was in town, trash his music to pay the bills, and he'd be all those things again because that's who he was. Happy in a world of friendships and rivalries, chemistry sometimes, jam sessions and gigs, jokes, drinking, dope, and music. Clichéd drummers and good ones, back-up singers, guitarists, producers, guys happy in love, guys chasing skirts and skirts chasing guys, guys who read every book under the sun and guys who barely made it through the sports pages, women with kids and women whose sorrow it was they'd missed out, careers taking off and crashing and parked. And now there was a glass wall around him, and everyone was on the other side, remote, their words and music thinned out as if he was on the point of fainting.

He got up and crossed to the window, but the little light there was in the room overpowered the moonless dark outside, so he switched the light off, went back to the window, and waited for his eyes to adjust and the stars to appear. Still it wasn't good enough. He opened the patio doors and made his way out into the garden. It was cloudless, and the Milky Way was visible – not its tormented heart but its imposing arch – and he stared at it for the hint of solace it gave him.

Things still weren't right. He went back inside, to the front room. Somewhere in the piano stool was a note, ah, there it was, to remind him of something he hadn't thought of for years. Ninety minutes of all kinds of music, thrown out a distance beyond his imagining, a wealth of surprises – and three pieces that particularly spoke to him. For a moment he imagined moving the piano into the garden and answering the pull of the stars with a cry of his own, and he savoured the impossible image before opening the windows of the front room – let the neighbours complain if they were mean-spirited enough – and began with the Bach. Not his choice of the forty-eight, but no need to argue. Then Blind Willie Johnson's extraordinary meditation, intoned over a slide guitar that of course no piano could match, but he had tried over the years and always something came over of the peace and desolation it contained. And then, roar it out, the not-so-subtle innuendo saying more about life in two and a half minutes than the spectacle beyond, Chuck Berry's 'Johnny B. Goode'.

Not that he could have said where, precisely, but it pleased him to know that somewhere, heading out of the solar system, the music had its silent, golden echo. Built to end its life in darkness, carrying a fragment of humanity into the constellation that was once said to commemorate the man who'd learned from snakes how to keep death at bay, and was killed by Jupiter, lest the human race become immortal.

Chapter 4

Late June 2018

Robert parked his car in the only spot he could find, next to a small, careworn green Ford. As he got out, so too did the driver of the Ford. He had an untidy red beard, dark, vigorous hair, and eyes that suggested an unruly temperament he was always struggling to control, but his quiet clothes and his clerical collar told another story.

"Who's dying and says they want you?" Robert asked.

"And who's died and needs you?" the man replied, with a grin.

Together, they walked towards the hospital entrance.

"So tell me, Father," Robert said, "don't you ever feel worn out watching them go?"

"Doctors get tired," the man replied. "Every time's a defeat for you."

"But at least we do what we can."

"I thought you were firmly on the far side these days."

"I've become a bit of a visitor, oddly enough," Robert replied, and he began to tell Father O'Coran about his visits to Josie Peters, even though she barely knew he was there most times, and he himself couldn't say why he was going, except that she seemed very troubled. The younger man listened calmly, a gentle smile on his face, and when Robert had finished, said only, "It's a kind thing you're doing,"

"Maybe," said Robert with a shrug.

They parted, and Robert made his way downstairs to his lab, and the steady stream of samples coming down in their sealed test tubes in sealed plastic bags from the wards above. It was routine to run the tests and reconstruct the illnesses from the results and the comments on file from the doctors looking to confirm a diagnosis but staying alert to others. Why is this one not responding to treatment? Can you confirm this one is safe to discharge? He took his lunch alone in the lab, as he usually did, while his assistants and the students went up to the canteen or out to the nearest Costa or Pret. It was the start of the course, and the students especially seemed a jolly, talkative bunch, which covered up their nervousness quite well.

"May I ask you a personal question?" It was Parvinda Pillai, small, quick and dark-eyed, her long black hair tucked mostly out of sight, back early from lunch.

Robert tipped his head to one side and waited.

"Some of us students were thinking, why don't you have lunch with us? Why do you stay down here all day?" And she blushed, suddenly thinking she'd overstepped her mark.

"Actually," Robert said, "it clears my head."

"You'd be very welcome," she said, and blushed again.

Have I become the sweet old man who needs help? Robert briefly wondered. "Then I'll come," he said. "Sometimes. When we're not too busy."

Parvinda, feeling her offer had been rebuffed, said, "I need the life. All the bustle, the noise, the hassle of finding somewhere to sit and eat. I don't think I could stay down here all day."

"Are you worried about the course?"

"No. I mean, this is interesting." She waved her hand around the lab. "And I've been to autopsies before…" Her voice faded, inconclusive.

"But?" Robert asked.

"I miss the people, I suppose."

"I might say we have the bits that matter."

Parvinda frowned, and Robert, hoping to rescue his remark, said, "It would be a grim joke. But diagnosis is the hardest part of medicine."

The other students came clattering back downstairs and the conversation, disrupted, spun round in Robert's and Parvinda's heads for the rest of the afternoon. Robert went from bench to bench, confirming and amplifying what his assistants had found, pointing out to the students the significance of what they were looking at, handing down opinions like a chess master in a simultaneous display. Checkmate in three months, even with best play. Checkmate in four.

At the end of the day, as the students hung up their lab coats, Robert found himself next to Parvinda. She looked at him, but said nothing, and left.

Over the next couple of weeks, as Robert got to know the students better, and even went to lunch with them occasionally, the lab developed a routine, as it did every year. This was one of the parts of his life that Robert enjoyed most, as the students learned to open up and share their observations and their questions with each other as well as with him. But Parvinda seemed to be increasingly withdrawn, to the point where she seemed to be avoiding him, until one afternoon when she came back late on her own from lunch, plainly upset. Robert watched as one or two of the students asked her if anything was wrong, and got no answers, and she shut herself off on her bench and worked harder than ever. As work finished and everyone was leaving, Robert asked her to stay behind. When everyone had gone, he waited for her to speak, which, reluctantly, she did.

"I went to see Mrs Morley," she said in a whisper. "I just sat there for a few minutes. I shouldn't have gone. I hope you don't mind."

"And?"

"It was awful. No one can do anything. I asked one of the nurses. She's really unhappy, and no one comes to see her. Except Father O'Coran, of course."

Robert asked for her hospital number and pulled up her details on a screen.

"It's worse than you said it would be," Parvinda said.

Robert, to his surprise and hers, could find nothing to say. After a time, Parvinda, in a quiet voice, said, "I thought you would say everyone's doing their best."

"They are," said Robert. "They are."

"But…" said Parvinda, searching for words that wouldn't seem critical of everyone and everything around her.

"The only reason for medicine," Robert said slowly, "the only deep reason, is that nature doesn't care for us.

Whether this person lives or dies, is born healthy or not, it doesn't care. Only we do."

"Krishna, we believe, brought the world to light so we could fight a terrible war."

"Is that what you believe?"

"My father is a very unusual man for India. He tries very hard to be a socialist, and an atheist, and that is a very difficult thing for us. His family despairs of him, but he brought me up that way. No temples, no shrines, just an endless struggle."

"That's tough."

"I'm not sure I can do it. Not all the time."

Robert pulled a couple of chairs over and sat down, but Parvinda remained standing.

"Is he a doctor?" Robert asked.

"No, he's a schoolteacher. He teaches mathematics."

"And is he pleased you're here?"

"He wants me to go back when I qualify. He says there are more people back home who need doctors." She paused. "And he's old now."

She tucked a stray lock of hair behind her ear and looked away.

"Why did you go to see Mrs Morley?" Robert asked.

"I don't feel we're helping anybody down here. I feel, more and more, everything on every course is science. It's so abstract, so remote."

"Didn't your father tell you that even mathematics is useful?"

"And look, we're in a basement here; half the time we're looking at things taken from dead people." She took a deep breath. "I don't think we're doctors." And then she blushed, and put her hand to her mouth, and said, "I'm sorry, I didn't mean that. Of course you're a doctor…"

"If it's any consolation," said Robert, "my family's never been sure."

A few days later, Robert found himself walking down a corridor with Father O'Coran.

"I've been talking to Mrs Morley," the priest said. "I gather you know her."

"A student took me to see her. I've been back a couple of times. How'd you know?"

"People talk about you. The pathologist who won't stay out of sight."

They walked on in silence for a few steps, then Robert said "She asked me to help her to die. She must have asked you."

O'Coran grabbed him by the arm and said, with sudden fierceness, "That would be killing her. Her cry's not for us to bring her an easy death but for help and love." Staring into Robert's eyes, he said, "For human and supernatural warmth."

What form of love is that? Robert thought, that denies her her final, thought-out wish?

O'Coran said "Can't we do better than kill the weakest among us?"

"Her only wish," Robert replied, "the only one that makes sense to her, is to die in dignity."

"We must try to bring love and peace to these people…"

"What love do *you* bring her," Robert said, "when she cries out for the only peace she will ever have?"

"I always think," O'Coran replied, "that the real test is could you do it yourself? You can ask other people to do difficult things for you, but could *you* do this? Take her life?"

"Within the law?"

O'Coran nodded. "With all the small print you people imagine."

"You've seen what we do," Robert said. "Stringing these people along, kidding ourselves we do no harm when we can see before our eyes… preventing them dying as they'd always wished. In peace."

"Someone you've cared for. Someone who's believed in you."

Robert shook himself free from O'Coran's grasp and said, "Someone who's known they're near the end, who only wishes to avoid pain and distress? Someone I've talked to? Yes. I hope I could. Yes."

He turned and walked away as fast as he could, O'Coran's voice echoing down the corridor after him that only God may take a life.

The next few days followed the usual routine, except that Parvinda was even quieter than usual, polite with the other students, but not sharing their jokes. On the Friday, as people left, Robert took her aside and said, "Come with me." Together, they made their way to the eighth floor, where Josie Peters lay in bed, half asleep. Parvinda sat in the chair by the bed and Robert pulled up another from an empty bed nearby. Josie opened an eye and said, "You again. It's no good you know."

"How are you doing?" Robert asked.

Josie drew a sequence of rough, shallow breaths and said, "I want to go home."

"Are they trying to find you somewhere?"

Another sequence of broken breaths and Josie said, "A real home. I have a real home." And then, seeing Parvinda for the first time, she said, "Is this your girlfriend?"

"I'm a student," Parvinda said.

"Every man should have a girlfriend. Keeps them out of trouble." And she winked disconcertingly at Parvinda.

"She's going to be a doctor," said Robert.

"You're too late, dear," Josie said. "It's always too late." And she closed her eyes.

Robert and Parvinda sat there for a few more minutes, and then Robert indicated that they could leave. Just as they got up to go, Josie pushed herself forward, grabbed Parvinda's hand and whispered hoarsely, "I've had enough. I've had enough."

Parvinda looked at Josie's grey, drawn face, her sunken, flickering eyes, and then over at Robert.

"Tell them, dear, won't you? I want to go." Then she sank back on her pillow, her disrupted breathing the only sound.

Robert and Parvinda walked back in silence down the corridors, Parvinda's mind filling with more questions than she knew how to ask, and when they reached the hospital exit and it was easier to talk, she asked, "She's dying?"

"Yes," he said.

"Why do you go?"

"I don't know. Maybe, *because* she's dying."

"Can't we… can't anyone…?"

It was a beautiful evening, the cloudless sky full of shades of blue that bent almost into white where it vanished behind the charmless outbuildings beyond the car park. A stream of people walked past them, heading for their cars or for buses or to the pubs. Three ambulances stood off to their right. The sunlight caught on corners of buildings, transforming them into youthful copies of themselves; it reflected off the windows of the hospital behind them and the windows of the cars in ways too bright to look at.

"One day, in India," Parvinda said slowly, "every hospital will be like this. Well-equipped doctors in white coats doing their best." She paused, biting her lips. "And it won't be enough."

"There are other countries. Where they intervene. At the end."

She paused again, looked at the ground, and looked at Robert. "I may have to go back to India. Very soon. My father… "

"Do you know when?"

She shook her head. "I don't think it will be for long. A week, maybe. One of my uncles will try to call me. I could study on the plane. On the flights."

"Just a week?"

"He's a kind man. And he's been so strong."

They talked a little more, and when she left Robert stayed there in the evening sun. He would sign the letter. He'd known that for some time, but that was the easy part. And Barbara – well, that wasn't the only thing that was not going well right now. But why was he thinking not of her, but of Jim?

Chapter 5

Mid-July 2018

Barbara sat there, trying not to say anything. Trying not to say "I'm not going to make this easy for you." Not to say "Tell me you've signed the letter." Trying to work out what she would say when he admitted he had, and the world would spin and she wouldn't know where it would settle.

Robert had been uncharacteristically quiet on their walk round Kew Gardens. Now they sat in nearby Richmond, in an old pub full of young people, it seemed to her, where they'd been lucky to get a table and a view of the Thames, and all through lunch he had still hardly spoken, until she guessed why and stopped talking herself. Now he pushed his chair away from the table, ran his hands over his hair and down to the back of his neck, and looked at his feet. He took a deep breath. Confession mode, she thought. He looked up.

"I have to tell you, I signed the letter."

"You didn't tell me you were doing it. Actually doing it," she said. Keep it cold, she thought, measured.

"We've talked about it. I know you don't want me to. But I've come to realise… "

"Realise what? What is it you've suddenly discovered?"

"I don't know. Maybe as you get older you… "

"Go on. You what?"

"The letter only asks that there's national conversation about what doctors should do faced with a terminally ill patient in great suffering."

"And now you think you should be allowed to… " She paused. Choose the next word with care, she thought, staring steadily at him. "End their lives."

"Only if the conversation goes that way. Only if the law is changed."

"And then two doctors can kill them."

"Of course not. No-one's asking for that. The patients themselves must… "

"Jesus, Robert. Sometimes I think you can't think at all. Did you think about me? About the children? What do they think about it? What will they think when it all unravels?"

"It won't. Why should it?"

"I give it five years before harassed doctors and mercenary private specialists and bullying relatives start coming to light. What are you going to say to us then?" Her voice rose, she could see people nearby glancing at her. Not another old couple who'd run out of things to say to each other, then. This was turning into a row.

He slowly shook his head, looking at her with an expression full of sadness that she didn't want to see.

"Where's your Hippocratic Oath?" she said. "Or is that just another piece of paperwork you signed long ago and want us to forget? To do no harm."

" 'To do no harm or injustice', if you want to know.

I looked the original up. 'Nor administer a poison or recommend such a course'. But that's not what I signed."

"How convenient. And what have you doctors written for yourselves instead?"

"That I must face the responsibility of taking a life humbly, aware of my own frailty."

"Isn't that humbug, really? Hubris?"

"There are so many people dying slowly and in pain…" His voice was rising now, she noticed.

"Robert, I don't care if the entire medical profession wants this. It's wrong. Really, really, simply wrong." And this is a public place, she thought, that's why you've decided to tell me here, so I can't scream at you, beg you to withdraw your name, for both our sakes. She stood up. "I'll be down by the river. You can pay."

She made her way through the crowded tables, down to where she could watch the Thames run softly by. Two white swans were drifting regally along it, dark-eyed with golden rims and golden beaks, occasionally dipping their long necks to feed. She watched them, quietly aware of each other, never moving too far apart, until a bend in the river took them out of sight. There was peace in the world around her, and pleasure in the sounds from the pub, and all of it was so far away, so different from what she felt, as if one or the other must be truly out of place: all that, or herself, alone.

Their journey to Bath the next weekend was fraught. Not because of the traffic, which was light enough, but because, since Kew, their conversations either died or were kept artificially alive, as if that could lead them back to the ease

65

they had once known. Each felt their lives together passing by as fragments, discouraging as they mounted up, and neither knew how to put them together. They found ways to be at home less, and to avoid each other when they were at home. What had had to be said had been spoken, and the well of trust between them was now fractured and draining away.

When they arrived, Scarlet took Barbara shopping in Bath, and Robert went shopping in Aldi for lunch. He wandered, a little lost, around the unfamiliar shelves. At a corner by chilled foods his way was blocked by a trolley containing a few vegetables and a cheerful, grubby two-year-old. A thin man in a long, combat overcoat held on to it with his right hand while picking out some vegan produce from the shelves with his left.

"Excuse me," said Robert, and the man turned. Robert saw an intense face, high cheekbones and raw red cheeks, just at the moment when the man shouted, "You. You're one of them murderers."

Robert backed his trolley away, looking for a place to turn it around.

"Mudwah" cried the two-year-old, as his father pushed his trolley after Robert.

Robert swung his trolley around, and headed rapidly for the doors. A security guard stepped listlessly forward and said, "You can't exit this way, sir, the tills are over there."

"This man's harassing me," said Robert, pointing at his pursuer. "You should be throwing him out."

"He's one of the murderers in that hospital," the man shouted.

"Then keep your frozen bloody fish," said Robert, and he abandoned his trolley and walked quickly out to his car. The man snatched up his child and ran after him, fast enough to catch up with him and prevent him from opening the car door.

"You're one of them murderers," he shouted again.

Robert could see the guard standing in the doorway about twenty yards away, unwilling to get involved.

"Tell me one thing," Robert said, barely able to control his voice. "Have you ever lost a loved one?"

"I know people who have."

"Have you?" Robert repeated.

'You're still a murderer. There's people who've lost loved ones what shouldn't."

"Who? No one. What do you know that I don't?"

A small crowd of customers was gathering, and the store guard had moved a little closer.

"People've died what shouldn't, in't that enough?"

"Who? Who? Give me one name."

The two-year-old was starting to cry. Robert pushed a step forward, managed to open his car door, and got in. As the man continued to shout, Robert backed carefully away, drove out of the car park, and stopped on the slip road, his hands trembling. Then, thinking he was still too close, he drove slowly onto the main road and took a turn off to a housing estate, and where he waited ten minutes before he felt able to drive back to Jim's.

"Come to the pub," Jim said. "It's a short walk and Scarlet says they do a good fish and chips."

Once there, they ordered their meals and took their drinks to a table outside.

"So you're getting this crap," said Jim, raising his whisky glass, "because of the letter?"

"The letter went on our website and some group made a scandal out of it," Robert replied, running his hands through his thinning hair. "It's faces now. It'll be home addresses next."

"You're worrying too much," Jim said, raising his glass. "Drink up, I find it always helps."

Robert raised his glass but didn't drink.

"It says you're not safe to be around," said Jim. "And nor are the rest of your lot."

"Forty people asking a question in a professional journal. Is that dangerous?"

"If you're going to run around ending people's lives…"

"It doesn't say that," Robert replied. "It just says we might consider, near the end, and with full consent… Nobody's creeping around in the dead of night."

"I suppose I'd rather I saw you coming," Jim said with an easy smile, "but I haven't thought about it," and he raised his glass again. Robert, unaware, looked disconsolately at his drink.

"I get other calls," Robert said. "From doctors, off the record, saying they've been there." He stopped short. Some said more than that. They spoke of what happens when you can do nothing, of invisible companions who whisper interruptions when people talk to you, who step between you and your family, who come and go and take away any sense of peace.

His phone rang. To his surprise, it was Parvinda.

"I'm back," she said. "I'm in London."

"How are you?"

"It was awful. So much pain. My uncles and aunts round his bedside all disagreeing, and the doctors doing their best when... when..."

"It must have been hard for you."

"On the flight back I was thinking about what you said, that nature doesn't care for us."

"No, nature doesn't care how we die."

"I think... I want to be a doctor. A better doctor."

"Your father would like that."

She was silent, until Robert began to wonder if she was still there, and then she said, "I didn't help. No one would listen to me."

"They will, one day."

She said nothing.

"Be in the class on Monday," he said.

Jim looked up as Robert put his phone back in his pocket and said, "You said that? Nature doesn't care?"

Robert took a deep breath, but before he could reply, Jim said, "It figures. I could go along with that. And you don't think doctors do, either?"

"Oh, we care. We care. The only way we can. Tablets of hope, injections, hospital treatments, even when we can see they don't work."

"Well, you're quite the ray of sunshine."

"I'm sorry, I didn't mean..."

"No, you've got McIntire right. And the others, I guess."

"They've got you through, so far."

Jim pulled a face and scratched the back of his neck.

"Could you have hurried our father out that way? He had a tough time, I believe. Or our mother?"

"There are laws against it," Robert replied. "You don't want greedy children bumping off their parents as soon as they get the chance. Persuading them to go."

"But just suppose, if the doctors had asked you, if it'd been possible?"

Robert looked down at his hands. "No, not then. I couldn't have asked them to do so then."

Jim raised his glass and said with a smile "I never thought I'd see you as Dr Death."

Robert grimaced and said nothing. Jim's flippancy annoyed him; one day he'd enter the terminal world and his denials would no longer work. Did he have no thoughts about it? Had no one sought to explain that it wouldn't be easy, or quick? He must have seen patients more advanced than him.

Jim stood up. "Come and look at the view," he said.

They reached the end of the garden without talking.

"You know," Jim said, "I thought living with this… condition would be worse. I mean, really worse."

Robert waited.

"Don't get me wrong," Jim went on. "The chemo was awful. But I can still lead a bit of a life."

"Play music."

"Play music. Eat, drink, and be merry." Jim paused for a moment. "And there's the gig."

Did his confidence dip just then? Robert wondered. How worried was he?

"We try to make it a chronic illness, not the scary thing it used to be."

"Not scary," Jim said, pensively. "I'm not sure about that."

"I'm not sure I'd be, either."

They walked back to their seats, and Jim let the conversation drift for a minute. Then he asked quietly, "What was it like when Mother died?"

"For her? I think she just wore out."

"You were there?"

Robert nodded, and Jim said, "And she knew what was happening?"

"She knew."

"I'm glad you were there. You must have made it less scary."

"I like to think so."

"You didn't know her when she was young," Jim went on. "You were just a baby. She changed a lot when our father came home to stay."

"I didn't know that."

"She was fun. I went to see her, you know. A couple of times. The last time was in ninety-six. Just before you came to say goodbye to me at Heathrow. She wasn't in a good way." He paused. "I think she thought I was you."

Robert nodded. "If you were lucky, you could catch her in a lucid moment. They came and went."

"Phone calls were worse."

One of the bar staff brought out their lunches, and Jim began to pick over his salad.

"Would you do that for me?" Jim asked. "Make it less scary?"

Robert, taken aback if only by the timing, said, "Yes. Yes, of course, if I can."

"That's what your letter's about, isn't it," said Jim.

"In a way. I mean, I'll do what I can."

Jim smiled. "Tuck in," he said. "I'm paying."

Over the meal he let the conversation dwindle, while Robert continued the uneasy dialogue that ran more and more often in his head, and tried not to ask himself what it was, exactly, that he'd just agreed to.

After lunch, they walked back home and sat in the living room, quietly swapping stories about crazy people. Jim relaxed into his repertoire of tales about talentless showmen with witless spectacle on stage and drug-fuelled egos off it, not even five minutes of fame and then a lifetime with only tattoos to show for it; Robert, unable to settle, drew from the arcana of unusual deaths, the satanist who choked on garlic bulbs, the vegan who ate nothing but carrots, turned orange, and died.

Then suddenly Jim lurched forward, grabbed the arms of his chair, and with every muscle tried to ride out a spasm of pain. He clutched under his ribs, taking short, shallow breaths, and tried not to speak, but then another spasm swept over him, and then a third, less severe than the first two. A giveaway symptom of the problems in the bowel, Robert thought. Jim took two codeines, and tried to sit it out. The pain didn't return but hovered in the background.

The doorbell rang, and Jim, looking at his watch, said, "This one's for me." He went to the front door and started a hushed conversation. Robert, his curiosity piqued, got up and took a cautious look. Jim was talking to a man in his fifties, with a rather obvious toupee, dressed in a maroon jacket with matching trousers that he was surely too old for, over a pale yellow shirt. Robert heard Jim say drily, "Of course, Harrison, you're always welcome." Something about his face was familiar, but before he could put a name to it Jim bundled the man out of the house.

"Who was that?" Robert asked.

"A local tradesman, that's all" Jim replied.

In the late afternoon Scarlet's car drew up outside. Jim stirred from a light sleep and said with a look "Don't tell Scarlet."

The two women came in cheerfully, and from her full shopping bags Scarlet produced a hatbox, which she gave to Jim.

"Open it," she said.

He lifted the lid, took out a Panama hat, and turned it around. Scarlet took it from him and placed it on his head.

"Now go and admire it," she said. "Use the mirror in the hall."

Robert watched. Jim sat forward, placed his hands on the arms of the chair, took a deep breath and pushed himself upwards. Robert saw a flicker cross his face, but then he stood completely straight and walked briskly out of the room. Scarlet followed him, and they stood for a while in front of the mirror, Scarlet adjusting his hair and tidying the hang of his shirt.

"See," she said. "Very handsome."

"Very handsome," he said. "Thanks to you," and he gave her an affectionate kiss on her cheek. They came back in arm in arm. He took the hat off, placed it on the table by his chair, and said, "Pity it's the wrong day for it," and sat back down. Robert watched his body relax and then curl a little, as if withdrawing slightly from itself. The performance was over, and he wondered if the audience had noticed.

"Should I have got you a Panama?" Barbara asked, turning to Robert.

He smiled and shook his head. "Summer's over soon."

Jim looked at Barbara. "There's a famous hat in the family, you know. Did he ever tell you about that?"

"I don't think so."

"The Malay turban?"

"I remember the turban," Robert said. "And the ornamental knife that came with it, but we weren't allowed to touch, or anything."

"Dad had been sent there after the war, God knows why," Jim said, with a quick look at Robert, who said nothing. "And there was this big, dirty, blue and white turban he brought back and kept hidden in a brown box tied up with string, and he'd make our mother put the turban on, or he'd put it on and he'd chase us round the room. If we'd been really good, we could put it on. It was the nearest he got to playing games with us."

Robert shrugged. "He liked everything to be very precise. Meals at the right time, us to bed at the right time, our few toys tidied away. Books neatly on the shelves in alphabetical order. A chessboard we were never allowed to touch, either." Jim's eyes flashed, but Robert merely asked if he knew where the turban was now, and Jim said he didn't.

"You don't make him sound like a load of fun," said Scarlet.

Robert paused. All he could think of was the chess club where his father had never taken him.

"Did he help you with school and everything?" Scarlet asked.

Robert shook his head. "He came to school only once to meet the teachers, and told me off for learning Latin. And that was it. Even when I went to Oxford, and they said they were pleased. No one in the family had ever been to university before. But they never came to visit me there."

To fill the silence that followed, Robert went on, "We went on seaside holidays."

"The same place every year," said Jim. "We went on the same trips. Did the same things."

"You mean, me tailing along after you, watching you go up to other kids, bigger kids, and join in their games, and them telling to me to play where I was told? Games of football where I hardly ever kicked the ball, games of cricket where I was out at once, and charges into the sea where I hoped no one would see I couldn't swim."

"You didn't try," Jim said. "You always wanted to be with Mother."

"That's not true."

"And even then you didn't see half of it."

"Like what?"

Jim waved his hand. "Go on, tell your stories."

"No, come on, what'd I miss?"

"Bit late now, isn't it, " Jim said, and stared pointedly at Robert.

To break the silence that followed, Scarlet said, "That's the first time I seen you be like brothers."

Jim smiled. "Go on, we're all listening."

"And then there were picnics," Robert said. "They were the worst."

Barbara stared at him, wondering where this outburst was taking them.

"You must remember picnics in the early sixties," Robert said, turning to her. "The long bus journey to wherever, and then the long walk. Somehow it was always colder than it was meant to be. There were nettles, and wasps. Jim kept charging off and getting lost. And told off."

"He's right about that," Jim said.

Wrapping the sentence in a smile, Barbara said, "I sometimes think you really were feeble as a child." And when no one laughed, she added "It's his excuse for not liking the countryside."

The doorbell rang. Scarlet and Jim looked at each other. She got up and went to the door. There was a surprised exchange of women's voices and Scarlet came back and ushered Lauren in.

"Look who's turned up," she said.

"I hope it's all right," Lauren muttered, and Jim, getting out of his chair, said, "Of course it is. Can I offer you tea, or coffee? Or something stronger?"

"Nothing, thanks."

"I've been here long enough to know that's British for tea," Scarlet said.

"No, it's OK, nothing. Really," Lauren said, and the conversation subsided into how she'd got here, how she could stay in the spare room if she wanted to, and how she had friends who would collect her tomorrow. Then Jim said, "Well, to celebrate this surprise, I think we should offer something," and went to the kitchen and came back with a bottle of whisky and five glasses. Barbara declined

– "I'll be driving eventually," she said – and the others accepted.

"Your father," said Jim, "was telling us how he went to university and wound up working with dead people for a living. I'm more and more interested, these days."

Robert, surprised, said, "It's not much of a story."

"Come on, Dad. Open up," said Lauren.

"Well, you could say they found *me*," he said.

"Yeah, right, like zombies", she said, extending her arms forward and dangling her fingers with, Robert now noticed, deep red fingernails that matched the tint at the tips of her hair.

"It wasn't planned, anyway," he said. "I went to Manchester to do a PhD. My tutor was a big-name American and it amazed me how much he knew."

"Did you, like, choose him? Or did he, like, choose you, or what?" Lauren asked. Something unsympathetic in her voice worried Barbara, and she looked over nervously at Robert, but he barged ahead.

"I was just assigned to him – but I trusted him." He leaned forward and drank his whisky.

"Then I went to see him, with an idea. I wasn't sure I was right, but I thought there was a chance. He just said it couldn't be right. For the first time, I didn't believe him. Didn't want to believe him."

He drank some more of his whisky and went on. "I spent three months getting nowhere, and then he showed me a new paper of his, just published. It was my idea, but bigger and better. And no mention of my name. Anywhere. I didn't know what to say."

"So what'd you do?" said Lauren, still pushing.

"Nothing. I mean, I tried to work on my own, but nothing came of it. I thought this was what it was supposed to be like, and I'd failed."

"So what happened?" said Lauren, probing again. "How come you got to cut up bodies?"

Robert finished his whisky.

"Rather late in the day," he said, "the department came to me. Things weren't going so well, they said, but there were always jobs in pathology if I was interested. With my existing qualifications it would be a one-year course, they could find the money, and I'd have a job."

"Why'd they do that?" asked Lauren.

"So I wouldn't be a failure on their books. Just a shift in career, happens all the time."

Jim picked up his packet of cigarettes and lit one. Lauren nudged him, he offered the packet to her, and she too lit up. Barbara started to speak but Lauren took a deep breath and slowly and smokily breathed out.

"And that's it?" Lauren asked. "That's how you got into bodies?"

"They weren't the first ones I'd seen. I'd been a medical student, remember. And besides, that's how we all end up."

Jim acknowledged the remark with a wave of his glass, and said, "Well, Lauren, there's your answer."

To break the awkward silence that followed, Jim began to talk to Lauren about where she was living and if she was listening to any interesting music. Scarlet asked Barbara about Robert and Jim's mother, saying Jim had never told her much about her, and Barbara began to say that Frances had wanted to help with Richard and Sarah but it got too difficult for her, suddenly aware that Lauren was soaking it all up.

"And then she got, well, very forgetful, and she had to be looked after herself, and we had to put her in a home, and that's where she died, and she was only seventy-two." Barbara stopped herself. "I'm sorry, I shouldn't have said that."

"Don't be," said Scarlet, "we've had some time trying to get used to it."

"I knew you'd put her in a home," Jim said.

Barbara, feeling judged, said, "You didn't see her in her final years."

Jim briefly lowered his head, considered his reply, and with an apologetic smile said, "It wasn't quite that simple."

"You could've found a week or two. You could've flown over. She'd have liked that. Before she got too old."

"I was in the States, eking out a living as an artist."

"He was too busy," Scarlet said. "He couldn't afford to turn down anything."

Barbara took a deep, angry breath and almost shouted at Jim, "You didn't even come to her funeral."

He looked back levelly. "No, I didn't. I've given you my reasons. But listening to you now, I do begin to wonder if she was my mother, or yours."

Barbara forced herself not to reply, and then found herself seized up with embarrassment. She looked at Lauren, but was unable to work out what she was thinking. Scarlet reached out a hand to her and said, "Come for a walk." She drew Barbara to her feet and they walked, arm in arm, round the garden.

"You'll stay for dinner?" Scarlet asked, and Barbara, anxious to make amends, said, "If you still want us."

"Of course," said Scarlet. "Of course we do."

Barbara, looking at a bed of tired oriental poppies with brown leaves, said, "They always need work, don't they."

"Men, sure," Scarlet replied. "Husbands especially."

"No, I meant these," Barbara said, pointing at the poppies.

Scarlet laughed. "Them too." And seeing that Barbara was embarrassed again, she went on "I try to look after the garden. It's one way of looking after Jim."

"I'm sure he appreciates it."

"No," said Scarlet. "No, don't be deceived, he's very much alone these days. An audience, any audience, will cheer him up, but mostly he's a long way away."

Barbara said nothing, and Scarlet led Barbara back to the house.

"Something I'd like very much," Jim announced after dinner, when wine had eased everyone's feelings, "is if you'd come sailing the Bristol Channel with us one weekend. Scarlet's found a great little pub we can stay in overnight."

Well, Barbara thought, as if putting Robert and Jim together on a boat, where presumably Jim could forget his worries and relax, was going to mend things long since broken. But the thought of being on a boat, a proper boat, crewed by someone who knew what he was doing while they lazily lived the grand life for a day had its appeal. She looked over at Robert.

"It could work," he said.

"Great," said Jim. "D'you want to fix up a date?"

"We'll ring you when we're back in London," Barbara replied, doubts entering her mind like drops of rain, and Robert nodded.

Barbara drove slowly up the hill and out of the village, Robert locked in thought beside her. It should have been just another opportunity to get to know the real Jim – but come to that, what was the real Robert? As if there was an essence locked away inside everyone somewhere that eluded the scalpel's careful search.

"Not the day we expected," he said.

"I shouldn't have said what I did," Barbara replied. "I really shouldn't. It's none of my business in the end." She stayed sunken in quiet for a moment, and then said, "I just couldn't stand him making all those excuses. He wasn't that busy. And what career? What bloody career keeps you from… ?"

"That bit about eking it out was just him being ironic."

"His parents? Your parents?"

Barbara drove on in the gathering dark, flicking the headlights as she overtook a cyclist. Robert took a deep breath and said, "Lauren turning up was a nice surprise."

"A surprise, anyway," said Barbara.

"I thought Jim and Scarlet dealt with it very well."

She rolled her eyes. "He did the naughty uncle number. It never fails. And she was rude, asking to stay out of the blue like that."

"They have a spare room. And she said her friends'll take her back to London tomorrow."

"And what was that about Scarlet teaching her to sing?"

"They were singing together in the kitchen preparing dinner," he replied. "I think Scarlet said something about practising together, and maybe Lauren could be a singer."

"You think she'll stick at it?" said Barbara, slowing the car down as they came into traffic. "It'd be a first."

"I think Scarlet really likes her," Robert replied.

"And did you mean to tell them," provoked, Barbara's voice was sharp, "all that self-piteous stuff about how you became a pathologist?"

He shook his head. "God, no. Not like that."

"You could just have said…" And she waited. Waited for him to say that perhaps Lauren's arrival had spooked him. But he didn't. Instead her told her about his encounter in Aldi.

"What did you expect?" she said.

"Not that. Not some crazy, ignorant vegan…"

"There's nothing wrong with vegans."

"All right, but you know what I mean."

"I don't," she said. "I don't know why you signed that letter."

"You mean you think he's right? He's probably never seen someone dying in his life. What does he know?"

"OK, maybe he doesn't know much. But yes, I do think he's right."

"And I'm a murderer?"

"No, you're not. But people will think that's what you're advocating."

"Vulnerable, well-meaning elderly being pushed to sign up by their avaricious children – I know what they say. But the letter…"

"It's Lily," said Barbara. "She's expensive to care for, she earns nothing, why shouldn't somebody, one day, maybe when we're not here…?"

"Nobody would."

"We've had to fight for her to get good care once already."

Robert nodded, accepting.

"If your letter catches on?" Barbara continued, "why

shouldn't somebody else think she's just a burden, and, and...?"

"No one's advocating that," said Robert. "No one will. That's not what the letter says."

"The letter. The letter," she said, shaking her head. "Robert, it's not gospel. If these ideas ever go through, they'll get rewritten, they'll get weakened. But it's not even that, it's trust. I don't want my sister to worry what her doctor's calculation is today. And when I get to be old and ill, nor do I."

"You might change your mind."

"I trust our children. I just hope I can trust you."

They stopped, each wondering whether to go on or to go back. After a time, Robert, attempting a joke, said, "Well, it won't be me. My patients are already dead, remember?"

She let the silence deepen in the car, took the left turn for Claverton Down, and followed the long curving hill back into Bath without saying anything until, after a time, Robert said, "Do you remember a doctor who was struck off ten years ago for prescribing all sorts of things to unhappy teenagers, and other stuff if they'd pay for it? He even got himself something of a reputation for doing drug advisory work with young people. Then there was a swoop on some festival and his name started coming up a bit too often. What was his name?"

"Martin? Martin something?"

"Martin Harris. That's it. Martin Harris. He came round this morning to see Jim. He calls himself Harrison these days. I thought I recognised him." He paused. "There was something odd about it."

"You think he's selling stuff to Jim now?"

"Or both of them." said Robert.

Barbara drove on for a while, then said, "That's not good."

She was silent again, and as they drove slowly into the town centre Robert said, "It's true, though, what you said – he didn't come to Mother's funeral. Or Father's, come to that."

"He didn't need me to go there and say so," Barbara replied.

She drove on without speaking until they were near the hotel, and then he said, "Why did you want to stay?"

"I couldn't leave just like that. And anyway, what were you so upset about?"

"I didn't like you telling me what to think about my mother. Telling Jim, I presume."

"She was a nice, sweet old lady."

"To you. A nice old lady. Who was in her fifties when you first met her." He glanced over at her, and she stared straight ahead, struck by the intensity of his reply.

"And not your mother," he added, when she didn't speak.

This was new. It wasn't his usual mix of affection and sadness for a woman to whom, he always said, life hadn't offered much. It felt like a fresh grievance, one she hadn't seen coming and, like all such things, unfair.

"She loved you," she said.

"I don't say she didn't."

He was insistent. A bitterness tinged his voice, hinting at a conflict that would edge out her own dismay.

"And the children," she added, knowing it wouldn't be enough to deflect him.

She pulled into the hotel car park and found a spot for the car.

"What did she have, after Dad was dead?" said Robert.

"Jim was off in the States. She had me, and she had her grandchildren. What else was she going to do?"

Barbara turned as much as she could to face him, thrown by the unexpectedness of it all, feeling cornered into saying, "She did her best."

"That's what I said. She did her best. And if you make me say it, then her best wasn't that much. And you know that, too."

She snapped back at him, "I'm not having a row in a car park."

"No point," said Robert. "Jim sorted it anyway. He made sure we stayed."

Robert put the bedside lights off. A faint light from the street seeped past the pleats in the curtains and cast images on the ceiling of the cars in the street, like so many pinhole cameras. Barbara sat in the only comfortable chair in the room, and said, "Is Lauren ready for this?"

Poor Lauren, Robert thought, the problem child we made for ourselves. Our way into everything difficult in our lives. He rolled over in the bed to face her and said, "She turned up, didn't she? Didn't have to be asked. Which is more than Richard and Sarah have done."

"Were you *ever* like her?" Barbara asked.

"I went to Oxford, I didn't come back. And didn't you, I don't know, push all the time?"

"Probably. You don't know about childhood till you've become a parent."

"That's like saying you don't know about your life until it's just about over."

"Maybe that's true too." She poured sparkling water into the glass she was holding. "What would you say if I said I don't want to come back again? That I'd rather stay in London? Would you mind terribly?"

He hadn't seen this coming. He waited, but she said nothing, and finally he spoke. "You haven't hit it off with Scarlet?"

"It's tough for her, I can see that. But I worry I'm just making things worse."

Robert pushed himself upwards, adjusted the pillows, and said, "You don't like *him*, is that it?"

She shook her head. "I hardly know him. We've managed fine without him…" Almost invisible in the chair, she added, "Was he always like this? Winding people up? Getting his own way?"

She drank from her glass and waited. Silence, she knew, worked on Robert. It wasn't easy, but if she could sit it out he would start to talk, stop seeing everyone he met – the living, and the dead he saw so often – as examples of some general types. The shell might soften, and he'd reveal more of himself.

"Of course," he said. "The big older brother." He was silent for a moment. "But I can't just walk away. Sorry, Jim, these visits aren't enough fun, I'd much rather stay at home and watch England beat India."

He could hear her pouring the rest of the sparkling water into the glass and drinking it.

"What are we doing with Jim tomorrow?" she said. "And the day after that? And the day after that? And why?"

They teetered again, he knew, on the edge of a row he did not want. He waited, and said as gently as he could "Come to bed."

She sat still, and said, "Would you mind if I don't come back?"

"I'd like you to. But it's up to you."

They stayed there in silence again for a while. Then she said "I don't think he even likes you."

"Why do you say that?"

She sat in the near dark with her empty glass, not knowing what to say or do.

"Come to bed," he repeated, gently. "We can talk in the morning."

Slowly she walked round the side of the bed, running her hand along the edge of the duvet to be sure she didn't bump into anything, and lay down. Soon she was asleep, and Robert lay there, kept awake by Jim's request. When Jim finally slipped beyond the reach of hope, what had he agreed to do for him? Drive him to the hospital for the last time, or home for the last time? Entrust him to the doctors in charge of his case, who would do what for him? Or had Jim, the thought lodged in his brain like a splinter, asked him to do more? To rise to Father O'Coran's challenge to advocate only what you are prepared to do yourself?

I've seen murders, Robert thought, suicides, accidental deaths. I've read signs of poverty, drugs, and folly. I read lives backwards. But I can't read this one. Because I am not ready.

Chapter 6

Early August 2018

The water lapped on the blue hull of the boat, which pitched gently in the slight swell. Huw Talbot, a muscular, heavily tattooed, sunburnt man in his early forties, navigated them away from the harbour, explaining with many reminiscences as he did so that he'd been a surfer until one accident too many convinced him he was getting too old for that lark and would be better off in boats. Jim sat near him, listening attentively, smiling at the glitter darting over the water like a shoal of mirrors. Scarlet and Barbara sat nearby, exchanging glances at Talbot's recital, and Robert sat opposite them, trying unsuccessfully to admire the view of the Somerset coast as it began to disappear behind them.

Huw took the boat out into the open channel and began to show Jim the navigational equipment and point out features of interest. Soon the two were in conversation about the pleasures and dramas of sailing, and barely perceptibly Scarlet began to relax. The sun was shining, there was a steady breeze, various boats and yachts around them added to the holiday feeling.

Perhaps, if Huw could keep Jim occupied, the day would pass off well. Perhaps.

The picnic lunch Scarlet had prepared passed with enough chatter about holidays. Jim was enjoying himself, telling his sailing stories, making everyone laugh, and that gladdened her, but Barbara was fussing around Robert, who was clearly uncomfortable and equally clearly unable to say so.

"Did your parents take you sailing when you were little?" Scarlet asked him. "I'm trying to work out why Jim's so damn keen on it."

"What's not to like?" said Jim.

"They didn't have the money for this sort of thing," Robert said.

"It wasn't just money," Jim said. "Our father would never have agreed to it. Not after the first time we went on a boat."

"That was a bit of a disaster," Robert said.

The boat rolled unexpectedly, and Robert grabbed the guard rail. Jim smiled. Huw started to steer the boat out of the choppy water, and talking stopped for a while. Barbara looked at Robert and asked in gestures if he wanted to go back down into the cabin. He shook his head, intent on giving the impression he was enjoying the trip.

Barbara looked across at Jim, who was saying something to Scarlet she couldn't catch. It made Scarlet laugh, she put her arms round Jim's neck and gave him a playful kiss. They stood there exchanging pleasantries, laughing, until Jim, with one arm round Scarlet, pulled them both down onto the benches that ran round the sides of the boat. Then he looked across at Barbara and grinned. "This is the life," he said, although the wind took his words away before they reached her.

Damn the man, she thought. If you forget everything about him that's making me worry, forget how ill he is, he's the only one here whose having fun. Who wants others to have fun. Who's keeping the whole foursome going. She smiled broadly back at him, and realised how easily she could be having fun too, and felt a shiver of a danger she was struggling to grasp.

Once they were in calmer water, Scarlet tried again to make conversation.

"It can't have been easy, having twins," she said, turning to Barbara.

"We managed," she replied.

"Robert's mother must have helped."

Jim looked over at them, suddenly interested.

"She'd been an army mum," Barbara said, "coping while her husband was away, telling you," she gestured at Jim, "brave stories about the man you must have barely remembered."

"I think that was her at her best," he replied.

"But when the twins came, he was dying of emphysema, and Frances was in the wrong place, wherever she was," said Robert.

Barbara got up, crossed to the other side of the boat, and took Robert's hand. Can't you read the signs? I'm not having us tell Scarlet that Frances, with so much experience, bound by love to you if not to me, had been nothing more than an extra pair of hands, hoping to do what she was told. How she'd held you as a baby; fed you, nursed you, washed you, attended to you every day, and now she was almost extra work.

She turned to Jim. "Do you remember your father coming home for good?"

To her surprise, his smile vanished, his eyes narrowed. He folded his arms and looked at her.

"Maybe not the actual day," he said.

No one spoke.

"I remember it," said Robert, trying to fill the silence. "I remembered it the other day, actually. I was at a funeral..."

"Whose?" Barbara asked.

"Josie Peters."

Barbara looked blank for a moment, and then said, "Homeless woman, TB?"

Robert nodded. "I was the only one there, apart from a student."

He leant back against the rail. That was what he did, he thought, sign people out at the end, work out how it was they got to pop up in front of him when it was too late, and wonder why it was they'd led the lives they'd had. "Anyway, I sat there, in the hospital crematorium, and I kept thinking of my father. Our father," he said, looking directly at Jim.

"And?" Jim said, staring back.

"I suddenly had this memory of our mother making you and me put on our best clothes and taking us to the railway station, which I'd never been to before. I must have been three. It was huge, noisy, and scary. It smelled of smoke, and the pigeons flew right at you. There were several other mothers and children, all waiting. And eventually a train came in and a whole bunch of men got off, shouting and waving as if it was a holiday, greeting the women, hugging and kissing them, and picking up the children and holding them high in the air. And there was a little man with a cigarette in his hand, kissing my mother and hugging you, and then picking me up. 'This is your daddy,' Mother said. And he said 'Remember me?' "

"And what did you do?" Scarlet asked.

"I think I said 'Did you bring me a present?' "

Scarlet laughed.

"But I do remember, very clearly," Robert went on, "Mother saying 'Having Daddy home is the best present you could both have,' and then him saying, 'Not Captain Parrish anymore.' "

Barbara smiled warmly, as she always did at the few stories Robert told about being a child, which came to her not as anecdotes but as secrets, patiently revealed.

Jim leant forward, picked a bottle of wine out of the cooler chest at his feet, and poured himself a glass. "It was a game changer, for sure," he said.

"I suppose so," Robert replied. We never talked about it. I mean, we talked about Dad and Mum, but…"

Barbara looked quizzically at him.

"Dad was a man of rules," Jim said. "That kind of gets to you as a kid."

Robert let the words sort themselves into a challenge. The wind was turning colder than he had prepared for, something about the way Jim sat there, his arms still folded, was annoying.

"You really caught it once," he said, falling into a story he realised he'd never told anyone. "Dad kept a chessboard at one end of the dining table, with a game in progress, absolutely not to be touched, and Jim stole a queen," he went on, turning to Barbara and Scarlet. "Dad noticed, of course, and locked him out in the yard in the rain until he admitted it and returned the stolen piece, and then Father beat him. Shouting, with each blow, 'Never do that. Never touch it again.'"

"I remember that," Jim said. "Not that I want to."

And you," Robert turned back to Jim, "went to our bedroom without waiting to be ordered, refusing to cry. So Dad turned on me and shouted for me to go too, and I went, but you wouldn't talk about it."

"I never did understand," Jim said, "why you didn't get into more trouble."

"Maybe I learned the lesson first time around, like I learned most lessons. Keep your head down, do what you're told. Wait until you can slip away."

"I don't think you see much with your head down all the time."

"You always won," Robert replied. "That's what I remember."

Barbara, alarmed at the way the conversation was going and new bitterness in Robert's voice, said "You didn't turn out so badly."

"I worked out," Robert went on, "Dad spent fourteen years in the army. All the way to Suez. Knowing he could be asked to lose his life, for his country, for what it says it stands for. And he believed in it. He came home having done his duty, and he wanted peace."

"Everything," Jim said, and there was coldness in his voice, "in its place, he used to say."

The boat pitched unexpectedly, and Robert grabbed again for the rail, spilling his drink. Barbara looked at him and shook her head. Don't say anything.

"I think I'd better go to the cabin," Robert said, and he cautiously made his way there. Barbara followed him.

"I admit it, it's a mistake," he said to her.

"It will be if you carry on like this."

"Maybe it's this damn boat," he said.

"Maybe, but we're on it for hours and we're better off trying to enjoy it."

Everything in its place. It tugged at him. He realised that with a little effort he could probably recall every room in every house he'd ever owned, all the way up to buying the current place when the twins were little, and the stories that punctuated his life: his childhood, his time with Barbara. Properly curated, that would capture more than half of him. Add a room resembling his lab at work and the whole site could easily be him, museumed. *These* things had brought him pleasure, or comfort; *these* marked the stages of his life. Some computer geek could doubtless arrange for the television to play selections of his favourite shows from the past. Whispered voices could summon up the big conversations and hint at happiness or pain. The children's rooms could be rearranged regularly to show what they had been like at different times, although his own childhood would be more of a mystery. Because now, Jim's return cast a suspicion of fraud over it. Yes, these things embodied the choices he and Barbara had made, but in what sense were they his? He had led this life, and taken pleasure and even pride in it at times, but now there was another way to see it. Not positive choices but negative ones, switching light and dark, turning moving towards into moving away. A house of what was not chosen, but merely happened. A life lived in retreat.

Visitors would come trailing bored children, meander through the few rooms, and stay for less time than they had planned, the more discerning beginning to feel that the whole elaborate, confected thing was somehow false, and something was missing. It tugged at him. Everything is in its place, and you can believe this had been a life, but the pieces have moved slightly, and look at how it holds together now. There was a story, and now he began to fear there was another story underneath, further back.

Jim stood framed in the doorway to the cabin, the mid-afternoon sunlight behind him.

"The sailor's life's not for you?" he said.

Robert shook his head.

"Come up on deck anyway," Jim said. "Scarlet and I think you'll want to see this."

Robert and Barbara followed him back up.

"Over there," he said, pointing off to his right.

"What are we looking for?"

"Can't see them? Try these," Jim said, and he took the binoculars from around his neck and gave them to Robert. He looked, and was about to say he couldn't see anything when, in surprise, he said "Dolphins?"

"Huw's trying to get us closer."

Robert passed the binoculars to Barbara, who said "Aren't they great?"

The boat rolled, and Barbara put out her arms to catch Robert.

"Better sit down," Jim said. "Huw says the next few minutes will be a little rough."

Steadily they began to chase the dolphins, which were swimming fast, leaping out of the water as if for the sheer pleasure of it, and for a time their pleasure was contagious. Huw brought the boat up close, and the dolphins briefly gave it some attention. Scarlet and Barbara had their mobiles out, attempting to photograph the elusive creatures, and to Jim's amusement they shared their pictures of noses, tails, and waves. Robert sat, quietly marvelling at the excitement until the pod suddenly switched direction, and Huw, with a shake of his head, indicated he wouldn't be following it.

"Now do you see what sailing can be?" said Jim.

"That was really good," Robert admitted.

"Mother knew how to have fun," Jim said. "When we were little."

He turned away and sat down at the stern. Barbara caught Robert's arm, and angrily shook her head.

Even before Huw took them back to the harbour, Jim was exhausted. Scarlet led him down to the cabin, wrapped a blanket around him, and sat with him. Robert and Barbara, out of place, could do nothing but watch the English coastline becoming visible off to the right. Time was up.

The next morning, they announced that they would be going back to London. They could see that only Scarlet was disappointed, and also that she understood why they were going. They left in a mist of pleasantries, and didn't talk much on the way home, each trapped in their own version of the weekend.

That evening, Scarlet rang and spoke to Barbara, who was in the middle of preparing dinner. They were getting serious about the gig, Scarlet said, but the guitarist they wanted was still on tour. If Jim's health would hold up for long enough they might try for a date in mid-October. Would she and Robert like to come? Barbara said she'd ask him, when he got back, but it sounded like a good idea.

It didn't. It grated on her that she would have to convey this loaded request to Robert, grated still more that he would want to accept it. He never listened to that sort of music – hadn't for what, thirty years? Nor did she. Lauren had taken all their rock'n'roll records on one of those occasions when she'd left home; probably they were now in some house she never went to anymore. It didn't matter, they didn't want to play them. Aren't there things that you just, well, grow out of?

"Of course we can go," he said. Then, seeing her turn back to peeling the carrots, he said, "You don't want to go?"

"It's not up to me, is it," she said. "It's what you always do — turn up. For things like this."

She turned back to face him, still holding the peeler in her hand. "Do you actually want to go? And listen to second-rate rock'n'roll in a pub somewhere near Bath? With a load of ageing hippies into crystals and spiritual realignment?"

"I'm not sure I'm as familiar with the scene as you are."

"I'm not going to argue."

Robert poured himself a whisky and sat down. She finished the carrots and put them in the stew. Then she topped up her gin, joined Robert at the kitchen table, and, when he said nothing, asked, "When did you last hear him?"

"You were there," he replied, "it was the first time you'd met. It was some 'authentically rural' pub outside Reading, and Jim arrived half an hour late."

"I was pregnant with the twins?"

"That's right. He splashed out on drinks only he could drink, and when the conversation flagged he got up and played the piano in the place."

She sat in silence for a moment, and then said, "And I tricked you into going back." Robert looked puzzled. "I said I must have left something behind, so you drove back, and he was playing a Beatles' song, and then something really fast. He was good, it was exciting. And then he saw me, and played something really slow and sad. I remember."

"Doesn't sound like it inspired a lasting love of his music."

"Wouldn't you be excited? The long-lost brother makes an appearance. Sheds new light on the family you've married into."

He took a deep breath and closed his eyes, as he often did when he was preparing to say something difficult. Barbara waited for him to speak.

"I have to tell you something," he said. "Jim asked me about the letter."

"And?"

"He asked me if I'd make his death less scary, and... I said I'd do what I could."

"Jesus, Robert. What have you agreed to?"

They stared at each other across a coldness that was new to them.

"I'll hold his hand," Robert said. "Maybe help him find a hospice when the time comes. That's all I can do."

Barbara suddenly felt a long way off, swept there by the silent questions she could never put into words. How disturbing it'd been to move in with a man, to marry him, and almost never to see his parents. To listen to his faltering explanations, how his father was ill and his mother had to look after him, how now was not the right time to visit and why he should go on his own, and never quite believe him. To find out, late in the day, that he had a brother he never saw and wouldn't talk about, when she saw her sister, Lily, every week. And now this brother was pushing him around, and pulling him towards what? A hint of alarm that she couldn't identify passed over her, as if the fabric of the house had briefly turned to painted cardboard, ready to be torn down. She drained her glass, took it to the sink, and rinsed it. "Is that what this stupid gig's all about?"

He gestured with his empty hands. "No. Maybe."

"You want to go?"

"It means a lot to them."

Without turning to look at him, she said, more forcefully than she meant, "I don't know. You might have to work this one out on your own for a bit."

When he still didn't reply, she said, "Ring Scarlet in the morning, tell her you'll go, whenever it is."

He headed out of the room. She looked at him. "I'll tell you something," she called out. "He played the same songs for us the other day, when we went to see him. He remembered."

That Friday, Robert had arranged to meet Lauren for lunch at a little Greek restaurant not far from the hospital, and to his surprise when he turned up she was already there, a Diet Coke in front of her.

"You're on time," he said with a smile.

"You're late," she replied, smiling back.

They chose a bunch of mezes, and while they waited for them to arrive, he said, "How was your stay with Jim and Scarlet?"

"It was cool. I like them."

"What made you go?"

"I dunno. I mean, like, he's my uncle."

"Still, no one asked you to," Robert said, and he reached out to squeeze Lauren's hands. "You know he's pretty ill, don't you?"

"Yeah, you said. They don't talk about it."

"I'd say, right now, that means don't ask. Your going there says a lot."

Lauren shrugged and sipped her drink. Hummus, falafel, and other standard delicacies began to arrive, and were divided between them. The conversation stuttered along, kept going with comments on the food, until Lauren explained that she had a new job, working for a small recording company.

"That's good," said Robert. "How'd you get it?"

"I think Scarlet put a word in," she said.

"I'm afraid we're not much use, your mum and me, at finding things like that."

"No. S'all right, though, it's not like I was expecting anything."

"Good to know we've done all we can for you."

Lauren managed a smile and a nod.

The baklava arrived, a little dry, and two Americanos. Lauren shuffled in her seat, picked a portion of the baklava off her father's plate, and said, "How're *you* getting on with them? With Jim?"

Robert scratched his forehead and let out a deep breath. "Don't know," he said. "Look, we weren't close. And now… now I feel people want us to make up. Be friends before it's too late."

"Who does?"

"Scarlet for one. She doesn't say so…" He looked at Lauren for confirmation, and she looked back. "You," he said, "the way this conversation's going."

"Mum?"

He stopped himself from saying that Barbara no longer wanted to see them, and said, "You'll have to ask her."

"What about Jim?"

Change the subject, Robert thought. Change the subject.

"I can't read him at all," he said. "Getting us back in touch was her doing. Now, he says he wants me around at the end, to make it less scary."

"Because of the letter?" Lauren asked.

"How'd you know about it?"

"Dad, lots of people know about it. I've had friends ask me if you're my dad because of it."

"Have you read it?"

"Yeah." A pause, then more warmly, "Yeah."

"It's nothing to do with Jim, you know."

"You still haven't said how you're getting on," Lauren said. "Except you have, in a way."

A waiter came up with the bill, and Robert automatically checked it. "I'm going back because they want me to. Because I want to. That's all I can say."

In the street they briefly hugged.

"It must be kind of weird, suddenly getting your brother back," said Lauren, and Robert shrugged and gave a rueful nod. Then they parted, Lauren going one way and Robert the other.

"Like it?" Lisa asked in Costa, showing her new arm-length tattoo to Lauren.

"No," Lauren thought. "Yeah, cool," she said.

"It's like this snake goddess protecting the tree of life."

Lauren sipped her macchiato.

"Well, since you're so chatty today," Lisa went on, "who's this older guy you're seeing in wherever?"

"Jesus, Lisa, he's my uncle."

"Sure, I believe you." And when Lauren said nothing, Lisa said "Hey, ease up, I really do. But what's the story?"

"I told you. He's just turned up. Even Dad hasn't seen him in, like, ages."

"So why go?"

"He's a pianist. And she sings."

"And so do hundreds of new guys a year. You been staying off Twitter or something?"

"No, he's good. He made a living at it, with her. And I like them."

"So you think... ?"

"No, I go 'cause I like them."

Lisa raised an eyebrow.

"Hey, you're the 'It's all rigged, it's just who you know' queen of Hackney."

Lisa's eyebrow stayed up.

"All right, she's helped me. But, honestly, I like them. So you can drop the cynical face."

Lisa obliged, and the conversation drifted on until Lauren got up to leave.

"Where you going?" Lisa asked.

Lauren shrugged. "A walk, maybe."

Outside, Lauren took a train, intending to mooch round Camden Market, but changed her mind, stayed on and got off at Hampstead Heath, walked up past the first lake and on to a run of trees with a view over the Heath, where she sat down, took out a small joint from the tin she carried with her, and lit up. Lisa was wrong, which didn't matter, she was a good friend. She'd have thought the same if it was Lisa going, well, weird. Hanging out with someone who wasn't even going to make it much longer, which she hadn't told Lisa. And wouldn't. But Jim and Scarlet? She drew on the joint and exhaled slowly. Why you two? No grand thoughts, OK. Nobody does grand thoughts. All that moral bullshit people just say and even they don't believe it. She finished the joint no wiser, and looked around. Perhaps all the people she could see were just as confused, waiting just as much for a door to swing open and close behind them. And them only. To go through, follow where

103

it takes you, because it won't come again. Hey, maybe the stuff was stronger than usual, Christ, I'll be floating away like one of Lisa's world spirits if I'm not careful. Ring Scarlet in the evening, nothing definite, just hi, how are you, I wanted to, to what? Lie back, get comfortable, watch the world go round for a couple of hours. And then ring.

Chapter 7

Late August 2018

Robert put his suitcase by the front door, ready early to go back to Bath for the weekend, and went out into the garden to say goodbye. Barbara tugged at the lapels of his light summer jacket, and said "You going to be OK?"

"Why ever not?"

"Be careful, is all I'm saying." She paused, wondering if she should say what was on her mind. "And now," she said, "you're doing the decent thing, like you always do. You do it out of kindness. And I've loved you for that."

She hadn't expected to say that. Not with its dangerous ambiguity. Hoping to hide it, she leant forward and kissed him.

"And I love you," he said, and turned away, picked up his suitcase, and drove off.

Agitated, she found herself remembering the first time he'd stood her up. They were going to see a film. She'd waited in the cinema queue for an hour, edging closer and closer to the ticket booth, unable to leave to find a phone without losing her place, not knowing what to do, looking for him all the time, and when she'd got to the head of the queue the man behind her had suddenly said 'I'll buy you a ticket, love,' and she'd said, 'No, no, two tickets, please, the expensive tickets, my boyfriend's coming, he's just running late,' and taken the tickets and stepped away. And stood there and waited until the film started, and then gone back to her flat, pinned the tickets to the cork board in the kitchen so he'd see them if he ever came, and started to drink, and at ten o'clock there was a knock at the door. And there he was, explaining there'd been an emergency at the hospital, someone's temperature had shot up and there'd been a chance if they quickly ran some tests, and it'd been touch and go for two hours and he couldn't ring it was so hectic. And then the man had died. No one with him, no family. Nurses and doctors, of course, and equipment and drips, and monitors, but no one who knew him. Just an old man whose daughter lived a hundred miles away and who couldn't have suspected, any more than they had, that he was about to go.

How sorry Robert had been. Sorry he was late, sorry he couldn't have got in touch. He'd asked if she'd seen the film, and she'd said no, she hadn't seen it, and suddenly she hadn't known what to think, and she'd realised at the very moment he'd let her down that she was going to trust him. He'd sat on her little sofa and stared at the floor and hadn't wanted to talk or make love, and seemed to be lost, and they'd slept together in her narrow bed and gone to work together the next day, and she'd thought he's a kind man, and I want a kind man, I hadn't known. I'd thought I wanted something else, but after all I wanted a kind man, and he is kind.

She remembered how, when the passion between them, the languorous immersion in the warmth of their skins, the playing at waiting, the speeding up and slowing down of their wonderful engrossing twoness, had dissolved into the daily business, the weekly business, of their lives, the ups, and the sudden, terrible down, she had loved him for his kindness. And she wished he was still there, so she could pull him towards her and put her arms around him; she would have run after him, but he was gone.

She began to attack a sprawling mass of bluebells that were threatening to take over the flower beds. She dug down to the roots and wrenched them out one by one, all the time thinking how he would often say to her we can finally do something about pain, and even death, and reject the useless talk about suffering, and God's understanding, and God's inscrutable way, and say 'No, we can do something about this, you needn't suffer, and this time you needn't die. Not as a child, or a mother giving birth, not in this accident, not with this disease.' And now he had signed that awful letter and hadn't even listened to her. Yes, death will mark you with age and infirmity, and patiently wait. One day you will see him in the stoop of your body and the lines in your face, hear him in the first hints of deafness. But how, she thought, could Robert do death's business for him?

To banish these thoughts she briefly gave up on the bluebells and sat in a chair in the garden. She thought of the births of Richard and Sarah, and her switch from being a secretary into jobs in human resources, where she'd taken decisions and instructed secretaries, who were now mostly gone, until now, where she works in a team juggling finances on a battered desktop machine connected to the hospital server somewhere. Where did they go? Where would she be, she thought, if she hadn't climbed upwards, encouraged by Robert, escaping a flood she didn't know was coming?

She went back to the bluebells, digging them out, shaking off the soil, cutting them out at their roots, wordlessly digging deeper and deeper, until just after twelve she stopped, annoyed with herself that she'd be late, went into the house, had a quick lunch, changed her clothes, and waited for Lauren to arrive. When Lauren was ten minutes late Barbara phoned her, but it went straight to voicemail. Five minutes later, just as she was getting into the car ready to go on her own, Lauren turned up.

"There wasn't a bus," she said.

"You could try leaving earlier," Barbara replied. "Get in."

Lauren did. "Isn't Dad coming?" she said.

Barbara drove off briskly. "He's down in Bath visiting Jim and Scarlet."

"What's he make of him?"

"Too much, frankly. They never got on as children, and now he's down there every weekend."

"Jim is dying."

"I don't want to sound unkind, but not any time soon."

"Mum, what's that mean?"

Barbara drove in silence for a while, trying to pick her words with better care. "Your dad has a pet project."

Lauren listened politely, and said, "That sounds like Dad. A conversation. What's wrong with that?"

"And he's said something to Jim about making it less scary for him."

"Like, hold his hand. Dad told me. That's nice." Lauren was quiet for a moment then said, "And you connect that to the letter – how?"

"I'm not going to argue," Barbara said.

"Mum, no one's going to be bumped off."

Barbara winced and said nothing.

"Seriously, they're not," Lauren said.

"I'm not going to argue," Barbara said again.

She stopped to buy some yellow and red roses, which she carefully gave to Lauren, and drove on until the grounds of the care home were visible on her left. She parked near it and they walked to the door and rang the bell. One of the carers came up, smiled and let them in. Barbara smiled back, and she and Lauren took the lift to the second floor, Room 28. She knocked on the open door and the woman in the armchair stirred from her reverie and looked at her.

"We brought you some fresh flowers," Barbara said. "I'll get rid of those," gesturing at the vase on the little table.

"Mum did," said Lauren.

"Can I smell them?" Lily said, and she buried her face in them. "They're lovely."

Barbara got rid of the old flowers, put fresh water in the vase, and, taking the flowers from her sister, put them in the vase. "Before I go, I'll ask someone to trim them so they look really nice," she said.

"They do look nice," said Lily.

"You look nice, too," said Barbara. "That green top really suits you."

"And so does Lauren," Lily said. "Those torn jeans are very fashionable."

Barbara perched herself on the end of the bed, took Lily's hands in hers, and said, "Now you must tell me all the exciting things you've been doing this week. I think someone's been to do your hair."

This was the ritual they played out every time Barbara came; that smiling, contented Lily was the busy one and she, Barbara, lived a quiet routine existence. And indeed, to hear Lily tell it, her life was full. She had people to talk to, and two or three days a week people came to play music in the big room downstairs, sometimes schoolchildren, sometimes the local church choir, sometimes just a pianist, and people would join in, and if by Saturday Lily couldn't quite remember who had come on what day, well, that didn't matter.

After a time, Barbara suggested that they go for a walk round the grounds, but Lily shrank back.

"I don't want to go," she said.

"Come on," Barbara said gently. "It's such a lovely day. Look at the sun streaming in through the window. I'll hold onto you all the time."

Lily let herself be persuaded and they went for their regular walk. Barbara watched carefully as they walked past other residents, carers, and visitors. Lily would never say if she didn't like someone, but she would stiffen up and stop talking if someone she didn't trust came by, and Barbara would have a word with a senior staff member about it if that happened. But today was calm, Lily leant on Barbara and walked with her very pronounced limp once round the garden, then they sat arm in arm on a bench for a while, and then they all went in and had tea.

"I like the cakes," Lily said.

"You must be careful," Barbara said, "Don't put on too much weight." Although much younger than her sister Lily was definitely weightier.

At four o'clock a singer turned up who was also a magician. He began at the piano and played and sang the Beatles' 'Yellow Submarine'.

"I like this song," Lily said, and she joined in with Lauren and some of the other residents.

Then the magician sang a couple of Abba songs, and finished this part of his act with a version of 'Goodnight, Irene' that Lily particularly liked. She smiled and held hands with Barbara and Lauren as they sang too.

But when the magician began to do his magic tricks, Lily turned to Barbara and said, "Magic's silly, magicians always have things hidden in their pockets for when you're not looking."

"I agree," Barbara said, even if she couldn't see how that helped.

"It's deceitful," Lily said, and she withdrew a little and didn't applaud when the tricks finished. Sensing Lily's discomfort, Barbara took them back up to Lily's room. She and Lauren settled her in, and she asked Lauren what she'd been getting up to.

"This and that," said Lauren. "I've got a new job, working for a recording company."

Lily seemed happy with that, even if Barbara didn't, and they all talked a little more, before Barbara and Lauren got up, kissed Lily goodbye and promised to come back soon, and Lily wished them both well and settled back into her chair to wait for dinner.

Standing by the car, Barbara said "Well, are you glad you came?"

Lauren nodded and said "Yeah."

"She's always happy to see you."

Lauren let that slip by her, and Barbara said "People think she's different, you know." She paused. "I did, when I was a child." She looked searchingly at Lauren, who looked back, waiting to see where this would go. "Then I realised she isn't. She's just like us."

"I know, Mum."

"I mean, not people where she is now." When Lauren said nothing, Barbara opened the car door and looked enquiringly at her daughter.

"I'll walk back to the tube station," Lauren said, and with a brief hug she was gone.

Barbara watched her go. How like her Lauren was, and how different; how certain and how uncertain. Making temporary choices she herself could never have made. Seemingly confident, Robert's daughter, oddly rational where she was instinctive, but underneath anxious and adrift. And that was the widening gap between them. Lauren could be forgiven, too young to hear winter in the wind agitating the leaves of the aspen nearby. But Robert, surely he of all people must feel it? Beneath his smooth surface, polished every day by denial, it now seemed to her, which she reached towards but could not touch, would not let itself be touched. The struggle between hot and cold, that ends in an emptiness not to be managed, still less brought about. No, that winter frightens her.

As Barbara drove away she found herself thinking of Paul, as she often did whenever she could not keep busy enough and had time to worry. A part of her life that unfolded inexorably, obsessively in her memory. Paul, the classic surgeon, super-confident in everything except how he's seen by his peers, the other surgeons in bigger hospitals with even bigger salaries, who boast you'll never see a surgeon in theatre hesitate at the start of an operation, it's "Shall we begin?" and the first incision is dramatic, swift, practised, just exactly right. The completed movement of the knife that signals mastery. Mastery over the patient anaesthetised in front of everyone, mastery over the condition that lies beneath the skin, mastery over everyone else in the room. That says, "Trust me, you are in good hands, the best there are."

She'd seen a lot of Paul because the lawyers were so busy with surgery: one of the junior surgeons was alleging that management had breached the Race Relations Act in repeatedly passing him over for promotion while promoting others less competent than him. Paul was adamant the decisions were correct, every time, and it had been Barbara's job to show that all the checks were in place and always had been. Training in the Race Relations Act had been given, interview procedures had been followed, advice given, mentoring offered and accepted, specialist medical training offered and accepted. Every 't' dotted, every 'i' crossed, she and Paul used to joke.

Paul knew everyone in the hospital, no one wanted this case to go anywhere, and he and Barbara had made sure it didn't. It was over in little more than the time it took to lead the judge through the huge pile of documents he'd had her get ready.

How pleased we'd been, she thought, and how pleased

the hospital management had been with us. We came out of court and it was snowing, it was beautiful, even in central London, but there was trouble with the tubes and the trains. Paul rang the hospital and got management to agree we could stay the night in a hotel because it was such a famous victory. Robert was looking after the children, and he was pleased, and Richard and Sarah were pleased, and said I'd won it on my own and Daddy was helping them bake a cake to celebrate, a chocolate cake. We went to a French place in Soho that Paul knew, and ate well and drank well and went back to the hotel and did what I thought I'd never do. And not just in London, but when we got back.

Oh God, Paul, how could I have settled for less, when just to have you touch my body sent me nearer to the sun? I opened up to you, ecstatic, alive as I hadn't been since Richard and Sarah were born. And when I said that we should end it, how painful it was that you were gentle, and respectful, and agreed. I'd wanted rage, granite refusal, for you to say we're bound together, it can't end, and certainly not then. All you'd given me were your practised hands, your skill, your years of experience, and now I was discharged, healthy and fit to go home. Everything will be all right, get back in touch if you have any worries.

Which is why I'd told you, Robert. I hadn't planned to. When I'd thought ahead I'd always thought I'd never tell you. Each time would be just one more lie in a sequence of lies, until the final lie that would tie everything up in a bag that could be left to be forgotten. There'd be an arc into the sun, and a descent that would be my secret sorrow, my sadder but wiser memory that I'd revisit when

I was old and such things wouldn't happen again, and I'd have learned to be glad of it. And you would never know. Instead, I was angry, and ashamed, and bitter, I wanted forgiveness and I wanted to punish. To punish you for not being a blazing sun, to punish myself for being so foolish as to smash everything we had.

And you forgave me. Not then, not at once. No, we juggled our coldness, our desire to hurt, to have the last word, juggled it past the children, or so we hoped, whispering to each other angrily in bed, eating lunch alone when the children were round at friends, throwing ourselves into long hours at work, denying that anything was wrong to my parents, and to your mother who even then didn't notice much. Juggling our emotions past the realisation that everyone knew, that that was what those glances and those muttered words were about. That we were this spring's gossip. Very little of it was true.

And you kept saying, "I love you, Barbara, not as I did when we began, but in a quieter way. If that's not what you want then you should leave, but truly I do." And I'd thought my last chance of passion was gone, I'd taken it and had only an invisible scar to show for it, and this kind, trusting man is offering affection, which he calls love, and I'd be a fool to turn it down, and I didn't want to be a fool again, and so I'd said, "Robert, I still love you. What I did is done, over, buried beneath a desert. But we love each other, or we can again, and I want that, and if you will have me back I will come back to you, fully." And you said you would.

And to prove it to ourselves, and to prove it to our children, and to everyone else, we had Lauren. Unhappy, aggrieved, insecure Lauren, so unlike the other two. Causing us worries even before you were born. Did you hear us in my womb arguing, did you hear me say to your father, "We can make this work, I'm sure we can," and feel us roll to face away from each other and fall into uneasy sleep? In the painful weeks before you were born, did you think already that you were heading into trouble? Did my blood bring you news, tiny chemicals carrying my fears like refugees shouting across the thin wall that separated us, that you took to your anxious heart and told you to travel light, be ready to move on, move away, trust no one? Because you were a runt, unlike the two big guzzling ones before you. Born early, with a thin face and staring grey eyes, who took time to suckle but then did so greedily, and slept only fitfully. Who snatched at things and clutched them hard, played often on your own, and shouted and cried. Who never settled in at school and had few friends, and somehow did OK, more than OK, although your teachers never knew what to say about you. Who patrolled the outer edges of the family, too young for the games we played with the others, too young for the conversations we had with them, but still sometimes shot down the shallow things they said, who saw too young the complexities, the other sides, the undercurrents of life.

And one Christmas I begged you "Please, Lauren, please, just join in. Sing in the hospital choir, the patients like it, everyone does, and there'll be other children to play with. And presents afterwards, at home – no, not the ones under the big tree in the main entrance, those are for the children in the hospital, some of whom are very ill. Well, one was run over by a car that didn't stop, isn't that awful, and some just came out of their mummies all wrong and there's not much anyone can do about that until maybe when they're older if we can get them that far, and some have very unusual illnesses that you will never have, don't ever worry about that. So it's right that they get those presents, don't you think?" And you listened gravely and said "And some of them will die and then Daddy will try to find out what really went wrong?" and I said, "Yes, but that will never happen to you." And I wanted to hold you really tight but you pushed me away and sat on a chair across the room and didn't say anything.

Back home, she took the savaged bluebells to the compost, and restless went back to the chair, moved it into the sunlight, and sat down. The time, to her surprise, was after six. Robert, she realised, will most likely be talking to Scarlet, Jim will be dozing lightly, there will be plans for dinner. It didn't bother her that Robert was spending time with an attractive younger woman, because she knew beyond question that Scarlet was devoted to Jim and had no interest in anyone else. She knew this because it was obvious, and this was part of what upset her. She wanted to believe that her own love for Robert was of the same kind, but she feared it was not, although she expected that after all it would last until they were parted by death. It was the dullness of the prediction, which even so fell short of certainty, that upset her. That Jim, whom she did not like, should have attracted a woman so evidently in love with him, while Robert, a decent, trustworthy man with, she was sure, fewer faults, had only her fractured love to see him out, little more, at times, than her sense of duty. Her own life, too was closing down, or rather emptying out. Not exactly ending, like Jim's, who's only sixty-eight. But there will be less and less of it. Yes, Richard and Sarah are settled, and will in a few years produce grandchildren, which she very much wants, but Lauren is a mystery. And it is Lauren who is the most alive to her, not because she is the youngest, but because she is the most unpredictable. She might have said, she has said to Robert often enough, that she has accepted this quiet stage of her life, and she's glad she's no longer young, although she privately feels a chill wind in everything she does. But Jim will not live much longer. His every breath whispered to her that the quiet years she so much wants may not be there. The chill wind may empty out into nothingness at any time, and that is something she had long ago decided never to believe. For who will look after Lily then? -- who is the kindest person she knows. And what will Jim do, as he nears the end? What, she wondered, will he ask of Robert then? A veil lifted, and she tugged it shut, afraid of the blackness behind it. Afraid of what Robert had signed up to? Surely not. No, she said to herself, surely not.

Chapter 8

Late September 2018

As Robert packed an overnight bag for his trip to Bath, Barbara leant on the frame of the bedroom door and said, "All I'm saying is, have you told Jim what you think of him? What you make of him now?"

Robert didn't respond.

"Damn it, Robert, do you even like him?"

He shrugged and carried on packing. "Where d'you want me to begin?" he replied. "We didn't get on as children. He doesn't need me to tell him."

"You can do better than that," said Barbara.

Robert got to the hotel two hours later than he had hoped, after a journey full of roadworks, tailbacks and delays, still picking over Barbara's parting words. He parked in the last space in the car park, and rang Scarlet.

"It's only me," he said, adding, although why he was still covering for her he didn't know, "Barbara couldn't come."

Did he detect a slight pause? Even a note of relief in her voice as Scarlet said, "Just you, then." A hint of irritation in his own voice as he said, "I'll have dinner here first, and come over when the traffic's lighter."?

"No," she said. "Come tomorrow. Jim's going to bed soon."

There was something abrupt in her voice that unsettled him, but he agreed, and hung up, the irritation spreading in him like the dampness in the air.

He checked into the hotel, ate an uninspired meal in the restaurant rather than go to the effort of finding somewhere better with a table for one on a Friday evening, and went up to his room. Although it was a double, it was a smaller one than usual and the bed nearly filled it. The mustard-coloured walls and curtains should surely be top of the list for redecoration. There was a dark green armchair, and a wooden chair by a small bedside table cluttered with the vacuous magazines you only find in hotels. He knew without looking that the drawer contained a bible and nothing else. There was a small television bolted to the wall, but none of the few films on the film channel were any good. He sat on the bed and began to read the novel he'd brought with him, but he wasn't in the mood for a demanding read and quickly chucked it aside.

He settled for an early night but fell asleep slowly; no position was quite right, the pillows were the wrong size, he couldn't decide if he was too hot or too cold. He tried resigning himself to a poor night's rest, and chased half-formed thoughts as each one dissolved into the next.

The phone rang insistently. The room was surprisingly dark, it took two more rings for him even to realise it was his phone that had woken him, three more to remember where the switch for the bedside light was, two to adjust to the light and to pick up the phone. What can it be that Barbara has to say at one in the morning? What can Lauren have done now that requires he be told at once? Especially when he's down here in Bath? What has happened?

It was Scarlet. The surprise jolted him, and he sat up.

"Robert, Robert, are you awake?"

He mumbled a reply.

"It's Jim." He tensed, waiting for something he dreaded, and she went on, "He's disappeared."

He swung his feet out of the bed and started looking for his clothes. "When?"

"I don't know. I came back late."

"Do you want me to come over?"

"Would you? Please. That'd be…" Her voice tailed off, she was quiet for a moment, and then, barely audible, she said, "Maybe it's nothing." Another pause and then, a little louder, "He's always turned up before."

The lights were on in every room in the Cotswold house when he arrived, the only house in the street with lights on of any kind. Scarlet was standing in the doorway waiting for him. As he got out of the car she came down the path to meet him, kissed him briefly, and said in a rush, "Thank you. Thank you for coming. We'll go in my car, I know where to look."

They set off without speaking. She drove fast, the car

following the headlights along the curving road, their beams catching hedges and walls and, on the crests of each rise, the ghostly shape of trees framing the road ahead. The full moon, when it broke through the clouds, picked out silver shapes in the fields.

To break the silence, he asked, "What are we looking for?"

"It's a white Ford Fiesta."

"Pubs? Lay-bys?"

"He had his favourite places."

She drove on. "Maybe he got drunk somewhere and fell asleep. That wouldn't be so bad." And after a time, she added "He's always come back."

Bradford-on-Avon was empty when they came to it; no one was walking, no one was driving. Scarlet pulled up at one shuttered pub and then another, drove around the empty car parks, and pressed on to Trowbridge. A white Ford was parked carelessly near a church, but it wasn't Jim's. The pubs were shut, the car parks blank. She drove on, through a straggling village and on to Westbury. At the first roundabout they came to Scarlet swung the car left, followed the road round to a T-junction, turned right and at big crossroads turned left, away from town.

She sped up, and in a mile she came to another crossroads, turned left, and in less than a mile turned off the road into a car park and spun the car round. There was a camper van, a battered white van, a dark blue car, and a white Ford. She drove up and stopped alongside it. "It's his," she said, and leapt out to look through its windows. "Damn, it's empty," she said, trying the doors, which wouldn't open.

"Then he's got the keys," said Robert. "He's here somewhere."

"I know where he is," she said. She went back to her car, took out a torch, and set off in the chill wind. She led him across the road and up a path, through a gate, and up a short steep slope. When it levelled off at another gate, she stopped. One path now went to their left, one to the right.

"It's an Iron Age fort," she said. "Really old. These paths go round it, it's real big, considering."

She shone the torch down both paths and in an arc around them, bushes and low stone walls briefly visible. She took the path to the left, and in fifty yards she said, "There it is."

It took Robert a minute to work out what he was looking at precisely, but there on the hill that fell steeply away from them was the outline of a giant horse. The path placed them above the back of the creature, its huge head many yards to his right, the slender legs following the hill downwards. It was remarkably clear in the moonlight, so much so that she guessed his next questions. "The Westbury white horse. They repainted it a few years ago. It's cement, I think."

"How old is it?"

"God knows. They say two hundred and fifty years. It doesn't have anything to do with the fort, but we all like to think it does."

Even in cement it was impressive, and they gazed at it for a time. Then Scarlet went further along the path, calling out "Jim! Jim!", stopping every so often to point the torch this way and that. Robert followed, and as they neared the head of the horse, which came almost up to the path, she shouted out, "There he is!" and began to make her way down the slope. It was difficult because it was so steep, but five yards down was the huddled body of Jim. She rushed up to him, and hugged him.

"Is he all right?" Robert called out as he came hurrying up behind.

"He's breathing," she replied. "We found him. He's alive."

Robert crouched round the other side of Jim and took his right hand. "He has a pulse," he said. "Quite a good one."

He fell silent. Something about the horse, and the moon, and the three of them sitting there in the moonlight reminded him of the old feelings of exhaustion in the face of death, and honour, and righteousness. He wanted the world to stand still, and the horse to be truly ancient, he wanted to sit with Iron Age ghosts, and to be borne away. Without even looking at her, he knew that Scarlet at that moment felt it too, and they sat there until a cloud scudded across the face of the moon and drops of rain began to fall.

"We'd best start getting him back," he said. Together they stood up, and taking Jim under his arms he started to pull him up to the path. As they got there Jim stirred and looked around him. Robert helped to keep him standing, and Scarlet stood in front of him.

"Go away," Jim mumbled, looking at her. "Leave me alone."

She reached for his arm and he stepped back and almost tripped. "Jim," she said, "we're taking you home."

He tried to push her away. "Go away," he mumbled again. "Leave me here."

She stepped forward, and with her face close to his, she

shouted, "You fool. You could've died. No one knew where you were." And then her voice cracked and she started to cry. "You could've died. I don't want you to die. You're not going to die." She kissed him, and kissed him again. "We're going home."

He shivered, and his barely focused eyes searched her face. "I need to be here. I want…"

"We're taking you home."

"Where are we going?" he said.

She put her arms round him. His shoulders dropped, his head slumped onto her shoulder. "Home," she said softly. "We're taking you home."

Robert woke at seven. The room was full of light streaming through the thin curtains. He looked at his watch, groaned, listened for any sounds coming from the opposite bedroom, and lay in the bed trying not to wake up. He found himself talking to Barbara in a room he didn't recognise. The conversation was very important, but he couldn't catch the words. Outside there was someone trying to get in, a younger woman; her face wasn't clear, but the house was locked. They couldn't open it and she couldn't get in. He was running from room to room trying to find a door, and so was the woman, following him on the outside. When he woke up it was ten o'clock.

He dressed, washed quickly and went downstairs to the kitchen. Scarlet came to join him. She was wearing fresh clothes, a white short-sleeved top over her jeans, and not much make-up. She looked drawn and tired, but she briefly managed a smile.

They drank coffee in the garden. Jim, she said, was OK, and fast asleep. They sat quietly for a while and then he said, "He wasn't just going to one of his favourite places, was he?"

He waited, but she didn't reply. He sat forward and looked at her closely.

"His clothes weren't that wet, and it'd been raining on and off all evening. He went there at night."

"Maybe he went there to get high. We'd go there quite often."

"He couldn't have driven there that high. He was totally out of it when we arrived. He took the stuff when he was there."

"What are you saying?" She stood up, not wanting the conversation to continue, but he wouldn't let her go.

"What's he taking?"

"Just weed. He has all his life."

"And wine, and whisky, and cigarettes." He stood up and reached out to take her arm, but she pulled it away. "Look, Scarlet, I have to know. You have to know. Has he ever been that far gone?"

She stepped away from him, her head dropped, she took a deep breath, and closed her eyes. When she opened them she said, "Once."

He waited for her to go on.

"It was in June. Early June. He was down, really down. When things are bad he goes deep into himself, he won't talk to anyone. He's always been like that. I'd gone into town to do some shopping. When I got back, he was in the living room. I thought he was fast asleep. I unpacked, pottered about, started to think about dinner. He wouldn't wake up."

She looked away, then looked back at him. "I got scared. I mean, real scared. I opened his eyes and I could see he was high. I thought he'd might have gotten some heroin, but he hates the stuff, always has. I went and looked at his medicine box. It didn't look like he'd popped loads of pills. There were no bottles in the trash. I didn't know what to do except to let him sleep it off. That's what you usually do. And he did. He woke up the next afternoon, with no idea of what'd happened. I had to put the TV on to persuade him it was Wednesday, not Tuesday."

"That was the only other time?"

She nodded. "The only one."

She waited, hoping he would speak, and when he did not she sat down at the table and said, "Why's it matter?"

"Scarlet, this is my job. I know all sorts of things that people take, in all sorts of quantities, and what they can do. When he drinks, he drinks a lot, which he shouldn't, but I haven't seen him get drunk. He doesn't get way too high by accident, either. What you saw wasn't him coping with pain, was it."

She got up and walked away, back into the living room. He followed her.

"Scarlet, listen."

"I heard Jim. I'm going to see how he is."

"You didn't, he's perfectly quiet. And perfectly all right, you know that." He grabbed her arm, she shook it free, he took it again.

"Scarlet, no one can do this on their own."

Her shoulders dropped, she looked without hope for a moment, and she sat down on the sofa. He sat down facing her.

127

"Yesterday, you weren't here all the time?" he said.

She nodded.

"You had a row?" he went on. "Did he get stuff from Harrison and not tell you?"

"How do you… ? No, we didn't. I didn't storm out and leave him feeling all abandoned," she said, and then more softly, "Really I didn't."

"OK." Robert put his hands up. "OK. And back in June, had anything else happened?"

"We'd been to see McIntire a day or two before. It really wasn't good." She looked at her lap, and then up at Robert. "It was really bad. But we'd talked about it, seen it coming. I thought he'd taken it real well."

"Nobody takes it well. Everybody needs time." He paused. "So, why last night?"

"I don't know." She shifted on the sofa, brushed something off her jeans, and looked upwards, over Robert's shoulder at the pictures on the wall. "He'd had a bad night the night before. I could see that. He went to bed all afternoon, and he hates to do that in front of me. When he came down, I kept trying to get him to tell me how he was." She stopped. "He threw me out. He said he was tired of me nannying him, I wouldn't let him alone. That was when you rang."

"What did you do?"

"I went." Her voice was weak with defeat. "He's never done that before. I should have stayed."

"You couldn't have. He wanted you out of the way."

She sat still, staring at the floor, unable to speak.

"When did you come back?" he asked, and when she could not reply he answered for her.

"It was late. He wasn't here, he wasn't in the garden. You looked everywhere, you looked up and down the street for his car, and when you saw it was gone you rang me."

"Something like that."

Robert tried to avoid sounding clinical, and was surprised at the sorrow in his voice. "When he doesn't want you around, it's because he's trying not to hurt you, any more than he knows he is."

She was starting slowly to cry. She didn't move. She barely breathed. The sadness in her face came from so deeply within her it was hard for him to continue.

"It's possible," he began, "he was…"

"Trying to kill himself," she broke in, in a voice a little louder than a whisper but which nonetheless filled the room.

Robert found he could only nod.

"It mustn't end like this," she said. "I don't think I could…"

"Don't say that. No one knows what they can do…"

"There are so many things…"

He stretched his hands towards her, but she stared past him, so far beyond the room that he could not move, and could only wait. Finally, almost to break the silence, he said, "He asked me – did he tell you, last time I was here – if I could make it less scary?"

"No. He didn't. What'd he mean?"

"We'd been talking about that letter I'd signed."

"But you can't… not on your own?"

"Of course not."

She drummed her fingers lightly on the arm of the

sofa, and said in a lonely voice "Robert, be careful. He starts very slowly, when he wants to."

She got up, walked to the window, and looked out.

"I made this garden," she said, almost to herself. "It was a mess when we came. I wanted him to have somewhere beautiful, and it was something I could do. He's never cared about it. He's flower-blind. He's brought me bouquets, and I've said, 'Lovely lilies', and he'll say 'Which ones are they?' " She turned to look at Robert, and her voice grew stronger. "I think when it's all over, I'll tear it all up. Bring in a tractor and wreck the place. I'll leave the cherry tree. It's older than any of us. Older than anyone I know."

Robert crossed to the window and stood beside her.

"The leaves are beautiful too, you know," she said. "Just before they all fall off, the whole tree turns a deep orange, as if it's on fire."

They stood together looking at the garden for some time.

"After that Wednesday," said Robert, "that's when you came to see me, isn't it?"

"Yes."

"I'm glad you did."

She turned and looked at him. "I thought I knew him real well," she said, "until I met you."

If he turns to me now, Robert thought, what would I say, other than the conventional things? I don't want to say the conventional things, because I know him better now, and not so well. Because we talk and we don't. Because he wants me and he doesn't. I'm waiting to find out what I can say and what I should do, not because I'm his brother, not because I'm a doctor, and not because he's dying, but for some unanswerable reason. A ball thrown high in the air, seemingly motionless at the moment before it begins its descent. Hovering longer than it should. Or a hawk.

Chapter 9

Late September 2018

Jim woke up again. This time the room was light. He looked at the clock by his bedside. Six o'clock. He knew he wouldn't get back to sleep, but he didn't want to get up so early just to drag himself through another day, so he turned on one side and lay there. Even now, with the illness so advanced, he had little idea how the day would go. But in some form or another it would mean music. Listening to it; on good days playing it. And if today, like so many others, has started too soon, still he has promised himself he will play, which makes him feel good.

After an hour, he went to the bathroom. Urine the colour of tea, but no sign of blood, which was reassuring. He washed his face and looked at himself in the mirror, trying to convince himself he didn't look tired and so he wasn't tired. His eyes and his skin were tinged with yellow, which disappointed him, as it did every day these days. He walked not so slowly downstairs, and went to the kitchen, where he sat for his first cigarette. The coffee didn't smell too bad; he filled a cafetière and waited for it to cool. He managed two slices of toast and marmalade and drank most of the coffee. It's been starting to taste too bitter, he thought, which is normal, apparently. It was still barely seven thirty, and the paradox of his condition returned to him. Just when it tears at you that you don't have many days left, each day you do have is in fact rather boring. Like waiting for a train when you don't want to go there anyway. He took his meds all the same. Make the man in the dark suit work for it one more time.

But today was going to be a good day. Sure, a morning spent with Stevie Wonder is always a morning well spent. Or Ray Charles for bluesier days, sexier days, more personal days. Or Allen Toussaint, a true New Orleans gentleman, or Dr John, and, man, you have to admire how he dressed. He bowed mentally to them all, knowing he'd make it through the day, because today he had plans to play.

The phone rang. Scarlet, of course, to say she'll be back by lunchtime after two days recording bullshit in London. He felt the house was empty without her, and in a way even with her. Three years, and despite all her efforts it still felt like they were passing through. But, and this is a difficult, ever-changing thought, she will eventually return to the life they knew. This stirred a small pit of resentment in him, which he knew he must push out of reach. She'd come with him after all. He would say, if asked, that what happiness he now had he owed to her. He would say he loved her. He would say that living with her was good. And that there were things best not said, best not thought. Being on his own wasn't so easy anymore.

And then, he found himself thinking, there's Robert.

Little brother Robert. The happy family man. All those school smarts and he's spent his life with dead bodies. Jim reckoned he wouldn't have guessed – but also that he wasn't surprised. Robert'd never been one for centre stage, always kept out of sight. Still, he was here, he'd come when he was called, and he needn't have done. Which raised a question in Jim's mind: would he have done it, if it'd been the other way round? Probably, yes, he decided: out of curiosity. Last chance to see. Still, Robert wasn't getting him at his best, and never had. That was the strangest thing. He'd missed the performance but come to the stage door to see him bundled off in a long black car. All because we share what? Nothing Jim wanted to remember. Nothing that mattered to him. Except one thing.

"Your life isn't your childhood," he said to the empty room.

But he gets to do the interview. Now you've retired, Jim, what were the highlights? Who did you play with? Tell us a story or two, and yes, Jim could tell Robert a story or two. About people like him, people his brother won't have heard of, which sort of spoils the story. And his favourite stories about the people everyone's heard of, if he hasn't heard them already, and with his life he probably hasn't. But actually, even those stories aren't that interesting now. They're gone, just album covers. Jim had always thought those stories were like trophies. Some people collect them, put them on the shelves and the walls, wall themselves up with them in the end. And some just chuck them in that old, battered suitcase and leave them one day in a cheap hotel somewhere. You were there or you weren't, and you can't be now. Work it out from that.

Jim went to the front room, and, with his now customary nod to the man in the engraving, sat at the piano. Playing finger exercises, scales, arpeggios, and chord progressions was now doubly reassuring for him: once because there was pleasure in making his way to where playing was a natural as speaking; and once because it was no longer certain he could every day. There'd been times when he could play with a clarity, a swiftness, and whatever he was playing became truly alive, and him within it. But these days there were times when it was like pulling the music uphill, it took an almost physical effort to focus on what was to be played. As if a fog had entered him.

After an hour, he moved on to the songs he liked to rehearse, improvisations he wanted to try, moving each song from one style to another: country to bluegrass to rhythm and blues to Cajun and back. Now he was tired, but there was something else he wanted to do. He moved over to sit in a chair until he heard Robert's car pull up outside. He let him in, and went back to the piano, took out a battered yellow volume of music from the piano stool, turned the pages, and found the ones he had in mind.

The first piece went well. He always thought it had a surprising swing. On another occasion he would go back and play up the swing, rework the runs in the left hand, and see where it took him. But right now discipline is the key. When he finished he turned over several pages and started the next piece. This too could easily be reworked, but he knew that wouldn't be right. There was time for only one more in this little gambit before he would be too tired, but almost as soon as he began the door opened quietly and Robert put his head round it. Jim nodded to show he'd seen him, but carried on to the end.

"Bach?" said Robert, obviously surprised.

Jim grinned. His little stunt was working. "Maybe not quite as our great master intended."

"Still," Robert said, walking up to the piano, "I didn't know you played him at all."

"Time was, I'd try to play them every day."

"All forty-eight?"

He went back to the second piece and played it without the trills and with the runs in the left hand turned into chords. Then he slowly changing the rhythm, making it more percussive, and asked "Recognise it?" Robert looked puzzled but suddenly went " 'Eleanor Rigby'!"

"Not that far apart, after all." He shut the piano and got up, starting to feel not tired exactly but muzzy, losing focus. "I need another coffee. You had breakfast?"

He walked past Robert, who nodded and followed him to the kitchen.

"You going to tell me it's not just three chords either?" said Robert.

"It is with that one," Jim said, putting the kettle on and measuring out the coffee. But the first one was C sharp major. You don't find much of my kind of music in that."

"And the last one?"

Jim grinned. "I win, 'Hello's F minor too."

"Hello?"

"Adele. It's on 25, and her 'Best of Adele' album. You'll have to do a better job of keeping up."

"Lauren's moved out. That's my excuse anyway."

Jim poured boiling water into the cafetière. He was

136

pleased with the way his plan had gone. Robert wasn't the first person he'd surprised this way; once you sat behind a honkytonk piano, people tended to assume that was all you could manage. His pleasure in his success was, however, being eroded by a familiar pain developing below his ribs on the right. Nothing too much, but it would be better to sit down than stand. He stirred the coffee, pushed down the plunger, poured out two cups of coffee, gestured at the milk jug on the table, and went through to the living room with his cup. Robert followed with his, and as they sat down Jim said, "She's fun. I like her. Scarlet does too."

"Fun's not the word I'd choose."

Jim sipped at his coffee, and abandoned it. "Ease up. She'll be OK."

"You never had kids of your own?"

"None I want to admit to, anyway."

He said it with a smile, and Robert took it as a joke. "How'd you think you'd have managed?" he asked.

Jim shifted in his chair, finding no position comfortable. "Never wanted to. I always said, best not to get started if you don't like the idea," he said, and before Robert could reply added, "She can sing, you know. Needs a bit of encouragement, a bit of direction, that's all."

"Can she make a living at it?" Robert asked.

"Sessions pay." He pulled a face, put his hands together as if in prayer, and gave Robert a look of shallow contrition. "Forgive me, Father, for I have sinned."

"It was that bad?"

"You've no idea. Cover albums, rerecording hits that should never have been performed in the first place. Disco 'greats'. Worst of all – Christmas classics. Movies straight to TV. TV ads with a seventies feel. I've so many aliases the FBI ought to investigate." He looked quizzically at Robert, and said, "Rock'n'roll's the new nostalgia, the soundtrack on exercise videos for the elderly. Who'd have thought I'd live long enough to see it."

They were silent for a moment.

"What do you really like to play?" Robert asked.

In a rough Chicago accent, Jim said, "I'm an old blues man." Then in his usual voice he added "It's real music. It was a people's music. Now people have forgotten it, they trash it."

"Not just dance music, then?"

"Traditional blues, Delta blues, Chicago blues. And it's swamp stuff, right? No-count rubbish. Kids' music. Dance music. Down and dirty."

"I seem to remember that's what even I wanted it to be."

Jim looked straight at Robert, and, with a hint of anger in his voice, said, "Then you weren't listening, you weren't thinking."

"Maybe because it was actually dance music."

Jim shook his head and said, with a vigour that surprised Robert, "And so much more. The music of a people. Take 'Love in Vain'. You know that one? Robert Johnson – or the Stones, to you."

"I think so," said Robert.

"It isn't just that it's true sometimes it's hard to tell when all your love's in vain. The train leaving the station with a blue light on for his girlfriend and a red light for his mind has confusion, sadness – it's a perfect image of a parting. I can see why good poetry's good – I just don't see why Johnson's words aren't up there too."

"Because, I don't know, it's entertainment? It's good, but—"

"It's the fucking 'but' I don't get. Out of a cauldron, a bunch of smart guys sometimes wrote the right words, set them to music that's lasted, forced its way into every corner where it hadn't been welcome, and now people write them all off."

Almost out of breath he let the words hang there, waiting for Robert to reply, and Robert said, "That was The Doors, wasn't it? The old blues man."

"Jim Morrison. You do remember some things."

"Lauren has some of his records."

"Yeah, some punky kids are really into him."

He slumped back in his chair, putting his hands up in mock surrender.

"You OK?" said Robert.

"Sure."

The doorbell rang, and Jim said, "That'll be the doc, you'd better go and hide in the kitchen." Robert did as instructed, and Jim let McIntire in. They sat and talked briefly, McIntire listening to the answers to his carefully memorised checklist of questions, Jim sounding upbeat, trying to balance, as he always did on these occasions, what a home visit said about his condition with the realisation that McIntire meant well. Whatever that was.

Finally, McIntire stood up. "I'm glad to see you're keeping going," he said. "Is it all right if I get a glass of water?"

Jim waved his hands and McIntire went to the kitchen. He saw Robert and stopped.

"I'm Dr McIntire," he said. "And you are?"

"Robert Parrish," said Robert. "I'm Jim's brother."

"They told me you were visiting." Then he frowned, and a coldness entered his face. "You signed that letter?"

"Yes," said Robert.

"I wouldn't have done," said McIntire.

"No one's asking you to."

"Of course you are," McIntire replied. "You're hoping for support for a position I believe would make my job impossible."

"You'll always be free to disagree."

"No. If you get your way, whatever I say, or do, people will know they cannot trust their doctors to keep them alive."

"It doesn't have to be like that. It isn't in places where it works."

"Doctor Parrish, keeping very ill people alive is our deepest bond. Everything else we do rests on that."

Robert decided not to reply.

"I'm a compassionate man," McIntire said. "At least, I try to be. If that became impossible, I would have to cease to practice."

"I respect that," said Robert.

"And your brother is my patient. Not yours. I'll thank you to remember that."

McIntire turned and, after a quick goodbye to Jim, he left. As soon as he'd gone, Robert rejoined Jim.

"How'd you two doctors get along?" said Jim.

"You heard."

"Compassionate. He's about as compassionate as fishermen are to fish."

"He visits," said Robert. "It's his job to tell you how it looks, even if you don't like it."

"I don't like it."

"I'm here, if that's any help."

"Strictly hands off, though. Now, if you don't mind, I do need a rest."

Jim let the conversation lapse, and drifted slowly half-asleep, recalling a night at Biker Joe's. The name on the door is Blues 'R' Us, and everything about it's as authentic as the name suggests. No one who plays there believes Joe was a biker, either, although he's big enough, tattooed enough, his face is lived-in enough, and he wears a bandana round his head. But he pays, he keeps the acts on schedule, and he keeps trouble to a minimum.

Tonight, there's sixty people. Should be OK, but three songs in and Wayne forgets the words to 'Big Boss Man'. No one notices but Cameron, the bass guitarist, Dannie, the lead, and me. Wayne gives us a sheepish grin when he finishes. He's new, he's a weedy runt, a college dropout for sure, learned what he knows from albums, and something's getting to him tonight; he would've dropped a whole verse out of the next number if I hadn't started to sing. Four more songs and it happens again. Wayne forgets the final verse altogether and the rest of us turn it into an instrumental. Not bad, but maybe not what the audience has come for. I try to look at them, but the stage lights are on us and the big room's dark and smoky. I can just see the two waitresses in their skimpy pink cowboy outfits flitting around carrying the drinks. Wayne's looking as if someone's just beaten him up, and we hesitate. Suddenly, there's a noise coming from the room, the waitresses turn to watch, and this big guy is pushing his way forward to the stage. It's hard to tell, but he's six foot four at least, and he's drunk and he's angry about something. And he's looking at Wayne.

"Same thing," he shouts, looking at Wayne. "Play 'The Same Thing'!"

I don't think Wayne knows what's going on, he's looking completely lost, but I know it. It's a Willie Dixon song, though it's not often covered.

"Call yourself a fucking blues band," the guy is shouting. "Can't play nothing."

I can see Biker Joe moving towards the guy. I look at Dannie, then at the drummer, and I start the song. The drummer picks up the rhythm. Eight bars of piano, and I start to sing. Fuck it if Wayne doesn't know this one. I let Dannie make up a solo, beckon Wayne over with a nod of my head, and whisper "Just sing along." We're about to start in on the next verse when I can see the big drunk isn't having any of it, and Joe isn't either. The big drunk wants to get on the stage, Joe pushes him back onto a table, he bounces back and swings at Joe who ducks and punches him in the stomach. Good blow, but this guy is big and it doesn't stop him. People are stepping back, knocking over chairs. The band retreats and we all make it louder. Two guys working the bar have come round and try to catch the drunk from behind, but he's unstoppable until Joe has the sense to let him try to climb the stage and he can hit him on the back of the neck with whatever he's got in his fist. The drunk slides to the floor, the bartenders get him under the arms and escort him out. Wayne and I finish the chorus. Wayne looks like he wants to bolt from the stage but I grab onto him and say, "This is where you step up." Joe, busy giving drinks to guys caught up in the fight, looks at us and says "What you waitin' for? The second coming?" and damn if Wayne doesn't go to his mic and say, "I guess we didn't make it clear – Biker Joe handles all our requests." Gets a laugh and off we go again. A good night after all.

Jim woke up when the front door made a sound, and opened one eye. Scarlet must be back. He managed an unobtrusive look at his watch. It's the right time. Scarlet bustled in to see how he was. He closed his open eye and mumbled something. She kissed him and went to fix lunch.

After lunch, while Jim dozed again in his chair in the living room, Scarlet and Robert tidied up in the kitchen.

"I saw Lauren," she said. "She came to the studio with me."

He stiffened and looked at her. "How come?"

"I spent two days doing a campaign of jingles. I thought she'd like to see what being a singer's really like." She finished wiping the table and put a bottle of milk on it for Robert to put in the fridge. "So I asked her."

"What'd she make of it?" he replied, without taking the milk.

"It was pretty gross. You ever been asked to sing 'more breakfast-y'?" She rolled her eyes. "She enjoyed it."

"Did you get her to sing?"

"I couldn't get her a contract. But I got her behind a microphone in a few of the down times. So she can say she's been in a studio." She started wiping the sink. "Doing jingles is a good way to learn to get to know your chest voice and your head voice, manipulate a mic. We even began to do a song." She looked over at Robert, sensing he was not too pleased by what she was saying. "You don't mind, do you?"

He picked up the milk and put it away. "God, no. I was just thinking… I mean, you're good, but… could Lauren make a living at it?"

She passed him some cutlery, nodded at another cupboard, and said, "Robert, she's twenty."

He looked unconvinced, and she added, "Sure, she can learn to sing, learn to do harmony. Why ever not?" She crossed over to him and lightly held his shoulders. "You worry too much."

He gave a rueful smile and they finished tidying up.

"I didn't know he played the piano so well," he said. "I wasn't expecting Bach."

"You got his party trick." She paused. "He was good?"

"I'm no judge. But yes, he was good."

"And did he turn it around?"

But before he could answer, a phone rang. Her phone, in her bag. She fished it out, looked at the screen, and said to Robert, "I'm sorry, I've got to take this." She crossed quickly to the hallway, without answering the call until she got to the garden, and through the kitchen window Robert watched her pace up and down, obviously interrupting and being interrupted in turn. When the call ended, she stood staring at the phone for several seconds before slipping it into the back pocket of her jeans and coming indoors.

As she came back in, Robert asked, "Everything OK?"

She stood at the kitchen door and said in a downbeat voice, "Everything's as I expected, if that answers your question."

She started to make coffee, and in an edgier voice said, "He's been thinking a lot about his life recently."

"I suppose most people do, in his situation."

"It's not like him. He never used to do it." She paused. "He was so in the moment, you know. Never look back, never look forward. I used to envy him. Now… it doesn't help him any. It makes him…" She gestured helplessly with her hands. "He always said what's the point? You can't go back. And he's right."

They heard Jim call from the other room "Scarlet, you around?"

"I just hate it," she said, almost in a whisper. "It's like he's writing his own biography, 'cause he knows it's over." She took her coffee and went to the living room, to see what Jim wanted, and Robert followed.

"Water'd be nice," Jim said.

Scarlet brought him a glass and settled into a chair next to him. "I gather you been impressing Robert here with your piano playing skills."

"I didn't do much. Just a little Bach."

She looked over at Robert. Jim, still pleased with the morning's success, found he was feeling talkative, and pushed the conversation forward. To entertain Robert, he recalled gigs he'd played and people he'd played with, like the one in a satanist blues club in Oklahoma, in a basement underneath the Church of Second Amendment Saints – "No, really, it almost made me like the musical". Always circling back to the blues, the people who'd played it and sung it, the people he'd played with, all the things it said when you listened to it, when you bothered to find out, because it was being forgotten again. The people who'd made the music had died, or were dying, and black kids these days were into hip-hop and didn't stick around to listen.

It was some time since he'd felt this loquacious, even if he was coughing quite a bit now, and he didn't notice Scarlet was getting up to collect the coffee cups, sitting down and immediately getting up to look at the garden, going to the front door to answer a knock only she had heard. Finally, as Jim again swung the conversation back to his better days, she burst out "You done your poetry number on Robert yet?"

Jim, surprised, said, "Sure."

She turned to Robert and said, "You had all that stuff about how wrong it is, everyone saying what those guys do is just the basics, over and over again?"

Before Robert could say it wasn't quite like that she turned back to Jim and said, "You're part of a great people's struggle trashed by the music business?"

"Hey, come on, Scarlet, you know—"

"You don't have to be so damn wound up about it."

"Their music. I play their music, that's all."

She got out of her chair and turned to first to Robert and then back to Jim. The anger that had gathered in her now radiated into the room. "Bullshit. You tell 'their story'. You want them to be 'heard'."

"And suddenly you don't? What are you saying?"

"Why don't you just say you played some songs? Made some records? Had some fun? Why'd you have to—?"

"I'm not talking it up. It's what I—"

"Instead yo' bin impressing brother Robert here with yo' tales of the South Side n'all."

"I just said they had a hard time and wrote some great songs."

"Brother Jim here," she said, turning to Robert, "brother Jim, he has lived. And now he telling everyone fool enough t'listen. Brother Jim here, see, he played with 'em all. He sang with 'em all. Yo' asking about Muddy Waters, Willie Dixon, Jimmy Yancey? He grew up wid dem. They painted a glorious chapter in the history of the free world. Now he painting it too. Y'ought know that, 'cause he bin telling everyone."

She stopped, and put her head in her hands. Then she looked up, crossed to where Jim was, and leant over him. "Jim. Jim, Jim, don't say this stuff. Don't make it sound so grand. It just sounds like you're not here anymore. Like you're gone, and we're talking about you. Like you're gone." She stood up. "Just be you," she said. "Just be you."

She watched Robert drive away, closed the front door, and went to confront Jim. Kindled perhaps by a burst of resentment at doing all the cooking, the shopping, the driving, which she hated to admit was deepening the more necessary it became. The peculiar anger that comes from not being able to get the easy stuff right, of failing long before the real tests of your life were in view; it's hard to practise love and forgiveness when you can't cope with not having tidied the kitchen and cleaned the sink. Only to find that Jim was taking himself to bed and refusing to talk about anything.

"You can't get out of it like this," she said. "You could practice much of the morning, play your trick on Robert, get on your high horse. Collapsing right now is just too neat."

"I'm really tired," he said.

"Maybe, but you always do this, sliding out of conversations you don't want to have."

"I'm going to lie down."

"We need to talk. I need to talk to you."

"I'm ill, remember. It can wait till tomorrow, whatever it is."

He walked past her, went upstairs and lay on the bed, obstinately pretending to be asleep until she realised she'd have to wait till the morning before trying again.

She slept poorly and woke up early. Jim had been like this even when he was well, she thought, as she sat in the kitchen and ate another unappealing brand of what the English called granola. His petulance when practising went wrong, his unpredictable fatigue and equally unpredictable bursts of energy, his misplaced enthusiasms, his ability to play the same track over and over, listening for what after a time?

When Jim came down she let him fix himself a coffee, and tried to talk about nothing for as long as she could. Then she said, "That was Ryan on the phone yesterday. And you know it was."

He looked at her.

"Well," she said, "you got nothing to say?"

He shook his head.

"That's it? You're real sick, your son calls, and you can't be bothered to talk to him."

"I'm damn sure he doesn't want to talk to me."

"And why d'you think that is?"

"I always said I wasn't going to be involved; I'd sooner live on my own. I told you so."

"Unbelievable."

Jim said nothing, and reached for the toast. She grabbed him by the arm.

"All these years, and I never understood. You're crazy, you know, messed up in your head."

"I told you all along, I never wanted kids."

"I beg him to come over, and he won't even say your name."

"We've been through this," he said, his voice rising. "Over it. Round it. What psychological shit d'you want me to say?"

"As if you haven't said enough over the years. Your father, it's your father. Jesus, Jim, is that all you can offer? And anyway it's crap. Your brother's got three kids."

"Maybe you've got the wrong fucking brother," he said.

She pushed his arm away and got up from the table.

"See if you can remember how to look after yourself," she shouted, and she stormed out, got in the car and drove off. Not knowing where to go, driving too fast until she nearly came off the road in the wet and into a ditch, which stopped her for a time. Then she drove off again, just to be out of the house, and away from Jim, and doing something, anything, for herself. She stopped somewhere for lunch,

149

went for a walk along darkly puddled paths wet with slippery fallen leaves, and looked at the dismal English landscape that was neither one thing nor another. All the time thinking about that phone call, how once again she'd begged Ryan to come over. The voices still echoing in her head, her saying "Jim's dying. You have to come and say goodbye", and Ryan saying nothing. Her saying "Come for my sake. I need you to do it", and all he could say was, "Mom, you know what I think of him. I can't". Her saying "Do it for your sake, or you'll regret it all your life", and him saying "He wouldn't have anything to do with me. All the time I was a kid. You two didn't really break up. He broke up with *me*". She went back to the car and drove off again, choosing right or left without knowing why. And found herself at the Goat's Head.

She sat in the empty back bar at Poker Martin's, drumming her fingers on the worn oak table and staring around, while Poker polished glasses and checked on the bottles, and the autumn light faded outside and the room grew dim.

"So he's all right, is he?" said Poker.

"Robert's looking after him."

"That's the brother, turning up after all these years?"

Scarlet shrugged. "Jim didn't want him. Till a couple of months ago."

"And he's a doctor, you said? Tidy, that."

"Specialises in dead people." She waved her empty glass and said, "Pour me another."

Poker came round from behind the bar, poured her a generous bourbon, and sat down opposite her. He knew Jim could be difficult, but he'd never seen her this wound up.

"So you just decided to get in the car and pop over?" he said. "Not that you're not always welcome."

She looked at her glass, drank a little, and stared back at him.

He put a hand on hers and said, "I heard him before you did, you know."

She said nothing.

"He did two things. Hard blues – he knew a lot – and all that Californian, Byrds, country rock stuff. He was good. And he usually got what he wanted.

She finished her drink and pushed the empty glass across the table.

"So who is this Robert? Who's Jim's brother?" asked Poker, getting up to put on a couple of lights in the alcoves.

She nodded. Good question. Who was Robert? For that matter, who was his dull, inquisitive wife? Strange who people end up with. But he'd turned up when she'd asked, back in June. And he'd come that night when she'd asked. Really asked.

"Four foot tall, church going, tin ear?" Poker went on. "None of your man's zest for living?" Zest, was it? Sure, Robert was quiet. But he hasn't missed much, and he's easy company. She shrugged. "He's OK. Can't say about the church."

She paused for a moment. "He's offered to make it less scary. Agreed to, I mean. Jim asked him to. Only now Jim,... I don't know."

Poker looked at her, but she found she could keep a nagging fear to herself. After a time, he said "His visits are helping?"

"In a way," she replied.

151

"A Cain and Abel way? Jacob and Esau? Prodigal son?"

"Poker, you gone religious because it's Sunday or something?"

"Where I'm from that's your whole education. You might as well hang on to it."

"You know it's not like that. Why you asking?"

"Fathers. Brothers go back to fathers."

"Jim never talked about his parents," she said, getting up and going to look out of the window. But Robert and Jim had, almost as soon as Robert arrived, when he and Barbara'd come the first time.

Poker came round behind her and put his arms around her. "I'm thinking you didn't come here just to get away from Jim for an hour or two."

She turned round and rested her arms on his, feeling weightless and far away. "You think I want to spend time with you?"

He stepped slightly forwards. She pushed back and broke his embrace. He renewed it.

"Ever been invisible, Poker?" she said. "It's easy. Live with someone really ill."

She pushed herself free again and stood in the middle of the room, looking round at the bar, the bottles with names she never remembered, the beer handles with their gaudy plastic labels, the pictures on the dark walls, scenes from a country she didn't recognise, and began to tremble. It was suddenly cold, the room and everything in it began to spin, and a desolate wind echoed in her ears. She jammed her eyes shut, clenched her fists and stumbled forward.

"I shouted at him, Poker. I shouted at him last night.

And this morning. About nothing. Told him he's no good. He's dying, he's frightened, and I told him he's…"

She fell into his arms. He led her to the settle below the window and sat her there, curled up, her head on her knees, crying, while he retreated to a chair opposite. The soft light vanished into the browns of the old room and her dark clothes, but it caught on lines in the table in front of her, and on her blonde hair, and her red shoes and her brooch, so that it seemed that the room embraced and accepted her. After a time she stopped crying, and hesitantly began to talk. Almost at random at first, and then slowly it came out. Ryan, her only child, the boy Jim refused ever to see, the semi-secret he wanted her to keep. Back there in Memphis, in college, and he wouldn't come over, not even now when Jim was so sick.

This time, in her own private photo album, he was eight. The age Ryan no longer believed the presents she bought him were from Daddy, all the way up in Chicago. The day he'd taken the elaborate model plane she'd so carefully wrapped up, and sat out in the yard and systematically, slowly, smashed it to pieces, and collected all the fragments and put them in a pile on the kitchen table and said, "Send it back."

"I'm not defending Jim," Poker said, "but where d'you think all that's coming from?"

"If I knew, Poker. If only I knew. In his head he's just not Ryan's father. I've tried so hard just to get them…" She looked desolately at him. "Is loving always like this?"

"Love can hurt," he said. "Love can hurt."

All her lies about love. Lies for Ryan's sake, never for Jim's. So Ryan could have a father, like all the kids

153

he knew, who loved him despite 'it not working out between him and me', until even he could see what was really true.

Chapter 10

Early October 2018

They were sitting on the patio. The sun had come out although it had rained most of the day, and it roused Jim from a prolonged, moody silence.

"A final flourish," he said.

"A good omen?"

"For the gig?"

Scarlet nodded, and they sat quietly for a while.

"You glad Robert's around?" she asked.

He looked at her dismissively. "He likes to think he's doing good. It was his way of trying to be liked as a kid."

She pulled her chair closer to his and said, "There's nothing wrong with doing good."

Jim nodded briefly. "Not put like that," he said.

"And he said he'll try to help you, when you asked him."

"Don't go there," he said.

She recoiled, and they sat in silence for a while. Then Jim said, "You want a drink?"

"If you do."

He went into the house, and after a few minutes came back with a whisky bottle and a small jug of water.

"You took your time."

"I was looking for something."

He poured himself a drink, offered one to Scarlet, and put the bottle and the jug on the table in front of them. "I think my dad killed it for me."

"Killed what?"

"Any sense of duty. He'd been in the army for years. I mean, from his time in the war all the way to fifty-six. He liked it." He took a drink. "Fourteen years. And for the first seven years of my life he was hardly around."

"The army life."

Jim nodded. "We did some pretty dirty stuff at the end of empire. Dad turned up for that."

He sat motionless for a few moments, then he poured himself another drink. After a time he said, "Fourteen years of that. Fourteen years of doing your duty."

"His choices." She leant over and took his hands in hers. "They don't have to be yours."

"I guess they weren't, either." He looked into her face and she knew he wouldn't say any more.

Next morning, when the doorbell rang, Scarlet realised she'd forgotten that Robert and Barbara would be coming. She went to the front door to let them in and found Robert, looking tidy as he always did, but no Barbara.

"She's caught up in something at work," he said, and before she could enquire about it he went on "Round here looks lovely in autumn, as if it's trying to be the perfect picture of England."

"Yes," said Scarlet, "and we have our maples in the fall, they look incredible too."

She led the way to the living room.

"How are you? How's Jim?"

"He's a bit rough. It's been a difficult few days."

"And you?"

"OK, considering," she said, and an awkward silence fell on them now that the pleasantries were out of the way.

"Actually," Robert said, "Barbara can't come because she's visiting her sister Lily. She's had a bit of a turn." As Robert began to explain, Scarlet became absorbed in the news.

"Is she going to be all right?" she said when Robert finished.

"Oh, yes. She's very sensitive, any kindness really warms her, and anything, well, even a little thoughtless is very upsetting." He paused, and then said "I sometimes think she's the person Barbara loves most in the world."

"Maybe, if we were all like that…"

"The world would be a better place?" said Robert. "I don't know. It wouldn't be a world that could look after its Lilys very well, that's the trouble."

"We're not doing too well with our Jims either," said Scarlet.

Robert waited for her to go on.

"Oh, nothing new," she said. "Or so he says. And I believe him, in a way."

"Do you want me to pop upstairs and see how he is?"

"Yes, do. I'd like that." She paused for a moment, not

sure what to say and he waited. "You'd better go upstairs," she said, and turned to go into the kitchen.

Robert knocked on the bedroom door and, getting no answer, opened the door gently. Jim was asleep in bed. His breathing was shallow, the room very warm, the air stale but not unpleasant. Robert went to the window and drew back the curtains. The windows were all shut except for one, which was only partly open; he opened it further and let the cooler country air gradually come in from the garden.

Still no response from Jim. Robert sat down on the edge of the bed.

Unable any longer to pretend to be asleep, Jim opened an eye.

"Oh, it's you," he said. "I thought it would be."

"You didn't feel like getting up... ?"

Jim opened the other eye. "There's no need to rush."

Robert took Jim's arm to feel for his pulse, but Jim snatched it away. "I've got enough doctors, thank you very much."

"You want to tell me how you feel?"

Jim said nothing.

"I think Scarlet's worried about you."

Jim said nothing.

Robert stood up, looked towards the door and back to Jim. "I'll say you're waking up," he said, walking towards the door. Just as he put his hand on the door handle, Jim said, "The women don't get on, do they?"

"Did Scarlet say that?"

"Neither in word nor deed. I noticed. You get used to looking at an audience."

Robert said, "Where are you taking this?"

"Nowhere. Still, it's a shame, the women don't get along." Jim struggled to sit up, and sipped his glass of water.

He waited for Robert to ask what he meant, but Robert said nothing, and Jim said, "You can go downstairs. Say I'm up, but I'll stay in bed and I don't want any lunch."

Robert went downstairs and conveyed the message, and Scarlet went upstairs and stayed there for about twenty minutes. When she came back down Robert asked how he was, and how she was, and got the same answer, "OK", to each question. They passed an uneasy lunch, the conversation turning as slowly as the weather. He asked about the pictures hanging in the various rooms.

"D'you like them?" Scarlet enquired. "The only one that's any good is the one Jim keeps by the piano."

"The guy in the street? The engraving?"

"It spooks me every time I look at it," said Scarlet. "All that black, I guess. What's he walking into?"

In the late afternoon, Jim came down and joined them. The conversation moved brokenly along, Jim asked about Lauren, and Robert said she hadn't been in touch. After a time, Jim got out a whisky bottle, put three empty glasses on a table in front of him, and asked what everyone would have. When the others declined, he pushed the bottle away and said, "Me neither."

Scarlet looked quickly at him and he smiled back.

"Don't worry," he said, "I feel fine. I just don't feel like a drink."

Robert and Scarlet talked for a while more, with Jim quietly watching, until it began to get dark and Scarlet got up to put the lights on. Then Robert saw the brown box perched in a corner beside one of the speakers. Jim saw him looking at it, but waited for him to ask.

"Is that what I think it is?" Robert asked.

"Bring it over," said Jim.

Robert got up and put it on the table between them. He removed the lid and took out the turban, picked it up to put it on, then changed his mind and offered it to Scarlet, who wouldn't take it. He put it down on the table.

"I thought it was lost," Robert said. "I didn't know you had it. How come?"

"I took it from Dad, in eighty-eight." He reached for the whisky bottle and poured himself a glass. "Not that I could tell you why."

Robert looked at him sharply and said, "I didn't know you saw him then."

"He didn't tell you?" Jim gave a slight smile. "I went up to see Mum. It was worse than I expected."

Robert, puzzled, said, "In what way?"

Jim sipped his whisky and said, "I got there later than I'd intended. Dad was there. He was telling her what to do. All the time. She tried to talk about when we were little, and he kept telling her what had really happened, even when he couldn't have been there. And she'd just mumble that her memory wasn't so good anymore. It was awful. I lost it with him. I told him he was a bully, and bullies are bullies because they are cowards, and he must have been a coward in the army to be a coward now."

"You did what?"

"He shouted back that, no, when it got dirty in Malaysia – you know he was there, right?"

"Training the Malay army, wasn't it?"

"More than that. Anyway, he said that one time when he'd got his orders he went to protest. They insisted he take part. Threatened him with a dishonourable discharge if he didn't."

"So he protested in advance. Isn't that something?"

"I could tell it was nonsense. So I made up some story about how what had happened was all over the American papers, and people were drawing parallels with Vietnam." Jim took another drink and looked levelly at Robert. "And he backed down. He admitted it. No protest, nothing." Jim let his words sink in. "He was a coward then, I told him, and a coward ever since." Jim's contempt was acid. "And I told him so."

Robert pushed his chair back and stood up. "You don't know. You weren't there."

Jim looked at Robert and said coldly, "OK, I winged it, but I got it right. And I know what you would've done."

He pushed himself out of his chair, Scarlet reached out a hand to support him, but he ignored it. "That's the man who brought us up. Who was never there. Who ran away from everything."

"He did his best."

As if itemising a list, Jim said, "He went to work. He came home. He played chess. With himself. What else?"

Robert looked around, as if the room was full of

161

testimonials and it was just a matter of selecting a few of the best. "He played football with us. With you. He was around. We watched television together."

Jim stared at him and shook his head. "I can't believe I'm hearing this. He shut down his life. He was never there."

"What did you expect? Nobody had hands-on dads. You've never had kids. You don't know what being a father's like."

Jim gave a hollow laugh that choked into a cough. "You thought you had a loving dad." He gave another, harsher cough, and leant on the arm of the chair for support. "He was a nothing. He gave nothing, he…"

"Since when were you the loser? Or is this your excuse for what you've made of your life?"

"You think you're the good son, the loving one who went to visit, always kept in touch. With people you never knew, out of duty." Jim felt behind him for the other arm of his chair and slowly sat down. "Nothing else." He took a shallow, exhausted breath. "Dad fucked up. In everything he did."

"You cleared off. I knew him better than you."

"For longer, maybe. Not better. You didn't know this."

Robert turned and walked to the door. "And if you just want to talk bullshit…"

"Our father, little brother. Our father. And things you ought to know about him."

"You know what?" said Robert, coming back into the room. "I can understand you taking Mum's side. But you mocked Dad's life."

"It's the lies that got me. One after another."

"Lying to us? We were little kids, we couldn't've understood."

"That lie. His lying to himself. The lie he gave in to. 'Do this, and keep quiet about it, because *we* don't do these things.' "

"I don't believe you. You don't give a shit about empire, or politics. All this anger is another one of your stunts, your endless fucking games."

"Maybe I don't give a shit about that stuff. But he did. And it fucked him up, and if I hadn't got away it'd have fucked me up. And Mother caved in, he had her this tight," and he clenched his fists together. "And all the time, you wanted their approval. Went crawling after them for something you were never going to get. It was painful, you trying to get Father to like you. I couldn't wait to get away."

Robert began to reply, but Jim interrupted him.

"And then you'd come trailing after me." He coughed again, but before Robert could speak he forced out in a quiet, bitter voice, "I remember Mother, when I was young, four, five, six. She was fun, we played games, she taught me to read. You were just a baby, or maybe a toddler, she'd take us to the park and chase us around, and take me to school and collect me and ask me what I'd done and what I'd learned. She'd tell me the names of birds and trees and things. And then Dad came home for good, and shut it all down."

"This from someone who didn't even come to her funeral…"

"You were too young to see it then. But you never noticed, that's what got me."

"Noticed what? That you weren't the centre of attention anymore?"

"He was a coward. He ran away from life, from

163

everything difficult. We were suffocating in there and you couldn't see it."

"And you've been such a hero?"

"He dragged our mother down, and he dragged you down. A doctor who turns up only when it's too late – what help is that?"

"If all you can manage is abuse –"

"I hoped, when you came back… but you know what, you're a coward too."

Robert stepped back, stared at him, and said, "Fine, manage without me. You've had years of practice."

He turned and left, with a cold look at Scarlet's frightened face. Exhausted coughs began to shake Jim's body, making him gasp for breath in short bursts before the next cough came. Scarlet sprang to his side, held his arm, and said, "Was that what you wanted?"

"He destroyed her," he said. "He destroyed her." And he stared bleakly ahead.

Chapter 11

Mid-October 2018

Scarlet walked slowly through Kensington Gardens in an open coat, jeans, and a new sweater to protect against the damp air. The clouds were an even grey that shut out the sun, the only people around were the occasional jogger and, off to one side, a dedicated Tai Chi practitioner. It was one of those days where she thought you needed a good reason to be out, and another to do anything with enthusiasm, and she was no longer sure she had either. With every step she took, the chill air on her face hinted that the whole thing had never been fully thought out, and that even now she should reduce it to nothing more than lunch with a friend. What had begun as something she wanted, even needed, to do, with the attendant restlessness to get it done, and an impatience with the days she'd had to wait, could still shrink down to, "I thought I'd like to see you." There wouldn't be many more opportunities.

Lauren was sitting on a bench in a shapeless, unbuttoned dark green coat and torn jeans, with a long orange and purple scarf around her neck, looking at her phone. Scarlet walked up to her, they kissed, and, at Scarlet's suggestion, went for a walk.

"How's Uncle Jim?" asked Lauren.

Scarlet stopped and said, "He's not getting any better."

"Sure, I understand," said Lauren, thinking that Scarlet would surely think she couldn't.

"Then there's the gig," Scarlet said. "It's all arranged: musicians lined up, we've got a good slot on a Friday evening in the Goat's Head, it's being advertised. And Jim's not playing, not singing, not ready at all. He's hiding."

"He'll be OK," Lauren said, aware again that Scarlet had no reason to believe her. "He, like, wants to do it."

"Yeah," said Scarlet, unconvinced. "Yeah."

"Could you, I mean, if…?"

Scarlet gave a flicker of a smile. "There'd be no point. There's only one thing it's meant to be."

Scarlet had promised herself she'd hold it together, almost persuaded herself it would be OK. She'd rely on her good sense of who to trust, and how far; now wasn't the time to get that wrong.

"I didn't know you had a mystery aunt," she said.

"Aunt Lily? Did Dad tell you about her?"

Scarlet nodded.

"I used to be scared of her as a child," Lauren said. "But she's sweet when you get to know her. She's not, like, hidden away or anything, she's just in a home. She's musical too, in her way."

"That's good."

They walked on, and Lauren, embarrassed at not having commented on it already, said, "I like the sweater. Is it new?"

"It's a gift. From somebody back home in Memphis."

"It's nice. Not too fussy."

"Not too cosy? Too Mel Tormé's 'Christmas Song?'"

Lauren looked blank.

"Mel Tormé, Nat King Cole?"

Lauren gave an involuntary shudder.

"You should listen to them, you know, if you want to be a singer. It's well-written music."

"I guess things have changed."

Scarlet nodded. "Uh huh." She hesitated. Hesitated too long, she thought, and set off down the path, past the Peter Pan statue.

"I've been trying to decide," Scarlet said, "ever since you turned up, if you're a Robert, or a Jim."

Lauren frowned.

"Stay at home or run away," Scarlet said. "That's everybody's question, isn't it."

"What did you do?"

"Ran away. Came back. Ran away. Came back."

"I never thought of life without a dad," said Lauren.

"Fathers are always difficult, don't you think?" said Scarlet.

Lauren shrugged.

"Well, I know some," Scarlet added. She stretched out her arms and said, "Keep walking." They headed off, with Scarlet's arm around Lauren. Scarlet side-stepped a puddle and said, "Jim really didn't like his father, I guess." She walked on, pulling Lauren with her.

"Hasn't he talked to you?" Lauren said, "about his parents?"

"No. Not much. Like I said, he always says he doesn't

167

do families." She turned to look at Lauren. "You carry it with you, you know, your childhood, wherever you go."

"God. Do you think?" said Lauren, with a shiver.

"Yours wasn't so bad. It's what you make of it." Scarlet hugged Lauren. "Have you seen your father recently?"

Lauren shook her head.

"Or heard about the row?"

Something in Scarlet's voice caught at Lauren. She tugged at the scarf around her neck, looked at the ground, and managed to ask what the row had been about.

"Their parents," Scarlet said. "Their father."

"He died before I was born," said Lauren. "What about him?"

Scarlet walked ahead, pulling her coat around her, and turned around, her back to the wind. "I don't know. It was crazy stuff, about when they were kids."

"Haven't you, like, talked to Jim about it?" Lauren said.

"He won't talk. Like I said, he's just… stopped."

"Have you talked to Dad?"

Scarlet forced herself to say, "That's the thing. He's not answering my calls. He's not been back."

"That doesn't sound like Dad. I mean…"

Scarlet's shoulders dropped, and her eyes looked far away.

"Don't worry," she said. "Don't worry, I shouldn't have brought it up."

"No. No, it's fine, honestly. I mean, like, Dad hasn't told me anything."

After a time, Lauren asked. "Where are we going?"

"To Bayswater, where Tessa lives. She's one of my English friends, and a back-up singer like me. Time to start teaching you what music really is."

They walked together in silence to the end of the park.

At that same moment, Barbara was on the tube heading to Sloane Square, worried she was late for a light lunch and a little shopping with Rhianne. She thinks of Rhianne as a salsa friend, the sort of person whose company you enjoy for as long as the music plays, but probably would never get close to outside the class. For a start, she's much younger, mid-forties, and disagreeable though it is to admit, much more dynamic. One of those women you suddenly discover runs a large business, or writes reports for governments or the United Nations. But for now it's a one-off deal to meet in Peter Jones, chat, and shop.

They had fixed this up a couple of weeks ago, but in a way it's unexpectedly timely because Robert is staying all hours at work, and when he's at home has moved beyond her reach. His last time with Jim was a car crash she'd been half aware she was waiting to happen, even if she couldn't have predicted when. Now Robert's retreated deep into himself, as if emptied out and refilled with a lethargy that cannot speak because it has no sense of the passing of time. He goes through the motions of cooking although he has lost all interest in doing so, and manages flickers of interest out of politeness. She cannot remember him ever being like this before. So in another way, the timing could not be worse.

What's difficult for her is to decide what she thinks about it. In her sorrow at seeing him like this she bustled around him, every suggestion an intrusion, every question, although unanswered, a wound. Pained, bewildered, but aware she does not quite understand why he has become so depressed. On those few occasions when she had expected, even wanted the relationship with Jim to end she had supposed it would be clean and abrupt. But yes, unlikely. Her rising fear now was that Robert would see Jim through to his final moments, and what that might mean was a darkness of contradictions her intuitions could not penetrate.

Sloane Square. She put her unread magazine in her capacious, empty bag and followed the crowd out to the exit, made her way to Peter Jones, up to the second floor, and scanned it for Rhianne. There she was with, praise be, a window seat. Apologies and pleasantries exchanged, she said "How did you manage to get a seat with a view?"

"I've been here since breakfast," Rhianne replied, and then put her hand on Barbara's arm and said "Only joking. I saw it as I arrived and made a frightful beeline for it."

They settled into compliments, and a little talk about the salsa instructor.

"He's rather gorgeous, isn't he," Rhianne said with a twinkle.

"A bit too young for me," Barbara replied.

"Oh go on, you quite fancy him. Everyone I've talked to does."

Don't go there, Barbara thought. Don't go there. "I admit, he can dance."

Rhianne looked at her and, when Barbara said no more, switched the talk to the other dancers, and then the choice of lunch and desserts, which came promptly. "Don't worry about calories, we're going to burn them all off," she said, adding "I hope Robert'll be coming back soon."

"Yes," Barbara replied, "but there's quite a crisis at the hospital, he doesn't know when it will end." That was the lie she'd worked out would cover everything.

"I know," said Rhianne. "It seems I read about the NHS every day."

"Is that what you do, hospital work?"

"Oh no, nothing so useful. I'm most of the way up one of those quangos giving out less and less money every year to countries we're otherwise trying to bankrupt."

Barbara didn't immediately know what to say, and Rhianne went on "You work in the hospital too?"

"Yes," said Barbara, "in HR. It's tough there as well. And Georgio?"

"Oh, don't worry about him. He does something to do with funding start-ups. I tell him he talks about unicorns in his sleep, but it's all way above my head." She paused. "That's how we met, actually. He was way above my head."

Barbara looked puzzled, and Rhianne explained "He was hang-gliding, and I thought it looked the most wonderful thing ever. So I did a little online search, found out where he'd must've set out from, and well, when he returned I thought he was pretty good too."

Barbara nodded in agreement, Georgio was a stylish dresser, and he could most certainly dance. "How long have you been together?"

"Four years. He's husband number two. Or number three, it depends on how you count."

"Any children?"

"No." Rhianne shook her head. "None for him, none for me."

Barbara decided she had nothing to lose, and said "I hope you don't mind my asking, but don't you want any?"

"Oh, yes we do," said Rhianne, "that's not a secret. But the whys and wherefores are a little complicated." She reached under the table for her handbag (Michael Michael Kors, Barbara noticed) and said "Come on, let's get down to the serious business of the day."

"Split the bill?" Barbara asked.

"Dear me, no" Rhianne said. "My treat, you can do it next time."

"Harrods?"

Rhianne squeezed her arm and said "We can do a bit better than that," and once the bill was paid she led Barbara off for what she called their 'R and R'.

The warm effects of the chatter, the trying on of autumn dresses and winter shoes, even hats (unsuccessfully), laughing at some of the prices as they bustled arm in arm up and down the King's Road in the dreary weather, lasted most of the way home, until she realised that most likely Robert would not share in her amusement at the day's retail therapy, which she had begun to feel Rhianne had somehow planned for her, and her anxieties began to ramp back up. "Oh, Robert," she thought, "where do we go from here?" and unable to answer her own question found herself asking it over and over again, as the clothes in her now-plump shopping bags lay in her lap like sleeping kittens she no longer wanted.

Chapter 12

Late October 2018

In a cold, wet month, the signs of autumn have appeared early, which Jim is denying has given him a sense of foreboding. But he has no better explanation for the fact that he is, as he puts it, out of sorts. Or, as Scarlet has just told him, out of sorts and a total selfish shit. He has retreated to his bedroom late this afternoon, leaving the living room to her, and now he is sitting upstairs and she downstairs united in an inability to do anything. Until one of them finds better words – and he hopes and supposes it will be her – neither of them will have much of a day. However, she is not yet in a state to find the words. Instead, she is staring wordlessly at the room, almost immobile, wrapped in an emotion that has encased her body, pressing upon her eyelids, her back, her stomach, her lower arms, her thighs. It is a tension familiar to her, which will not go away until she finds something to do that will lift it, which right now she is reluctant to do. She would rather prolong this moment than end it, as she would prolong most of her moments, eking them out as if they were her few remaining coins.

To her surprise, it was Jim who broke first, and called her in a weak voice. She went upstairs, and found him not in the bedroom but in the bathroom, sitting in his pyjamas on the edge of the bath, unable or unwilling to move.

"You in any pain?" she asked him.

Jim looked down at the floor, then up at her, and said, "A bit. OK, quite a bit."

"Any signs of bleeding?"

"You can guess."

"I'm going to phone McIntire," she said. "See if we can get you looked at. Just to be safe."

Jim, dejected, said, "Do what you have to do, doc."

He took her arm, stood up slowly, and walked slowly past her and back to the bed. She phoned McIntire, who said he couldn't be over before eight, and told her that that was probably good enough. She told Jim, and offered to sit with him, but he brushed her away, insisting that he wanted to be on his own, and she went back downstairs.

It was worse than before. Nothing was right, nothing held her attention. She made a cup of coffee then forgot it, and poured it away when she found it again. She kept thinking of phoning Robert, but it had been almost a month now and he hadn't been in touch. Jim was refusing to speak to him, and unless he changed his mind there wasn't much point in her trying. A lengthy hour of drawn-out fragments passed, until she heard Jim slowly making his way downstairs. She went to meet him. He was dressed, she was pleased to see, in a shirt and pullover, trousers, socks and slippers. He'd combed his hair but his face was still drawn. She offered to help him, but he insisted he was capable of walking, and made his way to the sofa, where he sat down.

"I feel better, now I'm up," he said, and he deflected any further questions about his health. Their conversation proceeded erratically, burdened as it was with good intentions, until his phone rang. He fished it out of a trouser pocket, listened quietly, said, "I will, I will," and put the phone away. "That was the doc," he said. "They're sending an ambulance. He doesn't know when it will get here, but I should pack an overnight bag." He turned to her. "Would you, please?"

"I'm sure it'll be all right," she said. "You'll be home tomorrow, feeling better."

Jim didn't reply. He brushed at a fleck of dirt on his trousers, looked at his hands, let his head sink forward a little, and waited for Scarlet to leave.

She came back downstairs with the bag and gave it to him. "When the ambulance comes, I'll follow," she said. "A & E or surgery?"

He looked up from the bag and said uncertainly, "I don't remember. I'm sorry."

"It's not a problem. I'll ask them when they come; it'll make it easier for me to find you."

A & E was busy. After a check to make sure he was no longer bleeding, they were put in a small, pale green cubicle at the end of a corridor with a narrow bed, where they waited an hour before a tall houseman of West Indian heritage who introduced himself as Dr Ambrose came to see Jim, but all he could promise was to come back and arrange for a CT scan as soon as he could. McIntire came by, and Ambrose popped in to explain what he had in mind, but neither had anything much to say about what Jim was going through. Best wait until we've had a closer look, Ambrose said, and McIntire agreed.

When they'd both left, Scarlet squeezed Jim's hands, which were cold although the room was very warm, and said, "You want your music? Your iPhone's in your bag."

He shook his head. "I'm not in the mood." He sat quietly, and then said, "Is there a glass of water?"

She went to get one, and came back with water in a conical beaker. He drank some and handed the beaker back, and she held it for a while until it became awkward and she went and threw it away, and went for a walk. Doctors in white lab coats, nurses in blue uniforms, and orderlies in green (she supposed they were) bustled about between the cordoned-off rooms, and she found their activity unsettling. Other sick people who required urgent attention reminded her just how bad it could be, and that Jim's condition was equally bad, and then that Jim was an emergency, needing extra treatment that could only last for so long, if at all. Which he was not getting. No one seemed to know what exactly was wrong with him right now, no one was there to explain what was going on. A sense of remoteness took possession of her, which could not be talked away and added to the confusion, the decisions and doubts that played in her mind like a second-rate double act.

She took out her mobile and called Robert, counting the seconds until he picked up.

"He's in hospital," she said. "I think he's really sick."

Robert was silent, she couldn't tell for how long.

"How ill?" he said. "What are his symptoms?"

So cold, she thought. So distant. "Pain. He's been bleeding."

"Where are you now?"

"In A & E. We've been here for hours."

"Which hospital?"

"The Royal United. It's out of Bath towards Bristol." Don't make me beg, please. Say you'll come. I don't have anybody else. She waited.

Finally, he spoke. "I'll ring McIntire, see what he says. And I'll ring you back."

"Will you, please? Please."

He hung up.

She went back to Jim, who was almost asleep, and pulled the chair up close so that she could hold his hand. He looked sleepily at her, and she murmured back, "No news. You get some rest. Someone will be here soon." He was too tired to argue.

Another hour went by. A nurse would look in, she would stare at her with wide-open eyes, and to her mute question the nurse would reply, "Someone will be with you soon." She went to the desk and was assured that yes, Jim would be attended to. It was obvious that a couple of people on the other side of the room needed a lot of attention; blue and white figures were coming and going with trays and towels. A dozen people with presumably less urgent conditions sat in the three rows of blue chairs that were bolted to the floor: drunks, people with bandaged arms and heads, an elderly, confused woman in a raincoat, a stoical woman in her sixties with a fussing husband, a stout mother with her eight-year-old, and a nearly bald young man with multiple tattoos and piercings trying to lie down and sleep. She went back to Jim, who really did seem to be asleep this time.

Her phone rang. It was Robert.

"I can't come," he said. "There's nothing I can do if I got there. I'm sure he'll pull through."

Before he could say any more, she hung up. No point in listening to words like these, no point in picking over them, although she knew she would. She wandered down the only corridor open to her, back to the front doors of A & E, where a cold hallway split into three passages, with a booth on a corner occupied by a tired elderly woman who smiled at her and went back to her magazine, frayed notices offering health advice were pinned to one wall, and where she could look out at the ambulances and the car park beyond. She told herself not to linger and found herself walking back and forth. A man and a woman approached the doors. A young couple, and she was guiding him as if he could hardly see. He smiled vacantly at her as they passed.

She went back to Jim's room, and found McIntire was there. She waited for him to speak.

"It's worth a careful look," he replied to her unasked question. "He'll get through this," he added, somehow making it clear how reluctant he was to tell her anything at all.

"Don't say that. Don't say it when you don't mean it."

"But I do mean it. He will get through this."

Suddenly, two orderlies came in and carefully moved Jim onto a trolley. "To the CT room" one of them said. Scarlet tagged along, and they wound along the corridors until they came to the room where the scanner was housed, and a tall Nigerian doctor came out and introduced himself to Jim as Dr Emeka.

"Hope you've done great deeds," said Jim, weakly, and Dr Emeka gave a big smile.

"Let's see what I can do for you," he said.

The scanner was a white metal tube like a section of a giant drainpipe, with a bed that slid in and out of it. Dr Emeka asked Jim if he could get himself onto the bed, and with some help from Scarlet he did. The orderlies left, and Dr Emeka let Scarlet stay for a minute or two while he started up the machine from his control room off to one side, and then he asked her to wait outside. A long twenty-five minutes later he came out and said it was all done and Jim could go back to the ward. Scarlet went up to him to ask if anything had shown up, and he said it needed an oncologist to be sure. Then Dr Emeka went over to Jim's side and said, "Do great deeds," and Jim smiled.

As the orderlies pushed Jim back, Scarlet asked him, "What was all that about?"

"Emeka's an Igbo name," he replied. "It means 'God has done great deeds', or maybe 'you are very strong.'"

"How in hell do you know that?"

"A drummer," he said, "in St Louis. We used to hang out, get stoned. He told me."

"And what did you tell him?"

"That James was an apostle of the Lord."

"Well, there's a thing." She was quiet for a moment and then said, "It's good enough for me," she said, leaning over to kiss him lightly as she walked. "Maybe you can stop being such a selfish shit after all."

"I can try," he said, and he squeezed her hand.

An hour later, back in their little room, Dr Ambrose reappeared, took Scarlet and McIntire aside, and explained that the scans had been sent to oncology, who said there was nothing urgent but they wanted to keep Jim in overnight and do some more tests in the morning. The bleeding had come from the bowel, which could mean the tumour had grown, and it could mean they might want to take a closer look, but that wasn't very likely. Then he stepped over to Jim and told him they were keeping him in so they could have a better look in the morning, but it was nothing to worry about, and they'd move him over to a bed in a ward if they could, but it might not be overnight if they filled up suddenly. Jim said that was OK, and Ambrose and McIntire said their goodbyes and left.

There was an awkward silence, then Jim said, "Look, I'm really glad you've come, but you don't have to stay all night. Nothing's going to happen." She looked at him, but he was inscrutable and it unsettled her even more. "I'd rather you were here in the morning," he went on. "I might need you then."

"Please, get someone to ring me if anything happens," she said.

"I'm sure it won't.

"I'll be along at eight."

She kissed him, and walked away. To her surprise, she caught up with McIntire at the door to the car park. She looked at him and slowly shook her head. "You don't mean it, do you?"

"No, I do. They just want to check."

In the cold hospital strip lighting, her clothes looked ill-fitting and in need of a wash. Her hair trailed untidily over her shoulders, and she looked much older than she was. She stared through the glass doors, trying to resist the question she finally had to ask.

"Will he be in pain? Real pain?" Begging him for the impossible.

"We can stop the pain. If that's the way it goes."

"Then why don't you stop it now?"

"He has to be in constant, unbearable pain, and then…" he paused, "the morphine will make him unconscious most of the time."

And then, she knew, it would be a race between the increasing pain and the rising dose, and the man she loved would be lost to her well before he died.

"But it might not go that way," he said. "We'll do what we can. That's what every responsible doctor's signed up to."

The coldness of the man, she thought. Why had he bothered to come? Surely not to be sure that Robert hadn't.

"I have to go," she said, "if I'm going to be any use in the morning."

She turned away, and walked to her car, thinking of all the things people say. That Robert, and the doctors, and certainly Barbara, and Jim had said. That she had said. That didn't agree, and couldn't all be right. And she told herself that nobody knew what was true anyway. Thinking of a song they sang, saying goodbye but meaning don't let me go, and now it had to be both. If it ever could be.

Scarlet came early the next morning and was sent to General Surgery, where she found Jim asleep in his bed. She went to look for the senior ward nurse, who explained that Jim had just been brought over and checked in. There was nothing in the notes about any more bleeding, and Ms. Turner would be doing her rounds soon and she could ask her.

Scarlet sat down in an uncomfortable chair and watched Jim stir in his sleep, almost wake up, then settle back down, his breathing shallow, and then open an eye.

"Can I get you anything?" she said.

"I'm not hungry."

"Just as well," she replied. "You're on nil by mouth."

Jim was reluctant to talk, so they rested, kept awake by the chatter of the nurses and the porters, the preparations for the ward round, and the more mobile patients walking about. At nine, Ms. Turner appeared at the end of the bed. She was a small woman, with a slightly red face, a shock of bright auburn hair that had clearly resisted strenuous efforts to control it, and a brisk, energetic manner.

She reassured Jim that there was no sign anything too serious had happened, the bleeding had stopped of its own accord, although, at his stage, it was becoming necessary to keep a closer eye on things, and she explained that they wanted to do one or two more tests to be sure that he could be discharged in the afternoon. "You're better off at home," she said to Jim, and she waited for questions. Jim and Scarlet had none, and with a few quick words to Jim, she was off to the next bed and its moribund occupant.

Just before noon, the nurses announced that oncology had called for Jim, and they wheeled him away, only to bring him back an hour later.

Another uncertain hour passed, and then Ms Turner came bustling up, a sheaf of notes in her hand. Scarlet stood up to greet her; Jim managed a brief smile. The tumour in the bowel had grown, she said, which is what had caused the bleeding. This wasn't a good sign, she didn't want to pretend otherwise, but it hadn't grown by much, and the oncologists were optimistic that a change in the medication would stop the growth from going further. But they'd probably want him back in a month to have another look.

Jim looked at her. "That's not all it means, is it?" he said.

"Nobody's giving up on you," she replied.

"Of course you're not," said Jim. "You doctors never like to let go." He shifted his gaze to look at nothing. "Sometimes I wish I could just fade away."

Scarlet leant forward, unsure of what she'd heard. Jim shook his head. "No," he said, quietly. "No. Despite last night. And one or two others. The gig's not over yet."

Ms. Turner turned to Scarlet and said, "You can go to the pharmacy to get his new meds, and we've got to sign you out. But you're going home."

"That'll be nice," said Jim. "It gets boring here."

It took another two hours for things to be ready. As Jim and Scarlet talked intermittently, Jim watched the other patients, one able to walk unaided, one on a mobile drip, some sitting up in bed trying and failing to read, and an old man with lined cheeks and sprouting hair lying almost immobile. It wasn't possible to guess what had brought them there, but anyway it was more interesting to wonder how they would leave. Who would walk out? Who would be going home, to a family, to a cold room and a television, to their old life if they were lucky, with nothing more than a warning? As he would be, this time. And who would make a different journey, one he'd sung about often enough, knowing it was no journey at all? How was that going to go? An unexpected chill passed over him that he hoped no one would notice, and he waited for it to pass, but it didn't entirely. It left a small scar in his memory, like a scratch in a recording you'd never noticed before and now couldn't quite forget.

By the time they were ready to leave Ms. Turner was back on the ward. She came up to wish them goodbye, and Scarlet took her aside and began to ask her questions. The doctor took her gently by the arm and steered her down the ward, speaking in a quiet, confidential voice. They talked for a few minutes, and as they parted Ms. Turner called out a few words after her, Scarlet turned round and said, "Thanks, Tina," Jim looked up with a grin, and Scarlet said "there's never anything wrong with Tina Turner's greatest damn hit."

Robert hung up, and answered Barbara's unspoken question with a shake of the head. Jim wasn't dying yet.

"They've discharged him," he said as he poured them their drinks and sat down for the dinner Barbara had prepared. Meaning that Jim had no claim on a bed, only that he'd slipped down one step and probably could not be pulled back up, leaving Scarlet to watch the man who was, and was not, the man she loved being eroded, broken down, slowly and unevenly ceasing to be the man he had been. Of course, you could say that had always been the case. But the damage to the bowel and the liver was not the benign business of age. Memory can compensate for imagination, skill for daring, help could come from the doctors – although it too would run out, and even as it did the toll on Jim would show up in other ways. It already was.

"Will you go to see him?" Barbara asked.

"Not for this," he said, realising as he did so that Barbara saw that as a question for him alone. She'd made it clear that she would visit only once more, to say goodbye, however Jim's last few weeks or months would go. He remembered his father, baffled by emphysema, less and less able to breathe properly, angry that he didn't know how to fight back. And his mother, more empty than resigned, apparently pleased to hear stories of her grandchildren even when it was clear she barely remembered them. He thought of Parvinda's anguish at her father's painful death, and her clarity about what should be done. Suddenly, Jim playing games with denial, showing off on the piano, being the imperturbable host, seemed so much better a way to go, selfish, maddening, unfeeling as he could be. A burst of anger surged over Robert, and trickled down into guilt. Jim was dying, after all.

"No," he said, adding almost without intending to, "they'll keep him alive down there."

Barbara looked up sharply, and his whispered thoughts faded under her glance. He struggled to recall them.

"I mean, he's dying. We ought to think more about that."

"What are you saying?"

He wasn't sure, and he tried not to notice that the other meaning of Barbara's question still disturbed him. Would he be going back at all? The consoling irony of his life, he often thought, was that the best and simplest way for him to show that he was, finally, a strong and independent man would be to say no when the right thing was to say yes. To refuse to help when he should offer it. No longer to try, with indifferent success he supposed when this mood was on him, to answer the call of others but to listen only to himself. And, of course, the only way out of the paradox was to do the right thing after all. But Barbara wouldn't even murmur if he never went to see Jim again; she had already stepped away.

And this time he had refused, he realised, hadn't seen Jim in hospital, hadn't said the right things. He put down the newspaper he hadn't really been reading and looked across the room. He saw Barbara look inquisitively at him, but he ignored her and she went back to her book. Jim's ups and downs could tend only one way. His doctors had known that for two years or more, which didn't mean Jim shouldn't try to seize the day. But there comes a time, further along, where it isn't living that's difficult, it's dying. Not the hanging on, but the letting go.

"You're worrying me," Barbara said, putting her book down.

" I don't mean to."

"What are you going to do, when Jim's time comes?"

"Try to be there, I suppose."

She reached out for his hands. "Promise me you won't… Promise me you know you can't…"

He looked at her, and waited, and she said, "You'll go back, I know you will. And when you do, think of me. Think of *us*."

"What'd you mean?"

"I think you're lost, Robert. I really, truly, think you're lost."

Chapter 13

Late October 2018

The sun had come out although it had rained most of the day, and it caught the cherry tree in a blaze of gold, matching the spirit of music and argument that filled the house. Not complete bits of music, and not long arguments, but fragments in each case. Jim would play eight bars, Scarlet would start to sing, and then he would complain she was taking it too low or too high, and point out that he had a limited range of notes he could still sing. Scarlet would say "If you call that singing", and he would call on any number of bigger names than him who had made a melodic growl work for them. They would sing together so she could cover for him if his voice gave him trouble. The real risk that, after what had happened, he might turn out to be too tired altogether was firmly ignored. There was only one way this was going to go.

Getting The Guitarist had been the key. He respected Jim, of course, for his years in the business and his knowledge of the music, and he respected Scarlet, too. But he didn't just play. He didn't just turn up. He would do a show when he was ready. When the vibe was cool. "It isn't just music, man, it's a whole other thing as well, or it's nothing." Nor did he rehearse much. "Kills it, man, kills it. You gotta be open, let it flow through you." You can say that, she thought, when you play like you do. Why he wasn't better known, why, damn, he wasn't famous was the biggest mystery about him. Why he didn't have his own band, why it wasn't out there, was something she asked him every time they met, and his answers made no sense.

But he had committed, and Poker had gone along with it at once. "People will be coming, my darling, and of course I'll do it. They'll be coming for Jim and The Guitarist – and you, to be sure." He moved an up-and-coming act nearer Christmas and up the bill, and people knew without asking that this was likely to be Jim and Scarlet's last gig together, which would be a draw in itself. Ringing round to get a drummer took Scarlet a bit longer, but the drummer for The Pupas, who were to be the warm-up act, said he was happy to join if he could use his own kit. A bassist would be ideal, but the Goat's Head stage was small, and the performance would be intimate at best, so she decided to leave it.

Now that The Guitarist would be playing and with Jim on piano there was a bunch of songs she could do. The question was what Jim could sing with her. And so they talked key changes, and who got what verse, and when would she join in, and how it would end. All the time she watched his strength, listening to what force there was in his voice, and hoping there would be no more surprises. Was that ever the wrong word… But he was enjoying this.

He could sit at the piano for quite a time and roll out the tunes, the intros, take it up for her voice and down for his. And she was enjoying it too, every time she could forget the reason for it and throw herself into the songs, listen to him improvise, play their old game of rapidly shifting the keys one more time.

The words were more of a problem. Jim could narrow things down to the songs he most wanted to perform 'on this occasion', but they were no longer the songs he usually sang. They would rehearse, only to find he might still let the words slip the next day.

"Couldn't you go for the ones you really know?" Scarlet would say as he missed another entrance. "Why've you gotta pick the ones with complicated lyrics?"

"Good lyrics."

"Good, complicated lyrics you can't remember."

"Trust me. I was singing these before you were born."

"God, are they that old?"

On the day of the gig, it rained most of the time, which made Jim uneasy. It'd been a good morning, an hour of warm-up exercises and a couple of run-throughs with Scarlet, but now it was a restless period of waiting. No music was right, no conversation came to life. It wasn't true, he felt, that he had absolutely nothing to say. But right now, nothing. He went to the window and looked at the neglected garden that the rain was starting to make look oddly unwashed. He went to the piano, but couldn't choose anything to play. He went to the kitchen for a drink, and wound up choosing a glass of water, which he then barely touched and poured away. In between he sat but didn't rest, and finally Scarlet said, "Jesus, do something."

"Like what?"

"I don't know. Yoga. Automobile mechanics."

He said nothing.

"Can't hurt," she said, but she smiled at him and held him and he was calmed for a while.

Harrison's visit the day before hadn't been a success. That's to say, it had gone exactly as they had planned, but not as he had privately intended. He'd paid for what they now had; a couple of weeks' supply plus enough for tonight. That was what he and Scarlet had agreed, and what Harrison had supplied, with his usual cut on quality. "Just can't get guarantees, man, it all goes to the kids these days, even I'm being ripped off. And you don't want those legal highs. Jesus, who knows what's in them? Horse tranquillisers? Who are you trying to kid?" That's right, Harrison the straight dealer, the ethical face of dope. The used car salesman, more like. But anyway, he had wanted to buy something else this time, that had been the intention. What had stopped him? The sheer unreliability? Couldn't be. This time it just had to be enough. Scarlet being there the whole time? Yes, that was the reason. But what really did it, the synthetic icing on the whole plastic, inflated cake, was Harrison's absurd toupee. He was beginning to think he could bow out, on his own terms, in his own time, even if it was running out fast, but there had to be a hint of well, damn, dignity about it. Not his usual state, admittedly, but this wasn't a usual plan. He'd order the long black car, and get in it, but the chauffeur couldn't be a laughing stock. That would bring the whole thing crashing down. Not just the final hours but the whole damn show. He'd often pretended to believe life was a cosmic joke, but it mustn't be a cosmic *bad* joke.

At seven Scarlet drove them over to the Goat's Head. The rain had stopped, and they were thinking how good it will be to be performing together again, how the choice of songs has worked out well, and how good it will be to play with The Guitarist. They were pleased that the place will be packed – Poker has assured them that all the tickets have been sold – "Oh man, you could've filled an arena, I've never seen such interest." And they were also thinking of what could go wrong. The sound system, the obliging but sometimes mediocre drummer, the act before them messing up. But not Jim's health. They were trying very hard not to think about that and banished every thought of it that arose. Tonight was going to be a good night.

She parked the car near the back door of the Goat's Head where Poker had kept them a space. The car park was filling up already. They made their way to the back of the bar, nodded at Poker, and went upstairs. The Pupas were there, giggling over *Spiderman* on a PlayStation, but the drummer, Jake, came over.

"Hi," he said to Jim and Scarlet. "Good to see you out and about, man. You doing OK?"

"Could do worse," Jim replied.

"And you," he said, looking at Scarlet, "you're looking great."

"I'm cool," she replied. "You too."

Indeed, in his leather jacket and trousers and

torn shirt, with his long, dyed-blonde, curly hair, thin moustache, and an earring in his right ear, he looked the part of a drummer in a disaffected band, much more than he looked the part in his day job as a care home assistant.

"No, I mean it," Jake said.

Scarlet had dressed carefully in a short-sleeved well-fitted cream top and tight jeans, her hair for the moment tied up at the back in a clip. After all, Jim, in his open-necked shirt and plain trousers, was no looker.

The drummer rejoined his mates, and Jim and Scarlet moved away to a corner and shared a joint. Soon, Poker put his head round the door and told The Pupas they were on in ten minutes or they wouldn't get paid, and with the usual collection of jokes about not getting paid anyway and what do you expect if you can only get gigs this far out of town, they moved noisily downstairs, leaving the room to Jim and Scarlet.

"No Guitarist," Jim observed.

"It's early, he'll turn up," said Scarlet, and she quietly began to sing one of the songs they had rehearsed.

"We shouldn't have come so early," Jim said after a while.

"Don't tell me you're getting nervous."

"No, not that. I don't like waiting."

"You never got used to it?"

"Sure I did. This is a new thing for me." He got up and walked around the room, which overlooked the car park. He looked out and said, "Filling up nicely."

"Good," she said.

They listened to The Pupas briefly tune up and then launch into their crowd-pleasing favourite 'Death Star

Maidens', a thundering drum and guitar thrash the music critic of the old Bristol Evening Post had once compared to the opening of Haydn's 'Creation Mass' without its underlying harmonic logic. Three pounding numbers later, just when the band was moving into the slower section of their set, the door opened and The Guitarist came in. He was a slim figure with a slim face; he had his long black hair slicked back in a ponytail, and wore a dark red shirt, black trousers, and black shoes. In his right hand he carried a guitar case. Without a word, he went up to Scarlet and kissed her, and turned to Jim and gave him a hug.

"Good to be here," The Guitarist said in his soft voice, "Going to be a good show."

"Hope so," said Jim.

"I know it," said The Guitarist. "I can feel it."

"The man's nervous," said Scarlet, nodding at Jim.

"Bound to be," said The Guitarist. "You just want to be out there playing, not hanging around."

"And listening to this?" said Scarlet.

"Hey, it's their music. It speaks to them. Like it's moving outwards, if you know what I mean."

"Could be, well, tighter?" she replied.

"Sure, but if you don't try to speak you never say anything." He paused, then said, "You could come round. I'm staying over in Bristol with some of my gear. A friend has a place out of town. We could play." He turned to Scarlet. "And sing. It'd be my pleasure."

"I'd like that," she said. "But let's see how tonight goes, first."

They carried on talking for a few more minutes, until Jim got up and said, "I'm going downstairs."

They followed him and made their way down a long corridor that led to the far end of the bar. They passed through what Poker fondly called the stage door and into a small space to one side of the improvised stage, where performers could sit largely out of sight until it was their turn. The Pupas were now into their 'No Fuckin' Hatred Blues', an eight-minute litany of everything wrong with the world that seemed to be meeting with general agreement. A barman came and gave Jim a whisky, Scarlet a dry white wine, The Guitarist a glass of water, said, "On the house, from Poker," and vanished. They drank a little and put their glasses on a narrow table in front of them. Scarlet leant forward, pushed aside the curtain that hid them from the audience, and said, "It looks full."

Jim said, "Anyone in particular?"

She looked again and said, "Hard to tell. No, I think not."

He looked winded, and stared at his feet for a few seconds. Then he got up, and looked over at the crowd, who were engrossed in singing the rudimentary chorus, three lines of "No hatred big enough". He stood there for a while, and then sat down, turned to Scarlet, and said, "Try again, towards the back on the left."

"Robert?"

"No. You look."

She did as requested, and when she sat down this time she said, "Well, damn, Lauren's come."

Jim, evidently pleased, said, "Just like we asked her to."

"She could've said she was coming."

"She wasn't sure she could get away. Anyway, that's kids."

She squeezed his hand. "That's one good thing anyway."

'No Fuckin' Hatred Blues' came to a loudly-applauded end, and The Pupas's lead singer stepped forward. "I know you think all we can do is play loud," he said, to general cheers, "but tonight, as you know, is a special night." More cheers. "So special, we're lending our drummer to carry it off." Jake thumped his drums to more cheers. "Like, it's Big Jim's final night." More cheers. The singer held up his hand. "No, like, he's played with them all, and Scarlet's sung with most of them." More cheers. "And he says he's giving up but we all want him to carry on playing great music. So, coming on after us is Jim Parrish and Scarlet." More cheers. "And to get you all in the mood for everything they can do, we're going to play this," and the band launched into Neil Young's 'Old Man'. Quietly, eloquently, so that the audience had to listen, and they did listen, and when the singer finished there was a moment of silence before the real applause began, and over it the singer said softly "Thank you and goodnight" and walked off the stage. He went up to Jim, hugged him, and said, "They're here for you, man. And you, Scarlet, sing 'em away."

The two of them got up and somehow knocked over the table, spilling their drinks and breaking the wine glass.

"No problem," the singer said. "Brings you good luck."

They waited while another barman came, tidied up the broken glass and swiped a large cloth over the floor. "Who'd 'ave ever believed it," he said, "health 'n safety back stage." Meanwhile, the crowd got up and surged around the bar to get more drinks, people went out to smoke, more people came in, and there was the usual search for seats. After ten minutes, Poker stepped onto the stage, took one of the microphones, looked at everyone's faces, waited for them to go quiet, and said, "Ladies and gentlemen – Bristol City supporters leave now – you've all paid for this, you've all waited for this, now you're all going to get it. No less than the great Jim Parrish, with Scarlet, and," he paused for effect, "The Guitarist." Before anyone could respond, the drummer again thumped his drums, and with a wave of his hand, Poker said, "And, standing in at short notice, Jake from The Pupas." Poker stepped away from the microphone, and The Guitarist, Scarlet, and Jim came on stage to loud applause, cheers and shouts and whoops.

Jim sat down at the piano and idly picked out a few chords. Then he adjusted the height of the nearby microphone and said, a little hoarsely, "Hello. It's good to be here."

People clapped, Scarlet adjusted her mike and said, "Yeah, good to be here." The Guitarist adjusted his mike and said, "It's a personal pleasure," and Scarlet said, "Just three songs tonight, favourites of ours, and I hope of yours."

Somewhere backstage, Poker checked his tape deck and video cam and adjusted the lights: a spot on Scarlet, another on The Guitarist, and lights on the drums and the piano.

Scarlet stepped aside for a moment, touched her brooch, and looked at the expectant audience. Some people had moved, and new ones had come in. Lauren was still where she had been, at the back on the right, but there, she was sure, pushing in on the left and coming round the angle of the bar, was Robert. She stepped back and whispered the news to Jim, who said, "Let's play," and began the opening chords of the first number. He played eight bars with the drummer, eight more as The Guitarist joined in, and then leant forward and sang, his voice firm but rough, and cheers drowned out the opening lines.

Jim had to admit he was surprised. It was working better than he'd hoped. He handed over to The Guitarist at the bridge, pleased that Jake was following his left hand better than he'd thought he would, and came back to sing the next few lines, looked at The Guitarist, who nodded at him, and away they went, his right hand dancing over the piano. Another nod, they repeated the second half of the song, The Guitarist added four bars, Jim replied with four, then up went the guitar and as it came down Jake gave the drums a final flourish. Jim was good for more, and so was the crowd. This was the right place, even if it was the wrong time.

Scarlet let herself linger looking at him, smiling like she hadn't seen him do in weeks, just waiting to start the next number, knowing this is what he loves. Then The Guitarist caught her eye and began to pick out the next tune, and Jim started to trace out delicate runs under the melody and track the chords in the bass. As Scarlet leant forward to sing, she remembered hearing this one for the first time, on one of Jim's cherished tapes, the band having broken up before she'd even met him. They were his passion before they were hers, his sorrow at times, and then sometimes everything would be in its intricate place and you would know where music could take you. And tonight she could see it was clear Jim and The Guitarist were locked in. She looked at Jim, he smiled, and they took the next verse together.

Lauren shifted awkwardly in her seat, uncomfortable because she didn't know this one. The first one she sort of remembered, and she could see it'd got the crowd of old guys going. But this number's an odd, sad thing, she thought. Nobody sings this stuff anymore, it's almost like folk music, and yet it means a lot to Jim and Scarlet. And they sing well, too; they're together, like they really mean it.

Robert sat in a silent argument at the back of the room, voices in his head asking him if he should have come earlier or not come at all. Sure, it's a big deal for Jim. Let him go ahead, have his last words while he can. But why did he have to put up with them? He's managed long enough; he can see himself out. He could hear Barbara saying, "And there you are, doing the right thing as you always do." As if there's no credit in it anymore. You just turn up. As if not turning up was the better option but he didn't know how to do that. Anyway, to do what instead, this Friday evening?

Jim looked over at Scarlet, who leant warmly towards him, and they sang together. Lauren stared at them, knowing she didn't get what this one was about. It's not a love song, it's not a break-up. No one's leaving, no one's happy to stay. Staring at them as they sang, and the guy on the guitar hit just the right chords for what her uncle was playing. Then they played solo again, and then it was Scarlet's turn, then the whole song came round again, and Jim came in for the last few lines. She turned up the volume, he was almost speaking the words. Lauren shivered, as if she had been let into a secret life.

Even Robert had to admit it had worked the way they must have hoped. Damn him. That repetition had left the audience not knowing how it was going to go and not knowing what it wanted. Even he hadn't, listening to this promise of the high time, the good life, that's just out of reach. He's good, he said to himself, even if I don't want to admit it. And she is.

The applause was loud, they knew they were on. Jim's voice was rougher than they'd hoped, but it was working. They looked at each other and as the applause turned to an expectant hush Jim said "This one's called an 'Angel from Montgomery', and as everyone cheered, The Guitarist played the opening four bars, and Jim began to sing.

Shit, thought Lauren, it's another sad one, like it's all these old guys want to be, and kind've upside down, too. Who's who? But now her voice, God, it says so much. I can live in that voice, it's like it's my voice, my secret, ideal voice I'll never really have, and I'm singing this old song from the end of a broken-down life. A voice that somehow floats, surges, pulls me out of myself. And him, too. The piano plays the voice back, like another chance, another time. Don't stop. Don't ever end.

Robert could feel himself trying to hold back, not wanting to like this, saying to himself it was only a song, it would be over in five minutes. Then he could go up and say all the right things and enjoy not quite meaning it. Say all the right things and say nothing, because the right things do say nothing. What else could you say? But there Jim and Scarlet were, in the moment, and he realised they weren't playing together for the last time, they weren't finding out how it feels to be truly at the end. They were here, now, waiting for the angel in the song and knowing it will never come, and in this moment they were alive, and the song will end because everything ends, but everyone here believes in them, is holding on to them until time returns and claims what it must, and the song is lost to them. Holding on, even as the voices fade away.

Jim looked at Scarlet as she came out of the song, and she looked at him, and they knew they had nailed it. The Guitarist, too. And Jake. And the feeling was so good. As people got up, clapping and cheering, The Guitarist stepped forward, and when they quietened down he said, "I want you to know, it's one of the pleasures of my life to have played with Jim and Scarlet tonight." And Jake stood up and waved and gestured to them to step forward. Scarlet put an arm around Jim and they almost took a bow, and people wouldn't stop clapping. They left the little stage with people still clapping, now in a rhythmic clap, almost a marching clap, and they came back out. People sat down, and when they were quiet Jim looked at Jake. He tapped the drums, Jim began the cyclical bass that held the number together, The Guitarist picked out the tune, and after sixteen bars Scarlet began to sing. People clapped along, The Guitarist took the first solo, Jim the second, they slowed it down as they neared the end, but the drums wouldn't let them and Jim and Scarlet surged back, singing that they're near the end. Don't let it be the end. Never do that.

Everyone was on their feet and people began walking right onto the stage to speak to Scarlet and Jim as soon as he stood up, Scarlet resting her head on his shoulder trying not to cry. Out of the corner of his eye Jim saw Lauren coming towards them, and, from the other side of the room, Robert. He wondered if he'd known that she was going to be here, and what she made of it. What will she think of her uncool dad, if she even asks his opinion? He could see Robert easily, pushing his way through the crowd, until Poker blocked his path, and he heard him say, "I'm Jim's brother," but Poker looked at him unpersuaded until he nodded at him to let Robert through.

"Sure," said Poker. "Jim told me you'd be here if you could make it."

"I'm glad I did," said Robert.

"You'd have to be deaf not to be," Poker said, making room for him to pass.

Jim and Scarlet were backed up against the door, Scarlet with an arm around him and a drink in her free hand. The Guitarist was over at one side with his own group of fans, and so was Jake. Jim beckoned Robert over. "You made it," he said.

"I'm glad I did," he said, repeating himself.

"You should be," Jim said with a grin.

"He was great, wasn't he," Scarlet said to him.

"You too," he said.

"Even if it isn't Bach?" Jim said, still grinning.

"Tonight was just as good," he said, and to his surprise Jim realised Robert really meant it.

"We took you away?" he asked, suddenly wanting to know his answer.

"The last one. Before the encore. The angel one."

"It never fails, that one," Jim said. "Unless it crashes. I know people who are afraid to sing it, in case they're not there with it. Be dishonest in that song and you suffer, for sure."

"I was hooked," Robert said. "I was with you." And Jim realised Robert was pleased, simply pleased.

"Here's somebody else," said Scarlet. She waved Lauren in and she pushed her way through the crowd.

"You were great," she said. "Both of you. Really great."

"Not too many sad old songs for a hip-hop girl?" said Scarlet.

"No," she said. "Not too many. I liked them. Really." Then she turned to Robert and said, "Hello, Dad. I didn't think you were into this sort of stuff."

"Never too late to become a fan," he said, and she looked at him in a way that said, "Yes it is, of course it is", and he said, "So are you a fan?" and she said, "No. No, it was really great."

"You guys want a drink?" Jim asked, and they said no it's all right but he waved at Poker who came over.

"Poker," he said, "drinks for these good people. They're family."

"You his long-lost daughter?" he asked Lauren, and she started to say "No I'm not," but Jim interrupted.

"Yeah, you know me, I've got so many. This one's called Lauren, and she'll have a generous vodka if I remember correctly," which made her even more uncertain what to say. Jim ordered double whiskies for himself and Robert, who pulled out his wallet, but Poker waved it away and disappeared.

"I didn't know you were coming," Robert said to Lauren, who started to say, "I don't have to tell you," but he cut her short, "It's a nice surprise. I'm glad you're here." He put an arm around her and kissed the top of her head. Scarlet smiled and said, "It's OK to kiss your dad, you know, on a night like this," and she turned her head up and pecked his cheek.

"We weren't sure you were coming," said Scarlet.

"I nearly missed the train," said Lauren, "I couldn't get away from work."

"How's it going?" Robert asked.

"OK," she said. "Interesting, actually. You meet some cool people."

"How did you know they were playing?" Robert asked, only to realise it was a stupid question even as he asked it.

"We asked her," Scarlet said quickly. "In case we needed our friends tonight."

"You must be pleased, though," he said.

"Yes," she said, "very. Very pleased, actually."

Poker reappeared with the drinks, everyone said cheers, and then Jim enquired, "You know the thing about the last number, the third one, if you were counting?"

Lauren and Robert said no, and Jim replied, "An angel from Montgomery is a state pardon."

"So he's in jail?" said Robert.

"Death row. Or her. But yeah, I think it's him," Jim said, and looked at Lauren. "You want to step outside, have a cigarette?" She agreed, and out they went.

Robert turned to Scarlet. "Is it really the last time?" he asked.

"The Guitarist wants us to play with him next week,"

she replied. "Just for fun, nobody listening. We might do that. But yeah, that was the last performance of Jim and Scarlet."

"You ended on a high note."

"We did, didn't we." She looked straight at him, still excited. "I can't describe it. It's not like being high. It's not like listening, even when you're right inside the song. There's so much you want to do, and things you hope to do. And when it all happens..."

For a moment there was a silence around them in the crowd of everyone talking, and when it passed she said, "I didn't think you'd come."

"I nearly didn't," he said. "And then I thought I couldn't stay away. I'd show the face, and probably just go."

"He wanted you here, you know. He didn't say so. But he wanted you."

"I keep saying it, but I'm glad I came."

"I'm glad you did."

They finished their drinks, and he said, "What happens to you next? Will you still sing?"

"I won't give up. They'll have to push me out and bolt the studio doors."

"And sing like this? Gigs?"

"You know, not for a while. Not for as long as... well, you know."

"People will want to hear you," he said. "I will."

"I'll drink to that," she said, warmed by his enthusiasm, and they clinked their empty glasses. "Let's go and find Jim and Lauren," she said, and as she did so Poker stood up and said,

"That was the last act, ladies and gents. The last act."

Chapter 14

Mid-November 2018

"I look like a scrawny waxwork. A shit-awful waxwork."
Jim leant forward, supporting himself on the bathroom
sink and looking in the early morning mirror. It had
become a ritual greeting, varying only in its tone across
late October and November: accepting, self-piteous,
comic, sad. Blues, country and western, bluegrass; blues
again. He knew what his future held. In a matter of weeks,
months at the most, he'd be eating less and less and losing
weight, nothing he wore would fit him, and he'd be lost
inside his clothes. Sleep was already difficult, no position
was comfortable, but pain and his growing tiredness
would prolong every day without giving him any rest.
He would doze, drift off briefly, and return to a passive,
utterly dull existence. Scarlet was already going shopping
and cooking different meals. Next, it would be endless
soups, all of them tasteless. If the last time was any guide,
he'd develop diarrhoea, he'd be unable to play the piano
because the meds would turn the palms of his hands
red and sore, and McIntire would try another course of

irinotecan injections every two weeks, which might halt the overall decline in his condition. But this too would bring no release, because Jim knew that it could not last, and every day would become more than enough for him to bear.

Robert was visiting when he could, doing his best to explain the explanations McIntire had offered Jim of what he was doing, and trying to shake off the feeling that McIntire was building a wall around Jim, and watching what he might be planning. Trying, too, to keep Jim's mood from turning completely dark, to be the person Jim could say anything to, and to shield Scarlet from some of Jim's despair. But some things do not need to be said, and some things cannot be said, and the house filled up with them until they were the air everyone breathed and settled into a silence that leeched away the familiar structures of their lives.

Jim looked emptily at the garden, clogged with fallen leaves. A cup of weak, milkless tea, which Scarlet had brought him, was now forgotten on the table beside him, and she was busying herself rearranging things in the rooms, putting away the dishes, dusting the furniture.

"Stop that, will you," he said.

"I'm just tidying up."

"You're not. You're pushing things around for the hell of it."

Something peremptory in his hoarse voice caught her, and she came over and sat beside him.

"I want to die," he said.

She looked at him and didn't know what to say. She reached forward to hold his hand and found she could not breathe. The moment was his to break.

He pushed himself into a more upright position and said more loudly, "I want to die."

"You know I love you," she said.

"It's too much," he said, slumping back. "I want it to end."

His eyes flickered towards her, but he couldn't hold his gaze. She looked at his face, trying to see the life in him, the energy that rose and fell, not with his breathing but to a slower, more uncertain beat, trying to catch it on the rise and hold it there.

"We can talk to McIntire. There might be new injections…"

"I don't want them."

"He might have something new, for the pain…"

He looked at her again. He squeezed her hand but he didn't speak. And now, when he didn't fight her, didn't spell out what he'd been trying to say, or force her to see how wilfully she was failing to appreciate what he was saying, she understood what she had not before. It'd never been his nature to hide from an argument: disagreement came so naturally to him, but now something had left him, and she saw him more keenly and yet across an empty space, as if he was lost like a ship in a distant ocean.

She'd thought she'd understood all along. He was dying, even if she'd almost never been able to say the word, even to herself. He'd been dying, she had known, the very first time he took himself to the family physician, before all the tests and examinations. He'd gone too late (and that was another word she could barely say), it was already too advanced. He was dying before the secondaries had been found, dying on the flight to England, dying every day as they settled in and played their gigs and made a few new friends. Dying though alive, though charming, full of humour, and smoking and drinking until recently. Outwardly, like his body, well worn, lived in, comfortable; inwardly, like his body, slowly being torn apart.

She'd known that, even before his first attempt, not, she thought, to end it all, but to howl, to protest, to beg some greater power to admit the grotesque unfairness of it all and to put it right, cure him completely, on the spot. Not with any hope, of course, just to cry out against it. And the greater powers had continued their eternal silence, and he had spat at them, and returned to his daily life. And again, by the White Horse, that phoney theatre he had surely seen as just another in the line of all those clubs and festivals and bars where, after all, he was most at home. Most himself. Ready and able to lose himself in the music. She'd known then, talking to Robert, that Jim was dying, known more clearly than before that dying is not one event, the drawing of a last breath, but a process, a descent, a passage from layer to layer, shelf to shelf in some darkening cave, where at each stage something must be given up. For some it is walking, for others the pleasures of food or drink, seeing friends, or hearing, even sight. And for some, she knew abstractly, hope. But never for Jim, never. He was too alive for that, and even in moments of despair hope would return. It always had, it always would. But now, as she looked at his exhausted face, she understood for the first time the falsity of that word. Nothing was for ever. What had been a simple abbreviation or a charming exaggeration was also a lie.

The rest of the day passed in broken silences; gentle words floated across an abyss, tentative movements towards each other as she got ready to follow him one further step down. Jim had said what he had to say and did not wish to push it any further. Their new routine continued; the pain, the tiredness, the sheer pointlessness of it all and the all-consuming need to be together, in an inconstant, disorienting mix.

When McIntire came in the late afternoon, making his weekly visit, Jim was well enough to be downstairs, a fact McIntire noted at once.

"Still well enough to get up and about, I see," said McIntire, pulling up a chair and sitting down, and Jim realised at once he'd made a mistake. Scarlet sat down opposite him, next to Jim.

"I don't want to be," said Jim.

McIntire sat forward and started to talk in a quiet, practised voice through the symptoms and the changes, to separate them into side effects and the progress of the cancer, to hint at what could be done, and Jim fell silent. Seeing this, McIntire paused and waited for him to speak.

"I want to die," said Jim.

"Well," said McIntire, "we can't arrange that, as you know, all we can do is manage it. And there might be better things we can do."

"I don't want them," said Jim, and the hint of fear in his voice made McIntire wait for a moment.

"You're a strong man," he said, "in a body that is slowly giving way. You need to understand what your options are."

"I haven't got any fucking options. It's tiring me out just talking to you." He stopped as a spasm of pain swept over him.

McIntire sat back, looked at Jim, then at Scarlet, and back at Jim. He leant forward again, and, in his professional voice, said, "There are always options. Perhaps none of them are what you want, but there are some. And choices must be made. I need to know what you are saying. You must understand, I cannot give you," he looked at Jim, "what you want. And on the other hand," he now looked at Scarlet, "the things I can do for you are not entirely exhausted."

"Like what?" she said, squeezing Jim's hand.

"We can manage the pain. And you have the right," looking at Jim again, "to ask me to discontinue the treatment."

Scarlet looked fearfully at him, holding her breath.

"It would hasten things," McIntire went on. "But that is all it would do. I still think—"

"What, you damn torturer?" said Jim. "What?"

"There are experimental treatments, new drugs. The results are promising, there are clinical trials that are sufficiently advanced for them to want patients. It would not, of course, be a cure, but it could set your cancer back and give you a few more months. I'm not promising, of course."

"Not interested," said Jim. "I want it over." But he caught a glimmer in Scarlet's eye, and stopped.

"I'd like you to think about it," McIntire continued. "I can call back in a couple of days, to see what you think. I wouldn't want to delay."

Jim refused to speak, so McIntire got up, wished him well, and walked with Scarlet to the door. When they got there, she said, "Did you really mean that? About the new drugs and taking part in a trial?"

"Walk me to my car," he said. "I have to be somewhere else, I'm running late." She followed him down the path to his car, which was parked by the gate. The dank November air smelled of fallen leaves, fires lit against the coming winter, and of retreat.

"He'll have to fit whatever it is they're looking for, and," he dropped his voice, "he would have to give his consent. His explicit consent."

"He's saying he won't."

"It's not for me to change his mind. But if you wanted to talk it through with him, he might get some extra weeks."

Scarlet looked around at the encroaching night and pulled her shawl around her. "And if he doesn't want it?"

"There's always hope. Try to persuade him of that." He opened the car door and got in. "There's always hope," he repeated. "Always."

He shut the car door and drove slowly away. Scarlet watched the red lights recede slowly until, at the turn in the road, they were gone.

The words of 'Love in vain' cried in her head. In Robert Johnson's voice. In Jim's voice. In her voice.

Jim and Scarlet did not discuss it the next day. It seemed too insistent a demand, and this was a quiet and peaceful day, which was rare, and not to be disturbed. So they accepted it as if they were in hiding, as if any activity would give them away. They took the day and asked it no questions, kissed each other good night and went to bed like children waiting expectantly for tomorrow.

The next morning in the kitchen, Jim stared coldly at a slice of toast and said, "I won't do it. No new trial. No new drugs."

She sliced up his toast, pushed the plate across the table to him, and waited for him to say some more. After a time, he said, "You agree?"

"I want whatever you want."

He chewed listlessly at a piece of the toast. "No you don't," he said.

"Yes I do. I've been thinking about it. I want you to do whatever you think is right."

And then she found she couldn't say anything, stopped by the familiar pervasive guilt of not saying the right things. Not even knowing what they were.

Jim got up, took his glass of water and shuffled into the living room, and she started to tidy up the breakfast things. Then on an impulse she followed him and stood behind his chair, put her arms around him, and bent over and kissed the top of his head.

"Am I being crazy?" he said. "I can't go on like this."

She sat on the arm of the chair and stroked his cheek. He gave a gentle smile, and she said, "Maybe, something new…"

"I'm tired of new things," he said. "They're turning up uninvited."

"You're going to say that to McIntire?"

"He's keeping me alive for him, that's what he's doing. The doctor saving his patient." A burst of pain low in his stomach spread out and faded away, and in a hollow voice he said, "End it, Scarlet. End it. I don't want this anymore."

He retreated into his shell, into the shameful fallacy of believing he could hide from the pain, that next time it entered the room it might not find him and would leave like a vengeful ghost to look elsewhere. She could see that and knew she had to leave him where he was. His world had opened up to her and closed, more certainly than if he was well but high, or asleep.

She closed her eyes and found that, as so often these days, her memories of Jim were solely of him as he was now: exhausted, untidy, almost immobile. She worried that they would be her only memories of him, that they'd burned out all the earlier ones. That, paradoxically, his final weakness would represent him, and not his life, like a few pictures salvaged from a fire. And she promised herself that she would not let his life be captured in these moments. Not just these.

When McIntire stopped by in the late afternoon Jim was asleep. Scarlet stopped him in the hall and said, "You must ask him, but he'll say no." He looked quizzically at her, and then nodded. She was surprised at how simple it'd been to say, after all, and they stood there silently for a moment.

"You'd better come this way," she said, "and wake him up."

Jim lay in his chair, in evident discomfort, and McIntire stood beside him, content to let his presence sift its way into Jim's awareness, and when it did and he opened both eyes to look at him, McIntire said, as always, "How are you today?"

Jim shuffled himself into a more comfortable position and said, "I've made my mind up. I don't want your new tricks."

"I respect your decision," McIntire said. "But there are still various ways we can proceed."

"Just one," said Jim with a firmness that surprised the others. "End it. End it now."

McIntire sat down, posture perfectly straight, and said, "You know I cannot do that."

"Come on, doc, there are these drugs. End-of-life drugs. You know that."

"I do, but by law I cannot administer them. I cannot end your life."

Jim was quiet.

"And you know that, Jim," McIntire said. "And your brother should know that too."

He looked at Jim's face and saw in it faces he had seen many times before: those of the angry man, the proud man and the defeated, the lost, the resigned, and the self-deceived. No one, he thought, is brave at this point, and no one should try to be. And no one can be helped – at least, not the way they say they want. He sat there, paralysed, protected by law from all of those he had sat with at this point in their lives, and knew he had to wait for the face he could speak to, whichever one it would be, when Jim was ready.

"Morphine. A morphine drip?" Scarlet asked, and McIntire thought the anguish in her voice was new. He took a deep breath.

"I'd have to be certain," he said, looking at Jim, "that you were dying. That there was nothing else I could do for you. And that you were in a level of pain which was so intense that unconsciousness was preferable."

"I'm telling you I prefer it."

McIntire stood up. "And I have to tell you that I still believe there are things medicine can do for you."

Was it anger he saw in Jim's face? Or contempt?

"Please, doctor," said Scarlet, "you've no idea. I don't want Jim to be in real pain. You've got to do something."

"I can, and I will," he said. "Jim, if it comes to it, I can have a district nurse come round and give you injections morning and evening that will diminish the pain. But you must understand, no one can do what you're asking me to do."

Jim looked away, down at the body that would betray him all too soon. He reached up with his hands and lowered his head into them, and seemed to be curling up inside his clothes. McIntire waited for him to speak, but he did not.

"Please, doctor," Scarlet repeated. "Please. You must be able to do something."

But Jim said nothing, so McIntire made his goodbyes, walked to the door with Scarlet, explained that any treatment was up to Jim, and left. Scarlet went back to the living room and sat next to Jim, and they stayed there as it grew dark, finding nothing to say.

Scarlet and Jim sat looking at the garden, and he said, "An overdose. Get something from Harrison."

216

Scarlet said quietly, "You know what I think. I can't." She reached out her hand and took his arm. "I won't."

"I'd see *you* out."

"They'll come for me," she said. "A guy too sick to leave the house dies of an overdose –"

"Who would find out?"

So he was going to push, force her to think about it in more detail than she wanted, to say out loud what she had hoped need not be spelled out.

"The doctors," she said, still holding his hand. "McIntire –"

"OK, he's all proper and up himself. So what?"

"So police. Dead bodies are inquests."

"I could just slip away when you're out –"

"It's not happening. I'll hold your hand right to the end, but I'll not go to prison for you afterwards." She looked into his tired face, trying to gauge the intensity in his sunken eyes. "I'll cry afterwards. I'll bury you here, or scatter your ashes wherever you want, and if you could see me you'd be proud of me – but I won't do that for you."

He made no reply, and they sat there, silent, until after a time she looked away, withdrew her hand, and there gathered within her a desperate, familiar risk. "And because…" she said, and he stared back at her, daring her to say it. "Because you can't let Ryan think…"

"He doesn't care about me…"

"… that he failed you."

Jim stopped in disbelief.

"You didn't think of that?" she said "His father kills himself, and he wasn't there even to say don't do it?"

"And why would he even…?"

She felt a rush of air about her face, cold and dizzying, made of all the futures there had not been, the memories of one hand holding another that should have shaped two lives, moments together hoped for but unshared, and found that she could only think of the obvious things to say: he's your son, despite everything he loves you, he refuses to be here because he is too young to understand himself, he will reproach himself forever if you die like that.

"You don't die alone," she said. "You die with us. You leave us."

"Yes I do. I die, you don't."

She stood up and turned away from him. She was there in the room; she hoped to be there at the end. She could shout at him now, for one of the last times, she could cry in his arms. He could end his life, and perhaps she could live with that. Was that the difference? That he could ask *her*, but not their son? How can it be, she thought, that you can know someone almost more intimately than you know yourself, know what he feels and thinks and how he will act, and in an instant they turn as opaque as a stone. You can care for them better than they care for themselves, and suddenly you have no idea what to do, and all you can do is hope the stone will release the one you love. One more time.

Two days later, when Scarlet was out shopping, Jim rang Harrison and he came over. They sat facing each other in the living room, Harrison nursing a cup of coffee.

"Sure, I can get it," he said. "You can get anything. It's ridiculous, the powers that be haven't got a clue. They run around busting dealers for ounces of shit they ought to legalise anyway, and it's all on the web."

"Don't they know that?"

"Not all of it, no. Bless the hippie geeks, they're all into security and hiding it from the man. I hardly have to do anything. But I'm going nowhere near it. You pay, I'll get it, but I'm out of here."

"Hey, man, I know," said Jim. "You're in supply, not mentoring."

Harrison nodded. "Cash," he said, looking at Jim. "I know you've got it. You've been saving up."

"You know, Harrison," Jim replied, "for a sleazeball you sometimes show business sense."

"Two mottoes: keep the customer happy, and get a monopoly. Competition's bad for trade."

Jim paused for breath, kept a hint of nausea at bay, and said, "When can you get it?"

"Two days. I can drop it off or you can do call and collect."

"Drop it off."

"Scarlet doesn't know?" asked Harrison, and Jim nodded.

Harrison stayed for a few more minutes, talking about people they knew, and then got up to leave. "One thing," he said. "Why not some other way?"

"Big thing about life," Jim said, "you've got to know what you really want."

"Ain't that the truth," said Harrison, and he left.

In another two days he returned, delivered a well-wrapped parcel, took the money, and departed. Jim, suddenly

219

exhausted by walking to the front door and back, put the parcel on the table in the living room and waited for Scarlet to return.

"What's this?" she said when she picked it up.

"Open it. Carefully."

She unwrapped it and took out a white plastic jar of tablets, a small brown bottle, and a hypodermic needle.

"Fuck. What's this?"

"They got names on?"

"Medical shit."

"That's what I paid for."

She sat down, realising as she did what it was and how it had come into the house.

"I won't touch it," she said. "I won't touch it."

"It's what I want." His voice was weak, but the intent was there.

"Throw it out!" She gathered it up in its packaging. "I'm going to throw it out."

"It's nothing to do with you," said Jim. "Wipe your prints off the stuff, burn the packaging. You've never seen it."

She looked at him, bewildered. "You can't do this yourself."

"And it isn't going to be you."

"Who then? *He* won't. I bet he can prove he was a thousand miles away."

"Sure. Not him."

"Who then?"

Jim looked at her with as much of a smile as he could muster, and said, "Robert, of course. My little brother, Robert."

"He won't do it. You're crazy if you think he'll do it."

"He goes around saying it's the right thing to do."

"But he can't. He can't even do what McIntire can, and put you on morphine."

"He will, he will."

Scarlet stared at him in disbelief.

"He will," Jim said, "because you're going to ask him to do it."

"I told you, you're crazy."

Chapter 15

Late November 2018

Scarlet went through to the kitchen to make a cup of coffee, then changed her mind and went back to the living room. Now that Jim had said he wanted to die, it was beginning to seem to her that everything had to be put on hold, and to live was an insult to him. Or, perhaps, that to put everything on hold, to reduce everything to rest around her, was her only chance of keeping him alive. Her mind flitted between these alternatives and kept her unable to decide on anything. Never before had she felt so reluctant to live.

Her phone rang. It was Poker, asking how she was.

"Same as ever," she said.

"And Jim?"

"Unchanged."

"Must be tough."

"He's not speaking much, not playing at all."

"It's an awful business, this waiting," Poker said after a time. "I've been there."

They talked quietly for a while, then she thanked him

for calling and hung up. She let time pass, picked up her phone and dialled.

"Hi, Mom," Ryan said. "How're you doing?"

"I'm coping. How're you?"

"Good, been better."

They talked about nothing very much for a while. Then Scarlet said, "Jim's saying he wants to die."

Ryan said nothing.

"He's your father," she said.

"I'll write to Doctor Freud about it."

"Jesus, Ryan, I want you to come. You *need* to come. I know about things like this. You need to get over here."

"Mom, I don't want to hurt you, but I can't."

Scarlet was silent, and after a time they said their goodbyes and Scarlet hung up. Doing nothing would have been better. She could go upstairs, see how Jim was. In an hour or so she could see what had to be done for dinner.

The salsa instructor looked around the class, and decided that his planned sequence of up-tempo numbers was working. Barbara looked at her current partner -- Robert still wasn't coming, saying he was too busy -- and with a nod from him they began. Quite well at first, and then she stumbled. He caught her, and she muttered "My heels." They picked up the beat again, and then she stumbled again.

"Do you want to sit this one out?" he asked her.

"No, I'll be all right." Then she shook her head. "Well, maybe. Do you mind?"

He said "Of course not," and she made her way to

the bathrooms. But before she got there, she froze. The incessant jollity of the music broke up into fragments, the call to dance, to warmth, to release splintered into shards stinging her all over her body, the rhythms that were there to surf turned to a rumble of thunder. Out of the corner of her eye she saw Rhianne and Georgio in the fun of each successive moment, unaware that she was barely able to breathe. She leant against a table in case she fainted, a chill spread across her body. When it passed, she made her way erratically to the door and slipped out, picked up her coat and went to sit in her car. The last tune jangled in her head. Something ominous that, only paper thin, it had failed to conceal, now made her tremble.

In recent years, it had become usual for the students on Robert's course to mark the final day with some note of recognition. Initially, it had been just a round of applause; more recently, a student would give a short speech with some of the dubious humour of a bridegroom at a wedding; sometimes there would be a present if they had been able to decide on one. It was, Robert recognised, a way for them to release tension after months of looking at the evidence of death and dying. Even the basement lab, however well equipped, suggested a tomb to some simply by being underground. Now they would move on to a short course on how to talk to patients, hosted in an airy room in Psychology Outpatients, intended to restore their spirits.

This time the honour of concluding the course fell to Parvinda. She held a neatly wrapped parcel the size of a small book, which she shifted from hand to hand.

"We'd like to thank you," she said. "We've all learned a lot about things we've never seen before, things we've never thought about before. I'm sure we can now do a much better job, especially if we ever need to get away with murdering someone."

The students laughed more than the joke merited, Robert smiled, and Parvinda relaxed a little.

"But one thing I think we've all learned," she went on, "is a particular lesson you taught us this year. One that won't be on the exam but I hope we'll all remember for the rest of our lives. And to thank you for that we'd like to give you this little present." She handed it to Robert, the students clapped, and then waited. He smiled, looked around at them, and said, "Thank you. Thank you for this, you've been a good bunch."

"Go on, open it," Parvinda said.

Robert tore open the packaging. He could feel a wooden frame, and at first he thought he'd been given a picture, but it wasn't. It was two panels of text, a large one above and a smaller one below. He couldn't immediately read the larger one, and he looked down to the end, which gave the place and date of publication of his letter – the letter. Immediately above it, he now saw his name and the words 'and thirty-nine others'. Looking back up he saw what he presumed was the text of the letter, translated for some reason into Latin. Enough familiar words stood out: mortem, mori, cura, ius patientis, conversationem. Underneath, in a smaller panel, were the signatures of the students. Every one of them. He didn't know what to say.

"We had it translated by someone doing classics," a student said. "A girlfriend."

"An ex-girlfriend," another student said, and they all laughed.

Robert looked around at them. "I've been trying to learn something this term," he said. "I don't think I fully have yet. Maybe I started too late." He looked down at the Latin text and back up at their smooth, untroubled faces. "It's not just the conversation. It's what you do afterwards. That, I believe, is something every doctor must learn. Maybe you'll learn it better than me, I hope you will, you've been good students. And thank you very much for this."

They murmured a collective thank you and began to disperse, clattering up the stairs to the world of the living. Parvinda stayed behind.

He waved the framed inscription at her and said, "Was this your idea?"

"No, actually. We've all been talking about it."

He pointed to the door, and she led the way upstairs.

"Are you any clearer on what you'll do next?" he asked.

"No, time will tell me."

"Something with living, breathing patients?"

"I have to know," She paused, "that I won't be afraid. When all I can do is cause harm, one way or another."

Robert looked at her and saw someone so unlike himself at her age that he had to suppress a grin. "Be easy on yourself," he said.

"I'll try to think of my father."

"Remember, everyone you meet is different."

Parvinda smiled and put out her hand. "Thank you for everything."

They shook hands and Robert stood and watched

her go. When she was gone, he wondered what he could do with the present. Taking it home would only annoy Barbara. Hygiene rules probably wouldn't permit hanging it up in the lab. For now, if it would fit, it would have to go in the glove compartment of the car and become part of his ongoing, private conversationem de Jamesis. That couldn't be right, but Latin wasn't the point here. Helping Jim was, and to do that he'd begun to realise he needed to accept that all too often he'd taken refuge in reflection, making a virtue of the simple, self-effacing things he did. He checked his computer to see that no urgent requests had come in, and as he did so the thought occurred to him that this might finally be the year in which he retired from his basement life. It didn't come with an argument for or against, or a plan for what he would do if he did. It just appeared, like a stranger at the door, waiting, hand extended, to be let in.

"I'm taking singing lessons from a real professional," Lauren said. "She's, like, really good."

"Not Scarlet?" said Barbara, putting the lunch plates in the dishwasher.

"No, not Scarlet."

"How long's this going to last?" Barbara asked.

Lauren put her hands up and said, "Christ, what's eating you?"

"You can guess," Barbara replied.

"How's Jim?"

"Dying, but not quite yet."

"You've been to see him?"

"Your father goes. You know him, he can't resist waifs and strays."

"It's nice he's like that."

Barbara shook her head. "You've no idea."

"Oh, come on, Mum…"

"More and more, I think he'd be a whole lot better if he saw real people every day, he wouldn't have signed up to this campaign…"

Lauren poured herself a glass of water and offered her mother one, which she declined. Barbara watched her drink it, then she took the empty glass from her, put it in the sink and turned to face her. "Who's paying for these singing lessons."

"I told you," Lauren said. "I've got a job. Working for a music company."

"Does it pay enough?" Barbara replied.

"I can manage."

"Not Scarlet?"

"Mum, why do you dislike her? It's like you think she's abducting me or something."

"And when Jim dies and she goes back to the States, leaving you behind, what will happen to you then?"

"Relax," Lauren said. "God, you really should have done drugs when you were my age, it'd have made you more sympathetic."

"Are you doing drugs?"

"I didn't say that."

"You sort of implied it."

"And be, like, supportive."

"I try. The world isn't the easy place you seem to think it is."

"I know that. You don't. You never had to struggle to get a job."

Barbara stared at her. "I'm going to see Lily," she said. "You can come if you're going to calm down, and you don't say any of these awful things to her."

"What awful things? She'll be happy to hear I'm trying to become a singer. You know she likes music."

"She'd like to see you. But you mustn't get her upset."

You're the one who's upset, Lauren thought, but she said nothing.

Jim came down for supper, a vegetable soup he sipped at and pronounced tasteless. "Although I thank you for trying," he said.

"I'm trying to keep you going," Scarlet replied.

"That's a loser's game," he said, but he gave her a weak smile.

She squeezed his hands. "You really don't feel like playing?"

"I want to quit on a high, and we had one, right?"

"We did. But just here, for me?"

He left his hands in hers, passive and inert.

"What's the first thing you remember?" she said.

After a time he said, "Pissing my dad off. I don't know what I'd done, but he was angry for sure. He didn't hit me or anything, but he was so cold, like he'd switched off completely."

"Come on, you can't have forgotten, you broke something, stole something..."

"I was, I don't know, four? Kids, right?"

She knew so little about his childhood that she trembled.

"I just remember the coldness. And the times after that, he could just shut down, like I wasn't there."

"Didn't your mother…?"

Jim turned round to face Scarlet and, puzzling about the memory, said, "He must've been on leave, back from wherever."

"And you wanted attention?"

"I was four. What I got was, he really meant it. You know, parents tell their kids off, but there's something else going on underneath, you both know it, that says we're still together. Nothing."

She imagined Jim, his angry father, his mother cross too, standing in a dark, narrow room cluttered with furniture, and tried to see Jim's round face. Bewildered? Truculent? She tried to see everything from his side, to lower the camera to his shoulders, but failed, caught instead a moment frozen in a baleful pearl of light that came more from the figures than outside, and then it vanished.

She caressed his face and said nothing, and he said, "My mother, you know, she used to sing to me. We used to sing together, when I was little. Just her and me. Then she gave up."

"Your blues guys didn't give up," she said.

Jim acknowledged the remark with a nod of the head and took a few more sips of the soup, then he got up and went slowly through to the living room. He shuffled through the channels on the TV and found nothing, and lay back on the sofa, wrapped in a blanket. Some time later she went for a walk and when she came back she heard the mournful sound of Jimmy Yancey's version of 'How Long Blues'. She stood in the hall and listened, and when Jim finished she went into the front room, tugged him onto his feet and put her arms around him. They stayed that way for some time. Slowly, quietly, dancing.

Chapter 16

Late November 2018

When the doorbell rang the next afternoon, Scarlet greeted Robert and Barbara with telling passivity. Robert had told her a few weeks ago that Barbara would want to pay a final visit 'when the time came', but Scarlet had almost forgotten. The embarrassment with which he'd said it partially made up for the emptiness of the words, so formal and correct they were robbed of any sense of belonging to what was happening to Jim. Seeing Barbara now only reminded Scarlet that she didn't mind. Might as well complain about the rain in winter, or that clouds are grey. Life has moved elsewhere, what there is of it.

Their hugs barely warmed Scarlet up. They followed her into the living room, Barbara went to the kitchen and made coffee, and Robert, sensing that Scarlet wasn't ready to say more about why she'd called them down, offered comments on the journey and what they knew about Lauren these days. Barbara came back in with the coffees and sat on the sofa next to Scarlet, who slowly said, in a weak and desperate voice, "McIntire's useless. He just keeps thinking of new tricks, but Jim only wants one thing. Can't he see that?"

"There's only so much any doctor can do," Robert began, but Scarlet interrupted.

"There must be something he can do."

"What's he said?" Barbara asked.

"Some nurse to come round when it's... necessary," Scarlet replied. "But Jim's said no to that."

"And what will the nurse do?" Barbara asked again.

"Some sort of injections. I think it was for pain, I don't think I really understood." Scarlet turned to Robert. "But it won't make him better, will it," and her tears broke out, she stopped talking, and sat motionless. Barbara pulled her slowly onto her shoulder and rested her head against her neck, until finally she softened and reached out to hold Barbara's free arm.

She found a tissue in her pockets and started to mop her face, and as she did so she breathed more deeply, and a purpose gathered within her. She pushed herself out of Barbara's arms, looked at Robert with tear-filled eyes, and said, "Jim wants to die... and McIntire won't help."

"He can't," said Barbara, looking over at Robert, who nodded back. "That's one thing he can't do. And we can't."

"I know this is really hard," said Robert, "but what do you want?"

Six months before, Scarlet would have thought the question absurd, almost insulting. She would have said "For him to get better, of course". One month ago, she would have said the same words, but more forcefully, trying to sound so sincere after all they'd been through that something would happen. Never let doubt creep in.

You have to hope, don't you, you always hope. But this time, she looked at Robert, and very quietly said, "I don't know. I don't know any longer." And as she said it, there came from her one thought: I've failed him. In the end I've failed him.

"You've done everything you could, I'm sure," said Barbara. "And more."

Scarlet turned away from Barbara and waited for Robert to speak.

"Then we start from there," he said. "Thinking what we can do. There are all the things you've been doing. All the cooking, and cleaning, and holding his hand, making his bed. He needs that."

"He wants to die," she said. "That's all he wants."

"He said that to Dr McIntire?" said Barbara.

Scarlet nodded, exhausted by an idea she could not accept, unable to see past it. All she could do was suggest the two of them go upstairs and see Jim for themselves. They found him looking tired but sitting up. He looked alertly at Robert, who sat on the edge of the bed, then at Barbara standing behind him, then back at Robert. There was a flurry of questions, which he fended off, waiting for the aggravating small talk to end, then he said, "I've made my mind up. I want to stop."

"McIntire can't do that," Barbara said, before Robert could speak.

Jim turned, grasped Robert's hand, and said, "I know my body. I know what I'm in for, and I don't want it."

"None of us do," said Robert.

"I don't want to live without music," Jim replied. "And to have to go through what's coming for me."

"I can be here," Robert began. "I can do what I can for you."

"But he's not your doctor," Barbara cut in. "You must understand that. McIntire is the only one…"

Jim pushed his body upwards, turned to Robert, and said, "No. Not McIntire. You. You can…" The effort of speaking glowed intensely in his eyes, and clearly he did not intend to speak again for some time. Robert remained perched on the edge of the bed for a while, holding Jim's hand in his, and then got up, and he and Barbara slowly went downstairs.

In the hall, Barbara looked at Robert, then across to Scarlet waiting for them, and said, "Do you want us to stay? We can get out of your way, if…"

"I think I want to be with Jim," Scarlet replied, "for a bit."

"We'll go for a walk," said Barbara.

Once they were out of sight of the cottage, Barbara took Robert by the sleeve, turned him to face her, and said, "How far gone is he?"

"I haven't sat down with the hospital notes," Robert said quietly, gathering his thoughts.

"So you don't really know."

"That's the optimistic way to put it."

"And how are you?"

Robert looked over Barbara's shoulders at the gaggle of houses that led down to the canal, and beyond to the rising moon, breathed deeply a couple of times, and said, "I don't know. He's on his way out and he knows that. But there's no timetable. It's weeks, I'd say, maybe months. All you can do is keep going, try not to think about it too much. And he doesn't want to keep going."

"I asked about you."

Robert looked at her, the lines in her face caught by the autumn light. He took her hands in his, looking at the liver spots on their backs and caressing the palms gently.

"I didn't think I was going to forgive him," he said, shifting his feet, trying to feel less cold in the wind. "I'm beginning to realise why doctors tell lies. I always thought *I* didn't. I just said what the samples said, or the body in front of me. But on the front line…" He released her hands and looked at her, and then past her again, at nothing. Something was a little bit clearer, if he could only hold on to it long enough. "It's because we're afraid."

"Of the patient?"

"Of not knowing. We can tell you what we can do. But we can't tell you how to live the end of your life. So we lie about it. We hold out hopes we shouldn't, just because it makes us feel useful."

"Is that what's happening to Jim?"

"I don't want to lie to him, Barbara. But I've got nothing else to say."

She put her arms around him, and they stood together in silence. Then, to end the moment, he said, "Scarlet's exhausted."

"I think," Barbara said, "if you fall really ill, I might garden all day. I don't think I could do much else."

It was the cue for a familiar routine, but before he could respond she released him and walked a few steps ahead. He followed her to the last of the houses and along a footpath that branched away from the road and ran beside a pile of tree trunks. She turned and looked at him, and said, "What if he's got the end-of-life drugs?"

"What? He can't have."

"Robert, you know they're out there. That's what he meant when he said "You can". He's got them, I'm sure of it."

Robert waited for her to go on.

"They're illegal, right?" she said.

"Oh yes. Absolutely."

"So what are you going to do?"

He stood still. He could so easily mark the moment with a small lie, a refusal only to tell the whole truth. How many things get done that way, he wondered, good and bad? Or he could offer a bigger lie. He could hear himself forming the words, "Tell them how risky it is. That they mustn't do it." And as he did so he could see that, of the two, only the bigger lie had a chance of success. To say only that he would go down again if asked would lead directly to the question, "And do what?" But somehow, at the moment Barbara asked the question, he knew he did not want to lie. Very softly, he said, "What can I do?"

Barbara almost sprang at him. "Jesus, Robert. You're a doctor, you testify in court. You could go to prison for years. Your reputation, everything you've stood for, trashed."

"I only know what they've said. What Jim said. I don't know they've actually got—"

"That's so much bullshit. You know they've got it."

It had been an evasion. He regretted it.

Barbara, much more confidently, said, "And tell the police."

He shook his head. "I can't," he said.

Barbara stared at him in amazement. Forcing herself

to try to sound calm, she said, "Then take your time. Think about it. Take a day. Then tell them you're going to have to tell the police."

Robert sat down on one of the severed trees, put his head in his hands and breathed deeply several times. Then he looked up. Clouds scudded across the sky. "It's not so simple," he said.

"It's perfectly simple."

Slowly, but with gathering strength, he began. "Jim's dying, he's in pain, and for a reason everybody knows I think is basically religious crap doctors aren't allowed to do the right thing, and…" Barbara started to speak but he raised his voice to drown her out. "And when I have the choice, the actual choice, I say keep the pain and oh, by the way, have some criminal convictions. How great is that?"

"Bullshit," she replied. "You have to tell them."

"I don't. I simply don't." He tried once more to say what he felt he had to. "He's my brother."

"He's what?" Barbara was almost shouting again. "He was a total stranger to you six months ago. You could practically have walked past him in the street and not noticed him. What sort of a brother is that?"

Robert gave a shrug. "Does it matter? We know he's in pain, we know he's dying. This is the way he wants to go."

"And you can't help. Tell him to get someone else, if he's hell-bent on it." There was contempt in her voice.

"It's not that simple," Robert repeated. "You need to get these things right or they don't work properly."

She looked down at him. "Tough. Tell him to throw it away."

Robert shook his head. "He's in pain –"

"Tell him to drink a bottle of whisky and take a bunch of sleeping pills."

"He'd just throw them up."

"Tell him – Jesus, I don't know. Just tell him you can't help." Her voice rising again as his began to drop. "I know he's in pain, but…"

Robert stood up, forcing her to take a step back, and said very quietly, "You don't know enough. You just think you do."

"What the hell does that mean?"

"It means," said Robert, his voice almost inaudible, "you think you summed something up but actually you've barely begun. I'm not saying you're unfeeling, or unkind—"

"What have I barely begun?"

Robert walked past her and further down the path towards the wood, and she watched him, realising that by staying silent he was trying to give her a chance to withdraw. But the sudden sense of not knowing what she was getting into, that she had not understood all along, that perhaps nothing would go as she had expected, swirled through her head like a swarm of insects. Surely there was palliative care. Couldn't McIntire put him in a hospice? There were morphine drips. She'd heard Robert say doctors bump people off with them. But the swarm howled that Jim would not consent, that McIntire would not consent, that they would be carried far beyond all the simple answers she had trusted. And that Robert – Robert of all people – would take her there.

She walked up and took his arm, desperate to talk, to persuade. "Robert, I'm sorry Jim is dying. I really am.

But you can't do what I'm really scared you're thinking of doing. You can't do it, and you know why."

"I'm not crazy." He looked at her in anguish. "Isn't prolonging his suffering crazy? Aren't people who want that to happen crazy?"

She let her voice drop. "Look," she said, "to be blunt… if Scarlet'd told us he'd died, we'd all be happy."

"Maybe not happy."

"Wrong word, but you know what I mean. Jim wouldn't be suffering anymore. That's what I want too. But we can't have doctors making up the rules, I've heard you say that a hundred times." She looked into his face, uncertain how to read it. "You need the rules, you've said that yourself. You have a contract with society… "

"And one with the patient."

"And one with the patient. And the two keep you in balance, so you can get home every evening as my husband, and not as a murderer, or a nervous wreck."

It's possible, Robert thought, for someone to say one thing sincerely and truthfully, and to mean something else, that was also true, but that they did not want to say, or perhaps not to be caught saying. To say something they mean and also mean the opposite by it. For both to be right, and only one choice to be made. He said nothing, and let Barbara conclude what she wished from that, and to put her arms around him, and say, "Robert, doctors keep people alive, and you, my husband, above all, you know why."

But what did it mean, the old injunction to 'do no harm', when only harm could be done? When the magician has run out of flowers from nowhere, produced the last card from thin air, turned all the emptiness he can into reality, and someone in the audience says "And now I need you to do one thing for me. Just one more thing"? When the rule says Jim's life will end, but not how it may be ended kindly?

Scarlet waited, as she knew she had to. Waited through the strained conversation about nothing with Barbara and Robert until their abrupt departure, through the rest of the afternoon, and the evening as Jim began to wake up, driven even now by some bodily memory of a life of gigs and late nights. She helped him downstairs and watched him drink a little soup, and they had dinner almost without speaking. It was oddly easy, becoming routine.

He poured himself a glass of water, sat in his chair, and said, "Well?"

She said, "You know what I want," and waited for him to speak. When he kept quiet, she said, "I need you to say it." And she waited again.

He shifted in his chair, and said, "Ryan. Your son Ryan."

"Our son Ryan. Your son Ryan," she replied, and when he said nothing she went on, "You can't duck out anymore."

He sipped his water. "Didn't work, did it," he said, in a low voice.

"You never tried. Twenty years, and you never tried."

"I never wanted him. I told you."

"He's your son, however hard you try to walk away."

Her anger washed over him, and he said nothing. There Jim was, dying for sure, with it all lined up, everyone doing what he wanted. He was planning the next performance, moving on. Getting away with it, one more time. If she let him, one last, unforgivable time.

She got up, walked to the window and staring into the dark said, "Why? He's a nice kid. He's always been a nice kid."

"I told you. I never… ."

"Don't fuck with me. I've heard you say "I never wanted a kid" more times 'n I can count. I've heard you say it to Ryan. How d'you think he felt?"

"Plenty of kids don't have fathers."

She turned round, glaring at him. "Who tell them to their face they weren't wanted?"

"He's never missed me."

"Unbelievable." She crossed over and stood in front of him. "Jim, I ask myself at times, why am I with you? There's a man I love, who is warm, and generous, and gifted, and when he plays music the whole air around us is better, I truly believe. The man who taught me to sing, and gave me life. The man I'll cry for. I'm crying now." She sat down on the arm of the chair. "And there's somebody so…" She searched for the word, "cold. To someone who's never done you any harm."

"It's done. It's who I am."

She pulled a mobile phone out of her pocket. "This is yours. I've put Ryan's number on it. You're going to call him."

"He doesn't want to speak to me."

"You're going to call him and have a good shot at saying goodbye." She put it in his lap. "As his father."

He did not move.

"Not now," she said. "When you're ready. You've got a

few days to think about it." She got up. "Because I swear to God, Jim, if you don't…"

He took the phone listlessly in his right hand.

"For him," she said. "For me. Damn it, for you."

He struggled to sit up. "Get me a whisky, will you, please."

She did so and sat on the sofa opposite him. He took a sip and put the glass down carefully, in his head a speech he didn't have the energy to say.

"I ask myself," he said, looking directly at her, "I went one way, Robert the other. How? Why? How'd you answer that?"

"Think about it," Scarlet replied, "because you've one last chance to tell Ryan."

"He won't speak to me."

She got up, surprised by the sudden clarity of her conviction. She had feared she would give in to him, because he was dying and for no other reason. Now she knew she would not. "Then leave a message on his answer phone," she said. "Something to remember his father by." His eyes looked up at her, and down to the phone. "I'll be back to take you to bed," she said. "Then I'm going out."

She left.

Chapter 17

Scarlet sat in the kitchen, finding things to do and reasons not to do them just now, telling herself she should be thinking about Jim, but knowing she was waiting for Robert to show up. And wondering if, when he does, will he say what she wants him to say, without her asking, like, "No, are you crazy, throw the stuff away, it's ten kinds of illegal? No one has the right, we're here to care, not…" Not what? That was what stopped her. You don't think it can go on like this, there's just so much a body can take. But it's like half Jim's body hasn't been told, it's not all on-side. There's no such thing as ready to go. Maybe he is, in his head, but not the rest of him, the bad boys, the bullies, that are dragging everything down. Hurting him – God, hurting him so much.

The kit was in the fridge. A lethal weapon, nothing else. Drugs, meds, guns, go down the list, it's not just what something's really for, there's always something else. But the kit was just exactly what it said it was. And that, she thought, was why she couldn't touch it. Because all it was,

was the end to Jim's life. It can bring him no comfort, because he will not be there, not there for the peace it's supposed to bring. And it will bring her no peace, even if she doesn't touch it. "Turn up, Robert," she said to herself. "Turn up soon. I don't know what to do."

The phone rang, but it was McIntire, offering to come round.

"No, not today," Scarlet said, and even as she said it, she felt that McIntire was suspicious. Perhaps it was the way he repeated the offer to talk about managing Jim's pain.

"No, we want to be on our own today," Scarlet said again, and he said he quite understood, although she was sure he didn't, and that he'd ring tomorrow.

"Thank you, do that," she said, and hung up.

She didn't like him, she never had, she realised, even though she couldn't say why. Because Jim doesn't like him? Because he's what, so proper, so scrupulous, so polite? Because he hasn't screamed and cried and raged? Because he hasn't called forth the spirits? She'd never believed that shit. He's listened, he's talked to the specialists, he knows his stuff, he's said he's sorry to see Jim like this. He wants to help. He thinks he's helping now. I know that, I know that. But not in the one way Jim wants. Instead, everything about him has said, "Come this way, walk with me a while, and rest here if you wish, I will be with you because I hold the door open to the emptiness of death." Everything he has done from the moment he first met Jim has said, "Once, on other matters, I could have been your friend, but on this, the greatest matter of all, do not be deceived, I have switched sides. I am an accomplice, and I must make their only excuse: I have no choice."

The doorbell rang. Scarlet went to the door and let Robert in.

"No Barbara?"

"She didn't want to come."

She waited for him to explain, but he said nothing. She took him into the kitchen, where she made coffee and they talked only to avoid bringing up the one thing they needed to talk about, each waiting for the other to even just hint at how they felt, as if it was a sign of weakness.

Finally, Robert said, "I'd like to see Jim. How is he?"

"He's awake. He's not eating."

"I'll go up, then," Robert said. "Does he know I'm coming?"

She nodded. "I'll come," she said.

Robert stood up. "No," he said. "Not right now. I need to…"

"You need what?" she replied, a pent-up force breaking out. "There's nothing he can't say to me."

"I need to be sure," he said, shaking his head. "If I'm to… I need to be sure." He paused, and tried to draw his words together. "I need to have this conversation with him alone. And then we'll talk."

Before Scarlet could reply, Robert turned and climbed the stairs. He knocked on Jim's door, got no answer, waited a few seconds, knocked again, waited, and then opened the door. Jim was quiet, but awake, and he looked at

Robert, who tried to decide what he could see in Jim's face. Exhaustion, but also a challenge.

"You're not so good today," Robert said.

"Scarlet tell you that?"

"Not in those words."

Robert sat, as he had so often before, on the edge of the bed. McIntire had told him a few things that the oncologist had told him, and added a few thoughts of his own, reminding him of a doctor's duty in these cases, essentially warning him off. Robert could see from his own experience that Jim was exhausted, but not near to death. He probably had months left, not just days.

"How do you feel?"

Jim shifted a little in the bed. "I could do with a good night's sleep."

"We should be able to manage that."

Jim breathed in sharply as the pain flared up and then receded. He waited, counting to ten, but there wasn't another burst. "Last night wasn't so bad."

Robert looked at him. How strange he seemed. How very different, and yet how alike. With so much in common, and so little.

"Are you ready to talk?" said Robert.

"Nothing to talk about," Jim replied.

Robert sat there for a while longer. They didn't talk, and after a time they started to feel comfortable not speaking. Jim closed his eyes and drifted into a half-sleep it would be easy to disturb, and Robert sat as still as he could for a long time, until he reached forward, put his hand gently on Jim's shoulder and fancied he saw a slight smile in return. He sat beside him for a while, and then he walked slowly out of the room and went downstairs to find Scarlet, who was in the living room.

"It's still in the fridge," she said. "I nearly threw it out."

"Did you know he was going to do it?"

"No. No. We had a row, but not about that stuff, exactly. I told him I wouldn't do it. The police…"

She waited for him to reply, but he sat down without saying a word. It was too much. "Christ, Robert, don't sit there like you're waiting for a bus."

He started to apologise, but she shouted him down.

"I don't get you at times. He's your brother, even if you haven't seen him for years. Maybe because you haven't seen him for years, you can't just sit there!"

"It's not like that."

"Don't you want to cry? To shout? To punch something. Anything to make it better?"

He felt a lifetime pressing down on him, a physical force he could hardly fight against, a living memory of who he truly was.

"Am I sad?" he said. "Yes. Sad for him. Sad for you. I'm not going to get angry about it."

"I'd like you a whole lot better if you were."

"Maybe I would, too. But I'm who I am. Maybe it's one of the ways you got the right brother."

"He thinks I got the wrong one."

Robert looked up, surprised.

"For real," she said. "He said so."

"He didn't mean it. He's not that crazy."

She walked over to the chair next to Robert's but didn't sit down.

"You come and go," she began. "Nothing seems to

248

get to you. You try to be kind, to be helpful. You've been helpful. But I don't feel I can talk to you at times. Say what I'm really feeling."

Robert looked at his hands, each one, separately, front and back. "I think I retreat," he said.

"And you're in control?"

He didn't answer.

She took a deep breath, sat down next to him, and said, "I wish I'd known you before. This'd be a lot easier." She was silent. Across from them, the sofa had a pillow and a neatly folded duvet for Jim's comfort should he come downstairs.

Robert slowly framed his next question. "If you knew the police wouldn't come for you? If they'd never find out?"

She shook her head, slowly and slightly. "I don't know. I really don't know."

"It's just," he said, almost thinking out loud, "if we're to proceed with this, I have to know what you really want."

"I don't think I can," she said, "if that's what you mean. Not with the stuff in the fridge."

"No one's asking you to."

"Then what are you saying?"

"There's where you want to be, and there's how you get there. I'm trying to keep them apart."

He waited. She looked down at the floor, then around the room, and then at him. She'd made choices in life, sometimes in an instant, sometimes after long periods of thought. She'd surrendered to place and time, too, and gone along. Accepted that was just how it was. But always with the thought, however faint, that it could be otherwise. This time, everything slipped away from her, as if it was too big to be grasped, like a dream in which she could never get ready.

"McIntire says he can do something about the pain," she said. "What's he mean? What would happen?"

"You could switch over to managing the symptoms. Keeping the pain down, helping Jim get to sleep."

"And… what would that give him?"

"He might die sooner than if you went for fighting the cancer with new drugs." He paused. "He might well be happier." He watched her eyes look past him, over his shoulder, and gaze emptily at the wall behind him. "But he will die," he said.

"He wants to," she said. And, after a pause, "He wants to die. Now."

"The question still is: what do you want?"

She shrank back, as if trying to hide. "Don't make me say. Don't make me answer that."

He waited without speaking. Again her eyes focussed on him, and slipped away, and came back. He was sitting forward, she saw, his face in his hands but turned upwards so that he could see her.

"I've loved him in many ways, you know," she said. "When I was young and I'd just met him, I thought he was gorgeous. I wasn't going to resist that. And over the years, when we could live together, and when we didn't, it changed. You must know that. And now here we are. He's the love of my life, after all." She broke off, pinched her lips between her teeth, and took a couple of deep breaths. "I must be stupid or something." She stopped, and repeated in a whisper, "The love of my life."

Very quietly, Robert said, "That's why I'm asking you."

"There are no happy endings, are there?"

"No angels from Montgomery, no."

She smiled, briefly pleased that Robert remembered the song. "Tell me what I should want."

"I can't. It has to come from you."

"He knows I can't do it. He's asked for you."

He sat back and looked straight at her. "And would you stop me?"

"Am I a coward, if I say no?"

"No. Anyone would understand."

"What's the difference? I do it, I ask you to do it. What's the difference?"

"Are you really asking me to do it?"

"Didn't I? When I rang you? Wasn't that asking you?"

Robert said nothing.

"Isn't that why you're here?"

Barbara's shouts, her rage, her contempt, hadn't swayed him. But then she'd stopped, and spoken quietly, and said what was incontrovertibly true. No one has the right to end another person's life. Whether or not he was found out, to end Jim's life was illegal. He could only argue for a right to die, to put an end to unavoidable, disabling pain. To carry it out, with no proof of patient's consent, no safeguards against abuse, destroyed the case he supported. "You will lose your job, the respect of everyone who knows you, you'll go to prison, you'll set back whatever cause it is by a decade." He had no answers. He could not say what he would do when he next went to see Jim. He would go alone, he accepted that. And her voice had been with him on the journey down, all the way across London, along the rain-washed

M4 with its sequence of tailbacks, along the country roads that skirted Bath. It was with him now.

Scarlet saw that he couldn't answer her, and instead said, "Tell me a story about Jim, when you knew him. When he was young."

He sat back, and remembered a story he thought he hadn't remembered in fifty years.

"It's a long story, this one," he said.

"I like long stories. They're the best," she replied, and so he began.

"I'm one of a group of children, standing on a beach. It's a long, flat beach and we've all walked quite a long way up it, away from all our parents. Out to sea there's a patch of water in front of us with a sandbar beyond it, and beyond that the sea stretches away to the horizon. It's summer, but in the wind it's cold. Were there any boats? I don't think so. Or any swimmers. We seem to have had this part of the beach to ourselves.

"Anyway, the patch of water in front of us was slowly filling up from where the sandbar ended over to our left. The sandbar itself was still one or two feet high, the sea was lapping gently on its far side. It was obvious it'd be covered completely by the end, and the water would have pushed a long way up the beach.

"The game we were playing was to run through the water to the sandbar, over to the sea, and back to the safety of the beach. We'd already done it once, all of us together. It wasn't too hard; the water was only a little deeper than it looked. But now where we're standing's already been reached by the incoming tide. We all take a step or two back. It seems to have been decided that this time we'll do it in turns. One of the big boys, Ed, I think he was called, shouted out a name and someone stepped forward and ran across the gap to the sandbar. The water came up to about his knees, he splashed through, over to the sea, and came splashing back. Ed called out another name, the boy went and came back, and then the group started shouting for Ed to go himself. He ran through the water, over the sandbar, and waded back. I remember seeing the water pushing against his legs."

"Where was Jim" Scarlet asked.

"He wasn't there, he hadn't been for some time. He was down the beach probably, or maybe in the dunes behind us having a pee, but I couldn't see him anywhere. So, two more boys go over and come back, and now the sea's reached us again and we step back another couple of yards. There's just three of us left, the younger ones, who've spent all day coming last. Before Ed could call out a name one of them shouts out, "I'll go," and ran off, into the water. He made it across, ran to the top of the sandbar, which is smaller than it was, over to the sea and back, but making it back to us was a real struggle.

"Ed had two of us left now, and he pretended not to know which one of us he'd choose, pointing at the other kid and then at me and then back to the other one.

"'You,' he said, and the other boy, who wasn't much bigger than me, ran forward into the gap, which had widened considerably. The water came right up his thighs and slowed him at once. You could see each step was an effort, and halfway across he stumbled. He got back up, but he stopped and turned round. The boys started to shout. "Go on! Go on! Go on!" Over and over, and I was shouting too. But he didn't move. Then the chant changed to "Coward! Coward! Coward!" And finally he turned back towards the sandbar, and he made it. We all cheered.

"He ran across the sandbar and came back and sort of threw himself into the water. He shouted something to us, but we couldn't hear it. He pushed forward again and stumbled and fell over, and the water carried him a couple of feet to our right before he got up again. We all cheered, and started to shout "Come on! Come on! Come on!" but the water was pushing so hard he was barely moving. Gradually we all stopped shouting. We could see the desperation in his face. All he could manage was one step at a time, until it started to get shallower and he got to the water's edge and walked slowly towards us, speechless and exhausted.

"And then Ed turned to me. "Your go," he said. I didn't want to go. I wanted him to say 'Forget it, you don't have to. Just kidding.' But he didn't. He just said, 'Your go. We've all done it,' and the other children, even the one who'd just struggled back, lined up in an arc behind me, repeating it. "Your go. Your go." I tried to say it's too deep, but he just stepped very close to me and said, 'We've all done it. It's your turn.'

"Then suddenly, Jim's forced his way through the other children and stepped between Ed and me. He's stockier than Ed, and he says "Cut it out. He's not going."

"And Ed said something, and Jim said 'He's not going. We're going home.' And Ed said "You do it." and Jim said it was too deep, and Ed called him a coward, and I think he pushed Jim, and Jim punched Ed in the stomach. He staggered back and Jim punched him again. Then he grabbed my hand and shouted for me to run. Before the other children had time to turn round in pursuit we've opened up a ten-yard gap, running fast on the wet sand. They gave chase, but we ran and ran and when we looked behind they'd given up. We slowed to a walk, and then Jim hit me hard on the back of the head. I stumbled forward, he pushed me over, I sprawled on the sand and he was on my back, hitting me anywhere he could. When he stopped and got off me and I struggled to my feet, he said, I remember it, "Learn to stand up for yourself, you useless little brother," and he walked off. We made our own ways back to our parents, and that was about it. When I took a last look up the beach the sandbar'd disappeared."

Scarlet said, "I don't think he thinks that now."

"I have my uses?"

"Don't write yourself off so much." She got up and went to the foot of the stairs, listening for Jim, but everything was quiet and she came back and went to the window and the empty garden. "I will, you know," she said, "I'll tear this place apart when he's gone."

"Don't do that."

"It's his. It can't be anybody else's."

"You'll go back?"

"To the States? Yes, this isn't my country. My life's over there, the people I know, my so-called career."

"Then why not let someone else have this?"

"Because… because I've left him before and I've always gone back. And this time I can't."

"Other people might need it, like you did."

Very deliberately and slowly she said, "It's not theirs. It

can't be." She let almost a minute go by in silence, and then very quietly said, "When do we talk with him?"

The next morning, after breakfast, Robert sat at Jim's bedside, trying to decide what to say.

"It seems to me," Jim began, almost in a whisper, "it's you who needs to talk."

Robert still said nothing, and Jim went on, "If you're worried about the risk…"

Robert shook his head. "Oddly enough, I'm not. It's because you're my brother."

"Not much of one, really."

"Well, you're the one person I get to decide about."

"I still think you need to be more sure."

Robert stood up and took a couple of steps away from the bed. "From the first time I came here, I've never known what to do, what you wanted from me. Even when I saw something like this coming, I didn't know. But I think I do now."

"What made your mind up?"

"Nothing really, no big revelation. Barbara doesn't want me to do it, and she's right, from her point of view."

"What then?" Weak though it was, something dismissive was creeping into Jim's voice.

"There's a lot of things as a doctor you have to work out for yourself," Robert said. "Maybe I've spent more time at this end of a life than most."

"What's that mean?"

Robert walked to the window and turned round. "Look, I have a reasonable idea of what you're in for, and

I can't see anything good about it, any more than you can."

"We were never close. Why do this for me?"

"Does it matter?"

"Maybe it matters to me."

Robert, surprised, waited for Jim to go on.

"Maybe I want *you* to help me with this," Jim said.

It wasn't just a request; it was also a challenge. A fleeting sense that Jim had won once again possessed Robert, and almost angrily he said, "Because you know I'll do it, tagging along one last time?"

Jim stared at Robert. "That's what I'm afraid of."

Robert took one breath, then another. He took a step forward, and stopped. Jim's plea was for him to get this right, he suddenly realised, not for Jim himself.

"Then if you must know," he said, "it's these last few days, seeing how you are. If it's what you want, if it's what you really want, I'm ready enough."

With a last flicker of energy, Jim looked at Robert and said, "Ready enough. That's going to see you through?"

"If it's what you want."

Jim relaxed. "My mind's made up," he said, and he closed his eyes.

In the late afternoon Jim came downstairs, helped, almost carried, by Scarlet and Robert. He sat on the sofa, getting his breath back, with Scarlet next to him, and Robert pulled up a chair to face him. When Jim was ready, he said, "You know what I want."

Scarlet took a quick breath and squeezed his hand.

257

Robert said, "There are things to talk about. Nothing but nothing gets back to Scarlet."

Jim nodded.

"And it won't be today," Robert went on. "Or even this weekend. I can stay a couple of days, or I can come back, but I need to know you've made your mind up."

Jim looked at Scarlet and back at Robert. "I have," he said. His voice was weak but firm.

"And you're not going to change it."

Jim slowly shook his head.

"You've thought through what you're doing?" Robert went on. "You've made your goodbyes? You're not just slipping out?"

"Scarlet's here. You're here."

"She's going to miss you. I'll miss you."

"Will you, after all?"

Robert looked straight at him, captured his gaze, and said, "Yes. Yes, I will."

Jim moved round a little and tried to find something to say, but failed.

Scarlet spoke. "Anyone else?" she said. "Anyone else you want."

"Who's going to miss me?" said Jim, sounding curious.

"Poker will. The Guitarist for sure," she said.

"And you need to think," said Robert, "if there's any last few things you want to do. Take a couple of days."

"Doctor's orders?"

"Just good advice."

Jim shifted again; Scarlet adjusted the pillow behind his head. He looked at Robert and said, "You can go through with this?"

Robert waited, then said, "I don't want you to suffer for nothing." He leant forward, and took Jim's other hand. "Make it work."

"I'll do what I can. It's not exactly up to me."

They talked on, more idly, as it grew dark, until Jim indicated he was too tired. Scarlet prepared a simple meal, helped Jim to eat a little, and then she took him upstairs to bed.

Jim had one request, to see Poker's music collection, and Scarlet drove him out there on Monday afternoon. Jim wasn't much interested in the wet, winter scenery, but he was pleased when they got there, and got out of the car. Poker greeted him, but the change in Jim's condition shocked him.

"You're not looking so good, man," he said.

"I've been better," Jim replied.

Jim began to walk to the barn, leaning on Scarlet's arm and with Poker's arm around him.

Poker unlocked the barn door, drew it aside, and flicked on the lights, which burst on down the rows and rows of recordings. The white walls and the glazed windows set off the muted colours on the racks, making it seem as if they were asleep, and, as ever, Scarlet couldn't help smiling. It felt like a time capsule, or a spaceship. It would endure. She held Jim tightly as Poker showed off some of his new acquisitions and talked about how the people digitising the collection were getting on.

"They doing the lot?" Scarlet asked.

"Except for the ones I shouldn't be having," Poker replied with a smile. "I do them myself."

Jim moved on to the tapes.

"You're in here, you know," Poker said. "You too, Scarlet. You want to hear some?"

Jim shook his head.

"Not much of your early stuff, of course."

"How come you got any?" Jim asked.

"You'd be surprised what people tape. I just have to hear about it and there's a copy. Deadheads, of course, but lots of bands, big and little."

"We weren't so little," said Jim.

"I'm not saying you were, and I've got the tapes to prove it. I'll probably be getting more, next time I'm in the States."

"I'll have it put on my tombstone: Part of the Poker Martin collection."

"You do that," said Poker.

"Better than putting Jim Parrish and Scarlet," said Scarlet.

They moved towards the chairs at the far end.

Poker looked at Scarlet and said, "What d'you think – he's going to be happy there?"

"He'll have enough good people to play with," she said, but she turned to Jim and kissed him and hugged him for a long time.

"You wanting to hear anything special?" Poker asked as they sat down. "You pretty much know the best things I've got."

"I brought something actually, if you don't mind," said Jim.

"It's your show," said Poker, and he led them to the seating area at the far end of the barn.

"I always loved your set-up," said Scarlet, nodding at the array of speakers.

"No point in having anything but the best," he replied.

They sat down and Poker said, "What've you got?"

Out of a coat pocket, Jim produced a CD and handed it over.

"Bach's two- and three-part inventions, Glenn Gould," said Poker, looking at it. "Good choice. Why this one?"

"You know," Jim said, "the stage I'm at, I like to hear him sing. He's so lost. So in the music."

Chapter 18

Early December 2018

Jim lay on the sofa wrapped in a blanket, his face drawn, the skin taut and tinged with yellow over the cheek bones. In his right hand he held a white plastic bottle the size of a bottle of aspirins, with a typed label on it that said secobarbital. When he shook it, it rattled.

"What is it, exactly?" he said.

"It will send you to sleep," said Robert, sitting opposite him. "I mean sleep. A deep coma."

Jim nodded, and then pointed at the brown glass bottle and the hypodermic.

"Pancuronium. It's a muscle relaxant, and it will stop your heart."

"But I'll be asleep? In a coma?"

"You'll never know. You won't even feel the needle."

Jim stirred in his chair. "I had a shitty night's sleep," he said. "You'd think you could go out on a good one."

"You could think a lot of things," Robert replied, relieved that he could briefly play the role of doctor as a mask for his feelings and, perhaps, a shield against his brother's. What his own feelings were, he could not at that moment have said; he knew no words for the combination of emotions, each mostly identifiable, that passed like a succession of filters between himself and where he was.

"And you're saying I can't have breakfast," said Jim, putting down the plastic bottle and picking up his whisky glass. "But you don't object to this?"

"I think, in the circumstances…"

"Yes. The circumstances." He sipped his whisky. "You won't join me?"

"Too early in the day for me."

"Even in the circumstances?"

Robert nodded, and smiled, and got up and went to the window. Jim followed him with his eyes. It seemed that there was nothing else he wanted, and he was silent for a while as Robert looked out at the abandoned garden and the sunlight.

"Can't say I'm in a hurry," said Jim.

There was a knock at the door. Robert picked up the medicines and said, "I'll put these away. Expecting anyone?"

Jim shook his head. McIntire had been told not to come. Robert put the medicines in a bag in the fridge and went to the door. It was The Guitarist. He had on a dark blue jacket, a dark blue shirt, and dark blue trousers and shoes.

"Come in," said Robert. "You were playing the other night."

"Had to be," said The Guitarist, in a soft voice.

Robert showed him to the living room and hung back as The Guitarist sat on the sofa beside Jim.

263

"I heard from Poker…" he said.

"Good of you to come," said Jim.

"I'm not sure I know what to say." He paused, uncertain. "I thought if I came all in black," he said, tugging at his jacket, "you might think I was Johnny Cash."

"I'm not that confused."

"Still, it's a shame, seeing you like this."

"My brother tells me we all wind up something like this."

The Guitarist turned round to look at Robert. "You're his brother? I didn't know. You a musician too?"

"No," said Jim, with a quiet laugh that turned into a hollow cough. "He's a corpse doctor."

The Guitarist looked puzzled, and Jim added, "He only deals with dead people. That's why he's here. He brings me whisky," said Jim, raising his glass. "You want some?"

The Guitarist declined and Jim made a joke of it. Then he took The Guitarist's hand and asked, "Where've you been playing?" and The Guitarist started to talk about his recent gigs and his plans, and Jim listened with a smile.

Robert left them to it and went to the kitchen. He was restless; nothing in the paper caught his attention, nothing on the radio came over as anything other than noise. There was nothing to do but wait. Wait for Scarlet to return, wait for Jim to say it was time. He examined the contents of the fridge. He made himself a coffee and drank most of it. He poured the rest away and washed the cup. He cleaned and dried the cafetière. He wiped the kitchen table. He was thinking of cleaning the sink when he heard Scarlet open the front door, and he went to greet her.

"The Guitarist's come around?" she asked. "I saw his car."

"He's talking to Jim."

"That's nice of him. He's very kind."

She put down a big bag, took off her coat, caught a glimpse of herself in the mirror, and said, "God, my hair. I'll just go and change. Don't tell him I'm back."

"He's guessed, I'm sure."

She ran up the stairs with her bag, and ran to the rack of pashminas, rejecting one after another. She slipped out of her shirt and jeans, pulled on some new, dark tights, tore open the shopping bag, and put on the new red dress, struggling for a moment to zip it up completely at the back. She turned to the line of belts, pulled out a gold one, then a white one, went back to the first one and put it on, pulling it tight. A look in the mirror and she went back to the pashminas, only to reject them again. Now the red high-heeled shoes that went with the dress. Then her hair. There just wasn't time. She brushed it quickly and firmly, decided to compensate by throwing a gold pashmina over her shoulders, pinned on her brooch, and went back downstairs to where Robert was still waiting.

"Does my hair look OK? There wasn't time to have it done."

"You look great."

Scarlet took his hands, looked at him, and said, "You mean, you think I look like a tart."

"It's not what I was expecting. But you look great."

She twisted her feet so that he looked at them, but he looked blank.

"Manolos." He still looked blank. "Manolo Blahnik. The shoes."

She kissed him on the cheek, stood back, tidied her

hair, and went to the living room. Robert followed. As The Guitarist got up she crossed the room and stood in front of Jim.

"How do I look?" she said.

"Best ever," Jim said. "I'm never going to forget it."

"You mean that?"

"Every word."

She turned to The Guitarist, kissed him on the cheeks, and said, "Thanks for coming."

"You look amazing," he said, giving her a kiss. And then, more quietly, "Hey, I had to be here."

Scarlet sank down onto the sofa where The Guitarist had been sitting, kissed Jim gently on his forehead, and lay there holding his hands, saying nothing. He turned his head to look at her and said, "You look really great." She remained lying beside him for a time, and then she sat up and said, "Do you want to stay for lunch?"

"I guess it's whatever you and Jim want," The Guitarist replied.

"Stay for lunch," said Jim.

"I'll fix it," said Robert. "Let you musicians get along."

Over lunch in the kitchen the conversation lurched from one thing to another, driven by everyone's desire to keep it going and make it seem like a normal day. Sometimes it was easy, sometimes one or other of the four of them seemed frightened by a moment of silence, as if it was a vacuum that would swallow everything they were doing and reveal their pretence. At one point Jim reached his hand forward, took a large piece of cheese, and ate it.

"Jim, don't!" Scarlet shouted.

"Damn it, why not? Can't do any harm now," and he

looked from her to Robert and back. Robert rolled his eyes and Scarlet shook her head and looked away.

After lunch, The Guitarist stood up and got ready to leave. He took Jim's hands in his and said, "Thanks for everything, man. Thanks for the music."

"Thanks for coming," Jim replied.

"We're all going to miss you."

Jim gave a smile and squeezed The Guitarist's hands. They stayed like that for a long moment, and then The Guitarist released Jim's hands. He turned to Robert and shook his hand. "Thanks for this. I'm sure you've done what you can."

"I've tried," Robert said. "Good luck. Take care."

The Guitarist turned to Scarlet and walked with her in silence to the front door. They exchanged a few words that Robert and Jim could not hear, embraced, and then he left and Scarlet shut the door. She waited a moment, and came back to the living room and said to them, "He won't go. He's just sitting in his car." Robert went with her to the front room and they watched discreetly until there was a squall of wind and The Guitarist slowly drove away. Then she turned and went back to Jim, and Robert followed.

"Are we ready?" said Jim as they came into the kitchen.

"Not here," said Scarlet.

"No," said Jim, "the living room. I want to be surrounded by my family."

Robert saw a spasm of... what? anger? pass over Scarlet's face, which she forcibly suppressed, and she said, "We're here."

Jim struggled to get up, they helped him, and together they led him back to the living room and his usual place on the sofa. They settled him down, Scarlet fussed over the pillows, and went to get him a fresh glass of water and another whisky. Then she sat on the sofa beside him, and Robert sat in a chair close by. Jim gestured for the bottle of tablets. Robert passed it to him, he unscrewed the top and poured some into his hand. "Ugly little orange things," he said, his voice weaker than he wanted. "Like maggots, somehow." He poured them back into the bottle.

"You can give me another, if I need one?"

"If you're still able to swallow," Robert replied.

Jim nodded. "And then you give me the other stuff?"

"I do."

Jim fell silent. Then he said, "I haven't got a speech."

Robert sat forward. "I'm going to leave you with Scarlet for a few minutes." He got up and left the room.

Scarlet leaned towards Jim and said softly, "I've promised myself I'm not going to cry."

"You know," he said, "I wouldn't mind."

"Well, I might have to."

Jim was silent again for a while. Then he said quietly, "I'm not much good at this, you know."

"You're doing fine."

"I mean, at saying goodbye."

She squeezed his hands. "I'm going to miss you."

"I'm sorry I have to go so soon."

"Don't be. We all go in the end." She kissed him gently.

"Would it be easier," he said, shifting around to hold her more closely, "if we believed…?"

"We'd meet again? Over Jordan?" She looked longingly at him. "I'd still miss you."

"I never could. And I'm not going to start."

"I'm going to miss you terribly."

He squeezed her arm. "It's been good. Better than I deserved."

They stayed silently together for a while, and then Jim said, "Go and get Robert." Scarlet kissed him again, whispered, "I love you," and got up. When she came back, Jim looked at Robert and Robert said, "I need to know... you're sure you're ready."

Jim caught something in Robert's voice. He looked at him with an expression Robert could not quite read – surprise? amusement? – and said, "Ready if you are."

Robert leaned forward and took Jim's hands in his. He looked straight at him and said quietly, "You're sure you want to do this?"

Jim looked back and said, "I want to end my life. I've made all my arrangements, and said what I have to, to Scarlet. I'm ready."

Robert took two secobarbital capsules and handed them over to Jim, who looked at them in the palm of his left hand. "Seems like this is the day," he said, and with his right hand he took the glass of water from Scarlet and swallowed the capsules one after another. He handed the glass back to Scarlet, and turned to Robert and said, "Thank you."

Robert nodded, and Jim said, "I mean it. It's not everyone gets killed by their own brother."

Robert nodded again and said, "Probably best to relax. Nothing's going to happen very soon."

"I'm on my way," said Jim. "There's no hurry."

It was almost an anti-climax, but something about the act gave it a solemnity that shaped the afternoon.

Mostly the three of them were quiet, sometimes memories shared between Jim and Scarlet made them smile, even laugh gently. Gradually Jim's tiredness took over and he stopped talking. Scarlet lay beside him, holding his hand, occasionally brushing his hair and his cheek, asking in whispers if he was comfortable, assuring him she was still here with him. She heard his words even as they grew fainter, held his whisky and then his water until he was too tired to want either, and she had to guess what he was saying when he murmured to her. She lay beside him almost motionless, stretching the time into one long moment, broken and restored like the motion of a calm, deep sea.

Robert watched. Watched for the signs that the secobarbital was working, that Jim was not in much pain, that his breathing was steady. After perhaps a further hour he got up and whispered to Scarlet that he was going for a walk. He took the door key from the hall table and walked down towards the canal. He stopped at the bus shelter, sat down, and suddenly, brokenly, began to sob. Tears blinded him, the world became a boat in the fog. All he could do was ride it out, and after a few minutes he began to see again. The road, the leafless trees, the empty cottages, the low hills beyond only a little darker than the clouds. A view that was banal and incapable of speech. He stood up, wiped his eyes, and walked slowly back to resume his place by Scarlet and Jim. There, he watched this man in his late sixties, whom he had come to know again over a period of six months, as his life now gradually ended, comforted by a woman who loved him. Watched his brother, for Jim had used the word, watched his brother, and thought of his childhood, his own children, his life with, and mostly without, the man before him, all brought briefly to life by a man now about to die.

Chapter 19

Early December 2018

The summer sunshine had filled the room, occupied every part of it with so much heat it felt as if everything was being recharged. The furniture had glowed, the walls had been warm to the touch, the air had been full. But the December sunshine merely hovered in the room, alighted weightlessly on the surfaces as if it did not belong, and disturbed nothing.

Now, as night fell, Jim rested on the sofa and Scarlet sat beside him holding his hand. His breathing was shallow but steady, his pulse rate low, his eyes closed, his face careworn but untroubled. She had sat beside him all afternoon, not exactly motionless but caring only for his comfort, her thoughts on hold. Robert had sat opposite them, drained, not knowing what might happen, trying for Scarlet's sake to appear calm.

Around nine o'clock, Jim's breathing became a little disturbed, and then, slowly at first, deeper. Scarlet looked at him, uncertain what to make of it. Robert crossed over to the sofa, and found that Jim's pulse was stronger. He looked up at Scarlet and shook his head. "I don't know," he whispered, "I just don't know."

Jim's breathing settled into a new, steady rhythm, punctuated only when his body gave a brief twitch. Again Scarlet looked at him, again all he could signal was, 'I don't know.' He brought her a glass of water, noting that she hadn't eaten since lunch, and put his arms around her shoulders. Without taking her eyes off Jim she said, "What's going on?"

"We'll have to wait and see," he said.

He moved his chair so that he could sit holding Jim's right hand. It was thin, the knuckles and metacarpals prominent under the surface, the fingers strong but cold. He found himself massaging it gently, warming what little life remained in it. Scarlet did the same, catching his eye with a slight smile before returning her attention exclusively to the sleeping man laid out before them. He found himself thinking, We are here, Jim, we are still here, and wondering at the same time what there was to receive this anguished, simple message.

This was the moment. Robert could see himself gently letting go of Jim's hand, observing as he did so that Jim did not notice, that he was indeed deeply asleep. He could go to the fridge, take out the pancuronium, prepare the needle, roll up Jim's sleeve, and slip the needle into his arm. In a minute, Jim would be dead. A death of his choice, that cut short the suffering of a dying man, that he had asked for with dignity and had been given with the support of the woman who loved him. He had seen people howl their way to death, tormented with pain and bitterness that no one would spare them, shards of their former selves, cursing those who brought them love. Men wasting almost paralysed to death, whose eyes asked only for release. Women for whom kind words and the gentle caress of a hand meant nothing but the failure to do the one thing they wanted. Jim would not have to die that way.

Something in the way Robert moved, even without getting up, caught Scarlet's eye. She looked up, across Jim's body, and stared at him. He nodded gently, and she looked relentlessly back at him. She looked at him as if he was her only friend, and yet, across a chasm, as if newly possessed of an unutterable truth. He stood up. She half started out of where she was sitting, unable to let go of Jim and yet wanting to keep Robert where he was.

"Don't," she whispered.

He waited, knowing it was not right for him to speak, knowing that at this moment Scarlet had to be alone. That after it she would always in some ways be alone. He stood there trying not to move. To let her live in the terrible freedom she had, and to accept it. Fully.

"Please," she said in the same hushed voice, unable to leave Jim's side, unable to let him go. Robert turned to sit down, but she shook her head and again he stopped. Except for her eyes, darting back to Jim and again to Robert, her face was rigid, her body set in one position, as if even breathing was too turbulent and only a perfect stillness could be endured. Life prolonged in eternal stasis.

Scarlet turned to look at Jim, bent over him, and kissed him. "We're here, Jim," she murmured. "We're here, we're here." Jim stirred again for a moment and settled again. Robert sat back down, and waited. An hour passed and then Jim opened first his right eye and then his left, and stared vacantly ahead. He looked to his right and saw Scarlet, and slowly gave a smile. She kissed him again and squeezed his hand. He closed his eyes, but seemed to be holding onto her hand. Her hair fell off her shoulder and brushed his face. She pushed it back, and he smiled again.

"Did you see that?" she said, breathlessly. "He's alive. He didn't die."

Numb with wonder, Robert took his brother's other hand, unable to think. If Jim is alive, how completely will he recover? Will he slip back into unconsciousness and this time not recover? What was it, after all, to give him those pills? The cancer hasn't gone away, the pain it has brought will return if he lives much longer. And yet he rests there at peace, breathing quietly, aware of his surroundings.

Jim, after that brief moment, fell asleep. Conversation remained suspended, as if it was frivolous and some obscure ceremony was unfolding in which their only part was silent attentiveness. Sometimes Jim would turn his body slightly to one side or another and they would try to make sure he was comfortable. Around midnight they moved the chairs around so that Scarlet could spend the night alongside him, and at her insistence Robert went to bed.

Sleep was difficult. He lay in bed, hearing every sound from downstairs: Scarlet walking to the kitchen to get a glass of water, or moving her chair, and every rustle from outside. He found the silences between the sounds more difficult than the sounds themselves. Had he missed something? Even now was Jim calling for him, in whatever way he could? Was Scarlet? Would she call him in time, if it came to it?

The sunlight infused the yellow curtains and shone coldly over the rail. He looked at the alarm clock; it was nearly eight o'clock. Memories trickled in, and thoughts about what he had to do today. He got up, dressed, washed his face, went downstairs and looked into the living room to find Scarlet lying on her side asleep, her high heels kicked out of the way. He went to the kitchen and started to make coffee but he could hear that the noise of the kettle boiling in the kitchen had roused her, and he padded back to the door to see how she was.

"Did I fall asleep?" she asked.

"You must have done. How about him?"

"Like a baby. Didn't even snore."

He offered her coffee, which she took by Jim's side, and he brought her two slices of toast. She looked exhausted, but she would leave Jim only to get washed and to slip on some comfortable sandals. Robert offered to sit by him while she got some sleep, but she refused, and they sat beside him quietly as the room slowly filled with light.

Shortly after nine Jim woke up again. He stirred in his sleep, opened his eyes, looked around, and began to push himself into a sitting position. Scarlet leant over and kissed him and caressed his cheeks. He looked at her and smiled. "You're here," she murmured. "You're back, you didn't die."

"I wasn't sure," Jim said quietly.

"You didn't. You're here."

"Maybe nobody wanted me."

"I do."

"I know you do." He squeezed her hand and then, with more effort, turned towards her and gave her a kiss.

Robert asked "How do you feel?" and Jim replied, "As

276

if I'm floating. Moving's difficult, and – I don't know –" he paused, and thought for a moment. "As if I'm not touching the ground."

"That's probably the drugs," Robert said, "now they're wearing off."

"And I feel…" he paused again, "… very calm. Does that make sense?"

Robert indicated that it might, more out of kindness than any degree of knowledge, and Scarlet asked Jim if he wanted anything. He thought about it and said, "No, nothing." Robert brought him a glass of water, which he sipped before returning it to Robert. "I think I'm dozing off again," he said, and closed his eyes.

When she was sure Jim was asleep, his breathing was steady, and he was comfortable, Scarlet let go of his hand and walked out of the room, down the hall, and onto the patio. Through the window, Robert could see her stand still as soon as she stepped into the sunlight, her head down, her body, her arms and hands tense. She brought her hands up, fingers clenched, and pressed her head into her fists. Then gradually she relaxed her shoulders, her hands moved an inch or two away from her face, then her fingers spread wide, she brought her hands back to sweep her hair away, and she lifted her face to the sun. She arched her back, took a deep breath, and another, spread her arms out wide and then slowly let them drop to her side. She gave a shudder, and then a softness spread through her body, out from her shoulders and down her back, and she gazed straight ahead. She looked around, turning her head left and right, and reached out to brush the wall beside her. Hesitantly, she took a step forward, and then another, until she was at the edge of the lawn. She stopped by the camellias, looking not at them but past them, slipped off her sandals and walked onto the grass. He watched her drift slowly towards the cherry tree, now robbed of its leaves, then randomly this or that way until, for no apparent reason, she turned and began her journey back. He could see now that her thoughts were far away, her face emotionless.

She crossed the patio to the kitchen door and he heard her draw up a chair and sit down. He waited for a time and then went to join her. From the doorway he saw her sitting by the kitchen table, her hands folded in her lap, nothing in front of her, her eyes closed. He was about to turn and go when she said, "No, join me. Be lost together."

They sat together in silence for a while, as if speaking was difficult, or, perhaps, unnecessary. She reached out a hand and stroked his arm with the back of a nail.

"Have we won?" she said, almost in a whisper.

"I've no idea," he said softly.

"He's back, though. He's back."

"For a while." He withdrew his arm. "And if he is, he's back as he was before. No different."

"I didn't suppose…"

He shifted in his chair and took her hands in his. "I think I'm floating too. I don't know where I am," he said.

"Me neither. Except I'm with him."

He held her hands for a moment, and then pushed his chair back and got up. "We are," he said, and then more quietly, "we are."

Scarlet looked around the kitchen. "Coffee. How about coffee?"

Robert made two cups, and they went back to be beside Jim. He lay there as quietly as before, and they sat with him as before. After another hour, he woke up enough to drink from a mug of thin soup. Scarlet helped him to push himself into an upright position, and then, with her holding the mug, he took small sips, and in between those moments he looked peacefully at each of them. He accepted a generously buttered bread roll, tearing off little pieces and chewing them slowly. With each sip of the soup and each morsel of bread, Scarlet seemed to grow in strength herself, to be living not for each moment as if it could barely promise to lead to the next but in the expectation of more time to come. Not holding her breath but daring now to trust that Jim was in fact coming back to life.

When he was finished, Scarlet brought a warm flannel to mop his face and wipe his hands. She started to do so, and without a word he took it from her, cleaned himself, and handed it back.

"He's getting better," Robert mouthed at her, and she mouthed back "More like his old self."

Jim sat up and looked first at Scarlet and then at Robert. "I had a dream," he said, in a soft voice tinged with surprise. "I thought you were trying to kill me."

"We were," said Robert, honesty mellowing his words.

Jim looked around, then back at Robert. "Were you going to come with me?"

"I thought I'd wait," said Robert.

"The long black train leaves every day," said Jim, and he closed his eyes.

For another two hours Jim dozed and woke, dozed

and woke. When he was awake he asked for nothing, accepted the water he was offered, and a little bread at lunchtime. But soon they could see that Jim's eyes were anxiously darting about the room, and gradually he became more agitated, trying to sit up but never finding a comfortable position. Scarlet, too, became concerned, but he said nothing and shrugged off their questions. He took short, shallow breaths, and seemed, despite everything, to be trying to get up. Suddenly, he pushed back the duvet that Scarlet had placed around him, pushed up with both hands, and stood up unaided.

Robert and Scarlet rose at once and she held Jim under his shoulders.

"The piano," he said, in a hoarse, desperate voice. "The piano."

Robert and Scarlet exchanged glances, and then, helped by Scarlet on one side and Robert on the other, Jim began to walk with difficulty across the room. He managed the first step, then the second, then the third, but then he stopped. He leant forward and held on to them.

"Who'd have thought it," he said, breathlessly.

"No hurry," said Robert. "Take your time."

Slowly, Jim managed another three steps, and stopped again, resting on Scarlet for longer this time. Then the next three, a pause for breath, and then, as if spurred by the nearness of the front room, the next two. His breathing was now rapid and shallow, his face almost vacant. When they reached the door to the front room, he turned his head to look at Scarlet, his eyes darting around. He squeezed her arm, and between breaths he panted, "Can't turn back now." He stayed still. Gradually his breathing slowed down, he shuffled his feet forward and stood less bent over.

"We could carry you," said Robert.

Jim looked at him, unable to speak.

"If you want," Robert went on, looking at Scarlet, who nodded in agreement.

"I can walk this bit," said Jim. He stood there with their arms around him for a minute, and then he set off for the piano in a slow shuffle, Scarlet supporting him.

When they got there, Robert stepped back and Scarlet helped lower Jim onto the piano stool, and then she sat beside him, one arm around him. With her free hand she lifted the piano lid and looked at him. He took several breaths before he looked at the keys. Then he slowly took his hands and placed them above the keys, ready to play. He was tired and uncertain, many expressions crossed his face but none settled. Now he reached up with his hands for the sheet music resting on the top of the piano. Slowly, he took down one score and then another, opening them, looking at them, letting them slip to the floor or into Scarlet's lap. Then he stopped, looked back at the keys, took a deep breath, and brought his hands down firmly. Once. Twice. Three times.

It was wrong. Terribly wrong. The chords were random selections of notes. None made any sense. Jim lifted his hands again, looked at the piano, let his hands fall back without any interest in the noise they made, and from his exhausted body there came a sound long, desolate, enormous in its grief. It echoed from the depths of him and clothed itself in his voice as it left, and as it left him his body fell forward. Scarlet caught him, and he lay in her arms until, at a nod from her, Robert stepped forward and between them they carried Jim back to his place on the sofa.

His eyes were closed, he was breathing more steadily than before, but it did not seem like sleep so much as unconsciousness. Once he was settled, Robert quickly took his pulse, but he couldn't say how Jim was, except that he was exhausted.

He stayed that way for several hours. They stayed beside him, barely talking, their shared anxiety rising and then gradually falling as Jim returned to the state he'd been in before lunch. As it grew dark, he woke up. He looked first at Scarlet, then at Robert, then back to Scarlet. Then, in an empty voice, he said, "All gone. All music, gone." A look of terror swept over his face, and was replaced by one of hopelessness. His eyes darted about, his mouth opened but no more words came out. Scarlet, alarmed, hugged him tightly, and gradually, unevenly, he became calmer.

Scarlet and Robert stayed beside him, holding his hands, talking in gentle words, soothing him as if he was a child, knowing all the same that there was no way back. Eventually, Jim fell asleep again, at first turning and groaning in his sleep but then slipping into it more deeply and securely until, finally, Scarlet felt that it was safe to leave his side. She leant over and kissed him on his forehead, stood up, and after a moment looked over at Robert. She was exhausted, her face drained and pale.

"You look like you should be asleep," he said.

"I will be soon. But I should fix you something to eat."

Robert shook his head, got up, went to the kitchen and came back with a bottle of wine and two glasses. "Red good enough?" he asked.

"Perfect," she said, taking a glass from him.

"Then I'll do my internationally famous Spanish omelette."

"Fine by me," Scarlet said, and she raised her glass.

They drank, and Scarlet said, "What does he mean, all music gone?"

"Maybe, just what he said."

"Can that happen? Music's his life. It's what he believes in."

"At this stage, sometimes… things just go. We don't know why."

A passion flared in her eyes and sank back. "It's who he is," she said. "You told me yourself; he was a different person when he learned the piano."

Scarlet looked at him, tired, bewildered, lost. He crossed to the chair where she was sitting, sat beside her, and put an arm around her to give her a hug. She didn't respond. They sat there for a time, until she turned her head to look at him and did her best to smile before she turned away again and looked at the floor.

"I'll make that omelette," he said.

When he came back twenty minutes later she was asleep, but only lightly. She woke easily, and murmured, "Ah, the international omelette. Thank you." She ate a few mouthfuls and said, "What did you put in it?"

"Pretty much anything I could find. Peppers, frozen prawns. Potatoes, of course. Is it all right?"

"It is, actually. Just what I want. But maybe not exactly Spanish."

They finished the meal in silence, Robert tidied up, and Scarlet got unsteadily to her feet. "Bedtime," she said.

"I'll sleep on the sofa. It's very uncomfortable, I didn't realise. See you in the morning."

"See you in the morning. And… I'll be here…"

"I know. I appreciate it, I appreciate it."

Robert walked slowly to the door, up the stairs, into the spare bedroom, lay down, and without meaning to, fell asleep.

Jim spent most of the night asleep and woke early in the morning. Scarlet stirred beside him, and looked at him. It took him a minute to be ready to speak.

"What time is it?" he said.

"I don't know. About six, I guess," she said softly. She turned around to look at her watch. "Six ten. You slept well."

"Did I?"

"Right through. You waking up?"

He didn't reply.

"I'll get you something to eat."

He took her hand. "Don't. Stay here."

They lay together in the dark until Jim insisted on going to the bathroom. Scarlet put the lights on and, to her surprise, he made his way there and back slowly on his own, and when he returned he pushed the duvet aside and sat on the sofa. She went upstairs and came back with a heavy pullover that she helped him put on. Then, when she went to the kitchen to fix breakfast, he got up and slowly followed her and sat in a chair while she bustled about getting him a glass of apple juice and herself a coffee. As they sat there saying simple things, looking at the emptiness beyond the kitchen window turn slowly into a pale, grey and white outline of the garden, Robert came down and joined them.

"You look worse for wear," Scarlet said.

"I fell asleep," Robert said. "Just like that. In my clothes. How about you?"

"Didn't sleep at all." She squeezed Jim's arm and said lightly "You kept me awake."

"I've been tiring you all out?" said Jim.

"Keeping us busy," said Robert.

Scarlet turned in her chair to look straight at Jim, and said, "You gave us a fright, yesterday." He looked at her, eyes raised. She stretched out a hand towards him, across the table. "About music."

"I dreamt something," he said quietly. "I don't remember."

Scarlet looked over at Robert, who quickly shook his head, but Jim saw him and looked anxiously at her.

"It was a dream. I thought... I don't know. I was in a storm. There was a great wind, somehow it was inside some big building, scouring the corridors, it had to be let out." He stopped. "Doesn't make much sense, does it?"

"Do you remember how it ended?" said Robert.

Jim slowly shook his head. "No. Why are you asking?"

"You were talking in your sleep," said Robert, looking at Scarlet. "You're right, it didn't make much sense."

Robert made himself some toast and a fresh cup of coffee for himself and Scarlet. Jim quietly sipped his apple juice, until, as daylight spread across the garden and into the kitchen, he said, "What happened?"

"To tell the truth," said Robert, "I don't know."

Jim looked at him as if he was reassured. "But I'm not better, am I."

"No," said Robert. "How do you feel?"

"Still in the air." He thought for a moment and went on, "I feel I'm somewhere else. As if this isn't me, just a copy. And there are some things I can tell it to do."

"That's good," said Scarlet. "That's good."

They were quiet for a time, then Jim stood up. "I never did like these chairs," he said. "Bloody uncomfortable," and with Scarlet besides him he shuffled to the hall. He looked at the doors to the living room and the front room, and slowly went to the front room. Sheet music was still on the floor where they'd left it. Scarlet bent down to scoop it up, but Jim took her arm and said, "Don't." He sat down at the piano and looked at it for a long time. With one finger of each hand he picked out single notes at random. Then he turned to Scarlet and said in a soft, accepting voice, "No. All gone."

"It'll come back," said Scarlet. "It'll come back."

"No," he said, more firmly. "All gone. No sense in arguing about it."

"How do you feel about it?" said Robert.

"Empty." He looked at his hands, turning them over, looking at his nails, which had grown too long. "I nearly insured them, once. Then I threw a party instead."

"The Memphis one?" said Scarlet. "That was worth it."

"Were your hands really at risk?" said Robert.

"Barroom brawls. General stupidity." He looked at his hands again. "No, I guess not. They made it."

"Doesn't mean…" Robert began, before calling it off.

"Aha, the doctor. You see," Jim said, turning to Scarlet,

"he was going to remind me a risk isn't the same as a guaranteed defeat."

"Success is the same, that way," Robert replied.

"Success," said Jim with a smile, "what, now, is success?"

Scarlet looked intently at Jim and he smiled again. "I got the words. Just not the music. How does that work, doctor?"

"No idea," said Robert. "The brain's a big enough place – pretty well anything can happen."

"A life in medicine, and that's what you learn," said Jim.

They went back to the living room, and Scarlet went upstairs to rest for an hour. Robert helped Jim sit down on the sofa and brought him the whisky he asked for. When he was settled, Jim, obviously puzzled, said, "Who am I, now I'm not a musician?"

"You were lucky with that. You had something you could really do," Robert replied.

"You did too. You still do."

Robert shook his head. "Maybe that's gone."

"Just because you tried to kill me?"

"That's more than enough."

"Even though I appreciate it." Jim pushed himself up a little and said, "Will people find out?"

"Maybe. It depends." Robert paused. "Do you miss it?"
"Music?"

Robert nodded.

"It was my life. But it's gone. My life's gone."

Robert waited for Jim to carry on. He sipped his whisky and went on, "I don't think I miss it. It just… *was*, that's all. And now, here we are," he added, more brightly.

"Waiting for anything?"

"No, nothing's going to turn up. I now feel…" Jim looked over Robert's shoulders, as if the words could be found there, and said, in an oddly calm voice, "as if I was running all my life."

"You were the active one. You left home. Ran away to America, almost never came back, played your music. Lived more than a little. Met Scarlet."

Jim took another sip of his whisky and said, "Jim the pianist. Sounds faintly Welsh, doesn't it? Was that me?"

"I couldn't have done that," Robert replied. "I was too timid."

"You were slow. I always thought that," Jim said, in a neutral voice.

Robert sat back and said, "Slow?"

"Oh, it drove me crazy." Jim sipped his whisky again, and his weak voice sounded a little richer. "You didn't want to live. You wanted to stay cooped up. That's what I thought."

Robert suddenly thought of the chessboard on the family dining table. What had started, that fateful day? What had been in plain view, if he had known then how to look?

Jim said, "You never did much back then."

"I stayed out of trouble," said Robert and, smiling, added "you ran into it." He waited while Jim caught his breath, then said, "You nearly killed me once."

Jim looked puzzled. "On the Broads?"

"Yes."

"You still remember that?"

"It was almost the first thing I remembered, when you came back in June."

Jim pushed himself up and looked at Robert with what disbelief he could muster. "It was just a game. With a football. I couldn't believe how much you hated football."

"I always had to play with you. Or older kids. Bigger kids."

"Anyway, I saved your life."

"And you knew I couldn't swim."

Jim sat back, and with a flicker of self-assurance said, "Well, you're still here," and raised his glass as an acknowledgement.

After a pause, Robert said, "What do you mean, you saved my life?"

"That time on that beach."

"You got me into that. You hooked up with those other boys."

Jim waved his right hand in dismissal.

"They were stupid," Robert went on, "and their stupid game could've killed me."

"So deal with it. I had to come and get you. That's what I mean, you always tried to hide."

Robert sat forward, rested his chin in his hands for a moment, looked at Jim and said, "I could have, should have, I don't know, pushed more. Taken risks." He gave a wry smile, and, when Jim stayed quiet, he went on, "What did you run away from?"

Jim tried to take a deep breath. "It's a terrible thing to dislike one of your parents as much as I did."

Robert sat forward, and, unsettled, said, "For what?"

"It never let up." Jim paused again. "You must have thought—"

"They were a let-down. Of course, all parents are. Ask Lauren. It's part of growing up."

"It never stopped with me."

His calmness upset Robert, and when he said nothing, Robert went on. "They loved us, in their way."

"No, they didn't," Jim replied. "I don't mind. I stopped minding a long time ago. But they didn't, and you're just saying they did."

On another occasion, in a time long past, Robert knew, he would have stood up and shouted his denial, but now all he could do was to shake his head and say, "No, they did. They made a home for us. They cared."

Jim shook his head. "You just want to believe it," he said, still in his calm voice, "But it was a lie."

"We didn't know them then. Children see the quiet phase, that's all," Robert replied, all the time thinking: Believe this please, for your peace of mind. Or is it for mine?

Jim continued in the same calm voice. "Father's lie. Do the right thing."

"I got the sense of duty. Not you. But Mother didn't lie."

"And he took the life out of her. I could see it, day by day."

"Maybe they just wanted quiet, and peace."

The hint of anger, or of desperation, in Robert's voice came across to Jim, and he held up a hand. "I've no problem with that," he said, "but they said they were happy, and they weren't. They didn't live, and they couldn't love." He took a couple of breaths. "He destroyed her, bit by bit. And that was our home."

Jim's matter-of-fact tone of voice pressed like a physical pain for an assent that Robert could not give. He looked at his exhausted brother, and all he could say was, "And so you ran away?"

"And you stayed. Explain that to me."

"I was more like them, I suppose. I wanted security. Not to have to count every penny. Not to have to worry."

"I'm not angry, you know," Jim said. "Not anymore. Not just because I haven't got the strength."

"That's good."

"Is it?" For a moment, Jim seemed completely still, as if asleep. Then his eyes brightened. "It's gone, anyway, he said. "We've done whatever we did." Then, checking himself, he said, "I have, anyway."

"It wasn't so bad, either."

"Even if you missed the best bits?"

Robert smiled. "Whose fault was that?"

Jim took the point. "Still. I'm grateful for your opinion. I'd say the same, if the roles were reversed."

"Thank you." Robert stayed silent for a moment, and then said, "I didn't think you thought that."

"Well, I do. I thought I'd say so. And now, if you don't mind, I'm very tired."

Robert leant forward and took Jim's hand.

"No, not like that," said Jim. "Not yet. I don't think so, anyway. You can let Scarlet rest, too."

Robert held his hand for a while longer, and then slowly got up.

"You must be tired too," said Jim.

"I can keep going for a bit longer," Robert said. "Doctor's training."

Jim nodded, and his eyes closed. After a time, Robert got up and walked slowly to the kitchen. He found himself almost mechanically checking what was in front of him: this table, these chairs, the taps by the sink, the bread bin, the fridge, the window onto the garden. In his work, he had stood in moments like this many times, but there was no puzzle now, no question to be answered. He had no thoughts; he felt only a swirl that moved him from one idea to another before they could properly form. Not an emptiness, exactly, so much as a wind, ungraspable and exhausting in its suggestion that it was hiding something from him. The bleakness and simplicity of Jim's judgements disturbed him, but he could find nothing to say to his brother, and, he feared, nothing he could say to himself. The child who'd left but not rebelled, who'd prided himself on being the better son. What had he not seen? What could he not see now?

Around lunchtime, the doorbell rang. It was Lauren. Scarlet let her in and gave her a hug.

"How is he?" said Lauren.

"Asleep," said Scarlet. "He's mostly asleep."

"Is Dad here?"

"I am," said Robert, coming out to join them. He hugged his daughter and they went to the kitchen. Scarlet made Lauren a coffee.

Robert looked at Lauren and said, "You know you might not be able to speak to him."

"Why? Is he...?"

"He's probably dying. It could be any time."

Lauren looked from Robert to Scarlet and back.

"There isn't a timetable for these things," said Robert.

"But I'm real glad you came," said Scarlet, and she squeezed Lauren's hands.

They fell silent, their thoughts on Jim in the next room, and without more words they went to join him. He lay on the sofa, breathing so quietly that at first it seemed as if he'd died. Scarlet took his hand and looked up to signal that he was still, just, alive. Robert gestured for Lauren to step forward. She sat down next to Jim, took his other hand, and said softly, "Jim, it's me. Lauren. I've come to see you." He gave no sign that he had heard her, and she looked up nervously.

"Stay there," said Scarlet. "Just stay. That's good."

Lauren shuffled into a more comfortable position, and said again, "Uncle Jim, I've come to see you." But Jim did not respond.

They stayed like that throughout the afternoon. Lauren and Scarlet held Jim's hands and talked gently to each other, to Jim, and to Robert. The three of them took it in turns to eat something for a late lunch, and settled down to wait.

At some stage, as slowly as the arrival of dusk, they began to feel that Jim would not wake up again. They could not say goodbye to him, but they gathered more closely around him and around each other. Unspoken questions passed between them, answered with nods, a touch of a hand, or a smile. Sadness filled the room like shadows. They waited.

Chapter 20

Early December 2018

Jim's breath grew slower and quieter, his chest barely lifting and falling. He lay curled over facing Scarlet, his head resting on the pillow below her arm, his eyes closed, his mouth partly open. After a time, his breathing deepened, and then, Scarlet thought, it stopped. Holding her breath, she rolled over slightly to look more directly at him. He gave a few shallow breaths, but before that could reassure her, he began to gasp for breath, a hoarse incoherent sound came from his throat, and then he stopped altogether.

"Is he… ?" she asked Robert.

Robert leant forward. He could see traces of foam on Jim's nose and lips. He nodded, and said very quietly "Yes. He's died."

Scarlet stayed absolutely still for a time, and then kissed Jim's cheek. "I'm going to miss you," she said. She moved back to rest her head on the pillow, and lay there, still holding Jim's hand. "As simple as that?" she said.

"In the end," Robert replied.

"Poor Jim." She lay there, overpowered by the moment,

only slowly finding her attention returning to the room where she was.

"What about you?" she said, looking at Robert.

"I don't know," he said, so drawn into himself that the whole room felt a long way away. "We'll find out."

Lauren looked at Jim and then down, biting her lip. When she was ready to let go of Jim's hand, she stood up. Robert got up and hugged her, and she turned to see how Scarlet was.

"I'm OK," she said, in an exhausted voice.

Robert walked to the window. It was dark, there was nothing new to see. He drew the curtains and turned to look at Scarlet and Lauren.

"Can I get you anything?" he said. "Either of you. From the kitchen, or… ?"

"I'll have a whisky later," Scarlet said. "To remember him by."

"I might join you," he said, and Lauren nodded.

Now that the mundane was filtering back, disturbing and disrespectful, Scarlet took a deep breath and let it out as if emptying herself of emotion. "What happens next?" she asked.

"We tell McIntire," Robert replied. "He does the rest."

"Will it be… ?"

Robert gave a small shrug and shook his head. "It should be nothing at all. He'll arrange for the body to be collected…" he saw her stiffen slightly, "and sign the death certificate. That's it."

A flicker of anxiety shimmered in her eyes. He walked back towards her, and bending over he said, "Give me your hands."

She gave him her right hand, leaving her left hand still holding Jim's. He waited, and reluctantly she let go and gave her left hand to Robert, who took it.

"It's a very natural death," he said. "Of a terminally ill man. You might say 'of natural causes'. There's no need for any examination. Or anything like that."

Slowly, she began to cry. Robert released her hands, and she searched around for a box of tissues and mopped her cheeks.

"He simply wore out," he said.

"He wore out," she repeated, very quietly. "Poor Jim."

She kissed Jim again.

Robert looked at her and Lauren and said, "You two go to the kitchen. I'll make the phone call."

"Can we… ?" Scarlet looked at Jim's body. "I mean, I don't think he's comfortable."

Robert gave a small, sad smile, and took a step back. Together, he and Scarlet bent down, took Jim's legs and turned him so he lay along the sofa. They gently straightened his curled body, and placed his arms across his chest, and Lauren rearranged the pillows and the duvet, as if Jim were only asleep. When they were finished, Scarlet looked at how he lay, and without a word left the room and went to the kitchen.

Robert and Lauren followed her. She poured herself a glass of water, drank a little, and sat down at the kitchen table with the glass in front of her. Lauren did the same. Robert turned and went to the hall and rang McIntire, who promised to come over at once. Then he went back to the kitchen, and he, Scarlet, and Lauren sat together for a while, saying little.

After a time, Lauren turned to her father and said, "How do you feel?"

"To be honest," he replied, "I don't know."

"And how are you?" she asked Scarlet, who turned her face towards her, inscrutable and distant. Lauren got up, stood behind her, and hugged her. "I'm so sorry," she said.

"Don't be," said Scarlet, reaching up with her hands to hold Lauren's. "You came. That's what matters."

"I'm so sorry," said Lauren again.

They stayed there together for a while, and then Lauren looked towards the living room. They went in. Scarlet knelt down to look at the body and briefly froze. Then she softened, and, turning back to look at Robert, said, "It's not him anymore. It's like something has left."

"He's so pale," said Lauren, and she looked quickly to Robert. He searched for the right, consoling remark, but none came. Was he to be the doctor, discreetly guiding the bereaved? But who lay before him, if not his brother? He knew very well how to be the expert; he'd been here before, many times. Many times in his imagination, too, as Jim had tended towards his death, he had asked himself what he would feel at this moment. But now he was possessed by a great emptiness, in which he floated, weightless and immobilised.

Scarlet looked at Lauren. "You can stay for a bit, if you like" she said. "Say your goodbyes, if you want to."

Lauren looked uncertainly at her, then at her father, and back at Scarlet. "Of course you can," she said, squeezing Lauren's hand.

Robert went back to the kitchen. Lauren stood still, and then slowly sat down on the floor next to Scarlet. "I don't know what to say," she said after a time.

"Anything. Anything at all."

Lauren looked at Jim's body, at Scarlet, and back at the body, so impossibly unlike the old man she had briefly known that it seemed false. So incapable of motion, of speech, of humour, caring, anger, warmth that it could never have been alive, never have been Jim. Jim who played music and seemed to drink all day and always had something to talk about even though he was dying, had been dying all the time she'd known him. She was seized by a fearful desire to push this cruel simulacrum away, but it passed, and she saw the body as it was, something remarkable but now stopped, broken down. Part of a world in which nothing lasts forever.

She managed to mutter a "Thank you," and got up and left.

Scarlet stayed, sitting on the floor looking at Jim's pallid face. After a time she said, "I used to think you were a fool. So careless. You didn't need to wind up like this. But I'm the fool. I chose you. More than once." She reached out and adjusted the duvet, brushing it away from his face. "And I'd choose you again. Every time. I've always known that."

She kissed his face, stood up, and walked slowly out of the room.

McIntire came over, looked at Jim's body as it lay on the sofa, and asked Scarlet and Lauren to leave. When they had gone, he proceeded to examine the body carefully, looking, Robert realised, for any sign of a recent injection, all the time asking Robert questions about the time and manner of the death, to which Robert, still trying to comprehend what had happened, gave simple answers.

His examination concluded, McIntire said, "I have to be satisfied you didn't intervene."

"I did not cause his death," Robert replied.

"You understand, I could ask for a further examination."

"I know that perfectly well. I also know you would be wasting your time."

"I have no wish to make things unpleasant, but I have a duty to perform."

"Which you will do amply by certifying that Jim's death was due to complications arising from cancer of the bowel."

McIntire took a death certificate out of his bag. "I try to be a compassionate man, Dr Parrish. I shall sign this, but I suggest you consider your position."

He invited Scarlet back into the room, and with a few words of commiseration agreed that the body could be taken to a funeral home later that evening, and left. When he had gone, Robert made the arrangements for the body to be collected, and to his surprise people came out within the hour.

Once Jim's body was gone, the three of them suddenly felt that the house was empty. It wasn't the coldness of the night air that they felt, or the practised condolences of the undertakers, but an absence. Jim had filled the house; without him it was a shell. Left like this it would collapse. Scarlet would leave, everything that had been here would go, the piano, the music, the pictures, the second-rate furniture, and, that evening, none of them wished to challenge the rightness of it all.

"What will you do tonight?" Lauren asked Scarlet as they sat in the kitchen drinking tea and soup.

"Do you want anyone to stay?" asked Robert. "It's no trouble."

"I'll be all right."

"What about us?" said Lauren to Robert.

"The hotel's still there," he said. "I can turn up any time. We can get you a room somewhere."

They fell into an uneasy silence.

"You know what?" said Scarlet. "I might come with you."

"You want me to check they've got a room?" said Robert.

Scarlet stood up, and then faltered, as if she could no longer proceed, only to find the energy to recover. "Let's just go," she said. "We can find somewhere, I'm sure. Let me just pack a few things."

She went upstairs, pulled a small suitcase from under the bed, and started neatly and mechanically to pack it with a change of clothes. She filled a bath bag with soap, toothpaste, a comb, a hairbrush, an old bottle of sleeping pills (half a dozen left) and other items from a mental list. She hunted out a pair of shoes from the wardrobe. There was a label on the suitcase for a place in Mexico where she and Jim had stayed maybe five years ago. She held it in her hand and realised almost abstractly that it stirred no memories, and felt only that it was all so far away. She checked she'd packed everything she needed, and looked round the room. Nothing. Was she so soulless? She tore off the label, threw it in a bin, and went downstairs. They looked round the house, switched off the lights in the rooms, locked the front door behind them, walked to Robert's car and drove into Bath.

The silence bore heavily on Robert and Lauren, and, in turn, they tried to break it, but Scarlet's replies were short; they could feel she had withdrawn well into herself, and they soon retreated to their own private, flickering thoughts.

The journey was short, but it felt like a journey to a different world; one of meaningless bustle and artificial light, impersonal, anywhere. The hotel had spare rooms. Scarlet said goodnight and, with a final hug to Robert and Lauren, disappeared into the lift.

Robert looked at Lauren and said, "It was brave of you to come."

She hesitated. "I thought I'd cry," she said, "But I can't. I thought you were meant to."

"You were fond of him, weren't you."

"Yeah. Yeah, and her. She's…"

"Cool?"

"Don't. It's not a 'you' word."

Robert put his hands up in mock surrender. "It's been a long couple of days." He lowered his arms and gave Lauren a hug. She wrapped her arms around him, and rested her head on his shoulder.

"You want to go for dinner and a drink?" he asked. "Somewhere where you won't burst into tears. It could be embarrassing."

She turned her head and looked up at his tired face.

"Dad," she said reprovingly.

"Or me. You don't want that, do you?"

"No," she said, gently disengaging from the hug.

301

"Uncool?"

"Like, yes."

"Well then, dinner out. You still eating Indian?"

"Vegetarian."

"That should be easy."

They walked towards the door of the hotel and pushed through into the street. The rain was still holding off.

"How long can you stay?" he asked.

"When will it be?"

"The funeral? That depends. Maybe in a week. You could go and come back, if you like."

"Could I stay? I'd have to ask the people at work, but I'm sure they'll give me a few days."

"Ask Scarlet. In the morning. Give her time."

"Will you stay?"

"I've got two days in court coming up. Then I'll be here again."

They walked on together, and stopped talking. After a time Robert said, "Penny for them," and Lauren said, "Nothing to say," and they put their arms round each other and walked on.

Chapter 21

Early December 2018

Robert woke the next day and lay in bed staring blankly at his hotel room. It was almost nine o'clock. He showered and dressed and went down to breakfast, hoping to find either Scarlet or Lauren, but neither was there. A waitress came up. Robert gave her his room number, asked for coffee and an orange juice, and wandered over to the buffet where he chose a cereal and a rather tired croissant. When the waitress came back, he asked if his daughter had already been down for breakfast and was unsurprised to hear that she had not. He drank his orange juice, made his way through the cereal and the croissant, drank his coffee and asked for more. What should happen next? He came to no conclusion as he drank his second cup. Only when he got to the lift did he decide. He went to Lauren's room and knocked on her door. When he got no response he knocked again, and then again. Finally, he heard a muffled, "What?"

"Lauren," he said, leaning against the door, "it's your dad. Breakfast finishes at ten."

"Uhh."

"It's your best meal of the day."

He waited until she said, "All right."

"Be there," he said. "I'll go back down."

He went back to his room and sat in the armchair. This was Thursday. Nothing was calling him back to London before Monday. He could ring Barbara and tell her Jim had died. He could tell her what McIntire had written on the death certificate and say that was the cause of death. He didn't have to say anything different. He could hear himself saying it. The 'after all' and the 'no, I didn't'.

His mobile rang. It was Lauren.

"Dad, where are you?"

"I'm coming," he said.

When he got downstairs, she was sitting by a window that looked onto the street, with a half-empty bowl of muesli, a cup of coffee and three apples in front of her.

"You don't have to stock up, you know," he said.

"It's free."

"I think I can run to the odd lunch."

She ate her muesli. He took one of the apples and started to eat it. She looked crossly at him, and he said, "There's more over there." She rolled her eyes and finished the muesli.

"Have you seen Scarlet?" she asked.

"No," he replied.

The waitress came up. He asked for another cup of coffee, and looked at Lauren, who shook her head. The waitress left and Robert and Lauren stared silently out at the street until the waitress came back with the coffee.

"Still thinking of staying?" Robert asked.

"D'you think I can?"

"Ask her. I think she might like it."

Lauren pulled out her mobile and said, "I'm going to ring her. Unless you want to."

"Maybe I should," he said, taking out his phone. He rang her number, and after a few rings, she picked up. Her voice was almost lost in a bustle of background sounds, and oddly nervous, as if she was both excited and caught out.

"I can't talk right now," she said. The bustle continued. "I'm OK. It's all right."

Robert hung up, and looked at Lauren.

She took one of the apples and said, "Where d'you think she is?"

"She could get her car and go anywhere." He thought of the White Horse, the midnight search for Jim, the sense even then of bonds drawing together and others beginning to break. He got up, Lauren took the other apple, and together they walked to the lobby, and then Robert stopped, suddenly, giddily, aware that he didn't know what he was trying to do. He looked around the empty lobby and muttered "Let's wait."

Lauren said she'd be back and went over to the lifts and back up to her room. Robert took a newspaper from the rack, sat down on one of the many vacant chairs, and tried to read. His eyes roamed over the pages, but he knew that even if he forced himself to read the stories he wouldn't be able to remember much about them half an hour later. The headlines, yes, but none of the details. He clutched the paper as a prop, unable to put it down and just wait. He'd sat outside courtrooms many a time, in draughty corridors with noisy teenagers and their worried, shouting parents, and sullen divorcing couples defaulting on their agreements, while he waited to be called and give his testimony in some other case. But that was prepared, documented, and seldom to be questioned. He was in control of all but the time, and now his mind was swerving erratically, drunk on emptiness.

He could lie to Barbara. He could say he had been there, in a forbidden place, he was guilty of that much, but only that much. Or that he had administered an illegal drug with the intention of taking a life. He wasn't certain at that moment of what he had done. Had Scarlet stayed his hand? Had he backed out at the crucial moment?

Was Jim his brother? Someone he hardly knew? Someone in pain, whose final wish he could not refuse? He remembered consigning people to worse fates, belonging to teams who had tried heroically – the usual phrase for those occasions – to save a life of inescapable pain and misery, and how he had gone home and had dinner and talked to Barbara and the children and planned a nice weekend. He wanted to say, "No, I did it because I had to. I couldn't walk away. Not this time."

Lauren came back and they sat together saying nothing, turning to look at anything that was going on. A young man rushing in with a briefcase, going up to his room and coming back in two minutes, still with the briefcase and, now, with a raincoat, and nervously brushing his hair. A young woman waiting like they were, going in and out of the swing doors until a young man appeared, embraced her, and took her away. Each time, Lauren sat forward, realised it was nothing to do with her, and sat back, tense. Robert reached out to take her hand, but she shook it free.

Suddenly, Scarlet appeared, and with her a young man who could barely be twenty and who stood a full six inches taller than her. They walked briskly towards the desk, but before they got there she saw Robert and Lauren out of the corner of her eye as they got out of their chairs, and stopped. As they came up, she turned to look at them, saw the puzzlement on Robert's face and the realisation on Lauren's, and reached with her left hand to hold on to the man who was with her.

"Well," she said, "you were going to meet him anyway, so I guess you might as well meet him now. This is Ryan, he's just flown over from Memphis." She paused, and added, "He's my son."

"Pleased to meet you," said Robert, more warmly than he might otherwise have done.

"And me," said Lauren, looking at him as if she already knew him well.

"This is a cute little town," said Ryan.

"It's very old," said Robert. "Some of it's Roman."

"Dad means it's shit old," said Lauren. "Like you wouldn't believe."

They fell into an awkward silence. Scarlet turned and began to walk to the desk and Robert followed her.

Scarlet hesitated. "Come for lunch," she said. "Give Ryan and me a bit of time…"

"We'll do some shopping," said Robert. "Everything went into the omelette."

She smiled and shrugged. "I was going to call you when we got back."

"It's fine. We'll be there," and he turned back to pick up Lauren. They made their polite goodbyes and left, and Scarlet turned to Ryan.

"Hey, don't start again," he said, "I'm real tired."

"Like I'm not?" she said, but she stopped herself going further, stepped up close to him and straightened his jacket. "What did I do to make you so tall?" she said.

"Fed me your mom's cooking?"

She looked up at his face, looking for a reflection of her own emotions, but saw nothing. Then he bent down and held her by her shoulders and said, "I'm here, Mom, I'm here," and she gave a shiver, as if time had stopped and started again, and leant against him to prevent herself from fainting. After a few moments she gently disengaged herself, stepped back, and reached out to brush some of his thick blond hair out of his eyes.

"You are," she said. "You done right."

Robert parked the car outside the cottage, next to Scarlet's. The blank windows were empty and cold, the front garden abandoned. Lauren looked at them, similarly reluctant to move.

"It's like he's there and he isn't," she said, and he gave the briefest of smiles. She sat still for a moment, and then said, "So I've got a cousin in there, right? And you've got a nephew? How'd you feel about that?"

"I honestly don't know."

With a shake of her head, Lauren opened her car door and got out, and Robert followed. They took the shopping bags from the back seats, walked up the path, and knocked on the door. Scarlet opened it and they carried the bags into the kitchen and started to unpack them.

"Where's Ryan?" said Lauren, putting a bag of pears on the table.

"Crashed out upstairs," said Scarlet. "Poor kid's been flying for almost a day."

"Why didn't he, like, come here with you?"

"Ask him." She put the pears on a shelf. There was a worn-out story she could tell one last time. "I didn't want to move him. He was all set to transfer to college in a year."

Robert checked through the bags and folded them up. "All done," he said.

"Shall I go and wake Ryan?" Lauren asked. "Or do you want to let him rest?"

"No, go get him," Scarlet said. "Or he'll be up all night."

Lauren went upstairs and Scarlet sat down and looked across the table at Robert.

"You guessed?" she said.

He sat down, and nodded. "Only when he turned up. Not before."

She picked up one of the bottles of wine and looked at the label without reading it.

"He couldn't stand Jim. You might as well know. He refused to see him, soon as he was big enough to get away with it." She put the bottle down but carried on looking at it, not at Robert. "Jim didn't mind. He never wanted to have kids. Wouldn't have anything to do with Ryan. Ryan's just paying him back."

"He's not the only one paying."

"He wouldn't come before. I called and called him.

309

Not even when he knew…" She looked straight at Robert. "Not even when he knew Jim was dying."

"He's here for you."

"Not when I wanted him. Not when he could've…" She tensed her hands as if trying to grasp something, then let them drop into her lap, and she looked away. "When they could've…. I was a fool, I guess."

"It's not always a bad thing to be," he said, struggling to catch up, to grasp what it could have been like, even to find anything to say.

"I just hoped, maybe, right at the end…" She spread out her hands, then let them drop, and her body sag. "My dad left me," she said, "but not like this. I mean, he left my mom, it wasn't about me. But Jim left Ryan. Can you imagine what that felt like, growing up?"

Robert waited for her to continue, but she had said all she could, and her silence wrapped itself around them more strongly than words.

They prepared a simple lunch, and Scarlet called to Ryan and Lauren, who arrived together, Ryan with a grin on his face.

"Hi, Mom," he said. "You didn't tell me Lauren's into R&B."

"I didn't tell you I've sung back-up for Alicia Keys either," she said. "Some things you're too young to know," and she tousled his hair.

"You have?" said Lauren, impressed. "What's she like? I mean, in person."

"I haven't met her," said Scarlet. "I just sang some

310

back-up tracks when her recordings came in. Right now, I don't know if they're going to use them."

She passed the salad round.

"What d'you want to do when you graduate?" Robert asked.

Lauren rolled her eyes, but Ryan answered "Business. I'm intending to go into the music business."

"What do you play?"

"Guitar, a little. I'm not like Mom; I want to go into marketing. Streaming, and web stuff."

Lauren took the chance to ask who he'd really like to promote, and Robert and Scarlet sat back and listened to her and Ryan swap opinions about singers and their songs – what made them stand out, made them the name on the album. Robert watched, seeing a side of Lauren he hadn't seen so clearly before, and looked over at Scarlet, trying to read the expressions on her face: at times entranced, and then annoyed, but often absent, as her eyes drifted away, and then she would force herself to listen again. But Ryan took over the room with the confidence of his opinions, the largeness of his gestures, the ease with which he set himself to impress Lauren and still attend to Scarlet. Lauren was wary, but Ryan was at home. And seemed not to see how out of place that was.

Scarlet scarcely spoke until lunch was over, when she stood up and said, "Clear off, kids, we'll tidy up."

"I can do it, Mom," said Ryan.

"OK, you do. I've got something I want to show Lauren, anyway," and she put an arm round her and led her out of the room.

Robert looked at Ryan. For all that he was tired, he was incapable of keeping still, with a latent energy that reminded Robert of puppies, or perhaps something more predatory. There was a shine to his face, a bounce to his movements, a sense that being here was not enough and he would soon be moving to somewhere better, and more exciting, to which he was somehow entitled.

"I'm sorry about your dad," Robert said.

Ryan gave a little shrug, and said nothing.

"It must be hard for you."

"It's hard for Mom."

"And you," Robert persisted.

Ryan lifted his gaze from the floor and turned to him. "I don't have a father. I never did."

"I understand…"

"You don't. You expect me to be cut up 'bout him? Well, I ain't." He stood up straight, his arms slightly raised in front of him. "I'm not so stupid as to cry over someone I never knew."

Robert put his head on one side and scratched the back of his neck. "I didn't know him either, you know."

Ryan looked back at him and waited.

"He left home when I was what, thirteen?" Robert went on. "I hardly saw him again till your mother called in the summer."

"So we're in it together, are we? You got forgotten too?"

"I wasn't saying that…"

Ryan started to walk to the door and stopped in the middle of the room. "Good, because he wasn't my father, and I don't need an uncle either."

"Forget about me."

"You know what it is to have a father? You think you *know*? Then bully for you."

Ryan turned and left. Robert stared after him, briefly angered before he found himself wondering what everything might have been like. A crowd of ifs jostled for attention: if Jim had stayed in England, if they had kept in touch, if they had been closer as children, all driving each other out. He was still trapped in these competing fragments when Scarlet came in, exchanged glances, and said, "He wasn't to know."

Lauren followed her into the kitchen, wearing the long scarf that Scarlet had found for her, and the matching hat.

"Wasn't to know what?" she asked.

Scarlet gave her a hug, turned her round, and pushed her out of the door. "Clear off," she said with a smile. "Take Ryan for a walk along the canal, show him some shit old stuff." She gave her a spare door key, and when Lauren and Ryan had left she slumped onto a kitchen chair. Robert pulled up a chair opposite her, and they sat there without speaking for a time. But she was restless, reluctant to enter the living room, where Jim had died, or the front room with the piano. So they too went for a walk, and talked at first like strangers thrown together for no reason and then about telling Jim's friends in England and back in the States, about Barbara, about Lauren, and Ryan, about her plans as a singer and his thoughts about what he might do when he finally retired, the cold weather, the wind, the clear skies, how few birds there were and how bare the trees.

The blandness was a comfort, like a cheap coat, until finally Robert was able to say, "Look, there's something

I have to know." He stopped, and Scarlet looked at him more acutely than before. "Lauren," he said. "You didn't tell her Jim was dying?"

She shook her head. "No. She just turned up."

"She doesn't know that…?"

"No, I didn't tell her." Her shoulders dropped a little, her face softened. "But I'm glad she came," she said. "It was very… I don't know. It can't have been easy. "

"She really liked him," Robert said. "And you."

They crossed the bridges over the canal and the river, and circled back towards the house. At a point where the path curved and there was a view down a bleak muddy field to the road, they stopped and Robert said, "How are you? How do you feel."

She stared over his shoulder, breathed deeply, and looked down at her feet. "Not like I'd thought I would. All over the place. I woke up in the middle of the night, and I felt around in the bed and he wasn't there. I put the lights on and I was in this strange room, I didn't know where I was. I was so frightened. I thought the bed, everything, had turned to stone, everything had stopped, like it was going to be like this forever. I sat up and put the TV on, but there was nothing, really nothing to see, so I switched it off, and the lights, and I sat in bed and listened to the traffic. And suddenly I was crying and I couldn't stop. It just took me over." She turned slightly, to look straight at him. "Do you ever feel that – that you aren't doing it, it's just passing through you? And I lay in the bed all curled up, my cheeks all wet, and I fell asleep."

"And you felt better? A bit?"

"No. I felt as if I'd been taken someplace and brought

314

back, and it wasn't really me who'd done it. It's been like that all day."

"Even collecting Ryan?"

"We have this complicated dance. He cares for me, sure. I know that. Deep down. But we don't talk about Jim. Not easily." She paused, and in a quieter voice said, "I can't cry in front of him. Crazy, isn't it?"

Robert's eyes were moist, whether from the wind or from emotion he couldn't tell. He took out a tissue and started to dab his eyes. She stepped forward, took the tissue from him and wiped his cheeks. He took her in his arms and she let herself be folded into his embrace, and they stood there together, arms around each other. Her blonde hair peeped out untidily from her hat and came down over her face. He gently pushed it back behind her ears.

"Do you think I've been a fool?" she murmured.

"I think," he replied in a soft voice, "that falling in love isn't meant to make sense."

She nodded. She pulled him tighter, and slowly released him.

"And this is the time for grieving," he said.

She took a slow step back, and, still holding his arms said, "How about you?"

"I'm twenty years behind you. Maybe fifty. I feel we've only just met, Jim and me. I never really knew him, first time round."

They walked on a little, side by side.

"I've been thinking," Robert said, "about what he said about our father. What did he hate so much? He was a teenager when he left, what did he even know?"

Scarlet said, "I didn't know any of that. I just got the unhappy kid who ran away from home. Nothing like that."

"I don't even know if all that stuff about the turban's true." He stopped, turned, and looked at her, puzzled. "But there's something about the way our father treated our mother, I've started to think, that did take the life out of her." He turned over a broken brick in the path in front of them with the toe of his shoe. "Maybe he saw that and I didn't. Maybe…"

"He told me your mother used to sing with him, when he was little."

"I don't remember that."

"And then it stopped, when your father came back."

"I'd have been, what, three?"

"I don't think he meant to tell me. He was falling asleep; I think he was talking to himself."

"You know, until Jim was seven, our mother was the only parent he really knew. It wasn't the same for me. Maybe he watched our father…" He couldn't frame the words, and he stopped. "It's my job, you know, to work out what's gone wrong. I never have with this."

He stood there without speaking, his thoughts emptying out into the winter air. She took his hands in hers and very softly she said, almost to herself, "Jim. Jim."

"He said they couldn't love us," Robert said. "So he ran away. But I was weak, and I stayed."

She shook her head and smiled. "I don't believe that."

They walked on. After a time, Scarlet said, "When Jim met things he really couldn't handle, he'd hide from them. It's a terrible thing to say, but I've sometimes thought he was really afraid of being a father. Ryan's father."

"How did you manage?"

"You get through it. You've seen the results."

"He'll be all right."

"Another fatherless child out in the world." She gathered her thoughts, and the voice to say them. "I was so young when I had him, and I wanted the best for him, for the three of us. This marvellous man, who changed my life, and this beautiful baby, and I thought it would all work out. I never thought... Jim just walked out, as soon as he could." She stopped herself from crying. "He could cut Ryan dead, I've seen him do it. And I loved him. I still do."

"You did what you could."

"When he was little, I told Ryan his daddy loved him, over and over again, he just couldn't be with him. Was that doing right?"

"I'm not good at saying things like this, but... things we do from love can't be all bad."

"I had choices. I could've said Daddy's left, I'm sorry, look around, it happens."

"But you loved Jim too."

"I lied to Ryan. I lied to him."

"And he loves you." Robert took her hands. "He's young, he can still change."

"Why do we lie to the ones we care about?"

The question had too many answers, none of them good, and Robert said nothing. They drew again into an embrace. They looked deeply and patiently at each other, their tired eyes, the bags under his and the fading make-up under hers, the wrinkles on his forehead and the slight plumpness of her chin. At the delicately varying colour of their eyes, at their lips, at the unexpectedly functional look that noses always have up close, at her neat eyebrows and his untidy ones, at their skin, at the small mole on one of her cheeks and the two or three liver spots on his. She pressed her face into his coat and sobbed, and when she had finished she stepped back and took his hand in hers and said, "We'd best get back. We don't want them wondering where we are."

They walked in silence for a while, hand in hand, and after a time, when the path rejoined the road and they could see the house, she said, "What will you tell Barbara?"

"I haven't decided yet," he said. "I thought I'd ring her tonight. Tell her Jim's died."

In the late evening, Scarlet rang Poker Martin and The Guitarist. Both calls were sombre and short, the consolation they offered proved short-lived, and she was suddenly restless again.

She got up and poured herself a glass of water. "Look," she said, "I know you did all that shopping, but would you mind if we went somewhere tonight?" And when Robert agreed she began looking around the kitchen for things to do, tidying the table and rinsing a couple of glasses. She looked over at him. "I'm not ready to let him go yet. This house is him. At least for a little bit longer."

"No one wants you to."

"I can't…" She stopped. "I think… Could you give me some time on my own?"

He went to the front room, took out his phone, and rang Barbara's number. When she picked up, he said in a quiet voice, "Jim died. Yesterday evening."

"I'm sorry," she said. "How d'you feel?"

"Sad. Lost."

"And Scarlet?"

"Utterly bereft. She's coping quite well. I don't think it's caught up with her yet."

"Poor thing. Give her my sympathy." She waited. "How… I mean, how did he… ?"

"Natural causes. He just stopped. Slowed down and stopped. Scarlet was there. I was. It was very peaceful."

"I'm glad."

He hesitated, and took a step nearer to what he might have to say. "Lauren was there, too."

"Lauren?" Barbara sounded surprised.

"Yes. She's been very sweet. She might stay until the funeral."

They were both silent. Robert switched the phone to his left hand and looked out of the window at the fading afternoon.

"Is Lauren there now?" Barbara asked.

"She's gone for a walk."

There was another silence. His eye was caught by the engraving of the man in the alley. He took one more step.

"Look," he said, "there's something you ought to know. I gave him the secobarbital."

"And that killed him?" Her voice was sharp.

"No. No, I don't think so. He lived for a couple more days, so I don't think it can have."

"And that injection, the pancu-whatever-it-is?"

"No, I didn't," he waited again. "But I was ready to."

"Jesus," said Barbara. "Jesus. And the other stuff, the seco… barbital. That didn't kill him?" Her doubts came out distilled, seeking like a lawyer to catch him in a lie.

319

"No," he said, wearily.

"Can McIntire find out?"

"No. He's signed it off," he said, tired of insisting on the point. "Jim died of natural causes."

"And no one else will look?"

"Jim's dead. He died of complications arising from cancer of the bowel." A certainty was forming in his mind. "And he was spared a lot of pain, whether it was my doing or not."

Barbara said nothing.

"I'm glad I did what I did," said Robert. "You have to know that."

There was a long silence, and then she ended the call. Robert put his phone away, sat by the piano and, after a time, tidied up the scores that had been scattered on the floor, closed the piano lid, and stayed there in the ebbing light from the window.

Scarlet was standing by the bare cherry tree, resting on a spade. As Robert approached she turned to face him, brandishing the spade like a weapon, and shouted at him, "Why? Why any of this?"

"There's no reason. None that makes the sense you want."

"Then why shouldn't I tear it all down?"

"I won't stop you."

"Why shouldn't I… ?" And she turned back to the tree and hacked a couple of times at the ground in front of it.

"I think Jim liked the garden, you know," he said.

Scarlet hacked again at the soil in front of her, saying between blows, "No he didn't. He didn't care."

Robert took a step forward. "He knew you did it for him."

"He didn't. He thought it was some weird thing I did just for me." She stopped hacking, left the spade in the ground, and turned to look at him.

"He knew you cared," said Robert.

"Didn't I, right? And for what? Nothing." Her voice dropped.

"You don't mean that."

"But it's true, though."

"Then why are you angry?" He stepped forward again.

"Why do you care? Jim lost. I lost. And all this…" and she waved her arms at the garden and the house beyond.

"You could've walked away, if you'd wanted to."

"I should've. I wish…"

He stepped forward until he could almost touch her, but she picked up the spade and shook it. "No. No. Not you."

He stepped back. She held the spade out horizontally in front of her, and slowly swivelled round, pointing it across the garden and along the back of the house.

"None of this," she said. "None of it."

She lowered the spade slowly, and when it touched the ground she let go and it toppled sideways. Her eyes roamed unseeing, and her breath was ragged. Slowly she fixed her eyes on the cherry tree, and then on Robert as he gently took her by the arm.

"Once you were here," he said, "once you'd come all this way? Knowing what you knew. Did you want to leave then?"

"Who've I given my life to?" she said, and almost in a

whisper she added, "And for what?" She stood still, as if a storm in her had passed, and she was waiting for the last drops of rain to fall. Suddenly she felt cold, and shivered. "Get the kids," she said. "We'll go and get something to eat."

Chapter 22

Mid-December 2018

On Saturday, Scarlet and Robert went to the undertakers, and were reassured that the funeral could take place as soon as Thursday afternoon. A determinedly meek young assistant director asked them if they would like to say their goodbyes to their loved one, and led them from his office down a long corridor and into a large room with, perhaps, a dozen coffins, all closed except Jim's, which was the nearest. He stepped back, and they took a step forward. Scarlet stood there, trying to find words to say, suddenly not knowing who she was trying to address. Jim lay waxen, slightly shrunken, and disturbing, like a copy that is not quite right although its creator doesn't know it. She reached into the bag she had brought with her, pulled out the Panama hat and placed it carefully on his chest. Then quickly, almost angrily, she turned away.

Robert saw her, and forced himself to look back at his brother. Suddenly, he felt confused and unprepared, as if he was rushing to catch up. He knew too precisely what was laid out before him, and his feelings split him in half.

His responses were doubled, conflicted; he wanted simple grief and he felt ashamed.

Scarlet walked to the door and waited for him to follow. She'd done what she'd promised herself she would to do, but the place was so tidy and so constrained that the falsity of it filled her head like an illness. If there was ever to be a chance to say her final words, it would have to be some other way. She stretched out an arm to Robert and pulled him away.

Back at the cottage she began to tell friends in England and America of Jim's death, each letter painful in a different way. More distant friends could be told in emails. Jim's solicitor back in Chicago, domineering but not exactly competent, would have to be instructed to wind up the contracts and chase outstanding payments. The woman who owned the cottage would have to be given notice, which she would turn into a problem as Christmas was drawing near. What property they had would need to be sold (the piano, the cars --- but how?), given away, or shipped to Memphis. Clothes, likewise. Flights booked, but when? When would it all be over? English friends asked to be ready to sort out any loose ends once she had left. And on, and on.

Scarlet found it a whirlwind. Unable to do anything or choose anything if time was free, she found it a relief to have something to do, but then she found it almost insulting. Her love for Jim had turned her into a secretary ticking off chores: write these letters, address these envelopes, stop for a cup of tea and a gossip by the water cooler – even if in her case it was a whisky in the kitchen – all the seemingly endless details of arranging the funeral. Then she found it caring. She was doing it for Jim. And then it became empty, formal, pointless, like everything after his death. Then she rallied, only to feel that this diminished what she was going through. She had loved him, she loved him still, but found her way to none of the gestures she had expected and began to believe she showed no true signs of grief to ratify her true love.

She'd friends who had keened and wailed, Jewish friends who had sat motionless for a week looked after by their family and had then got up and walked into a new life, a friend who had almost succeeded in throwing himself into the grave. Friends stranded forever, it seemed, and friends who had taken up a new existence and in one case never been seen or heard of again. All of them, whatever her relationship with them had been, were people she had thought about at their time of extremity. But she felt she could not think about herself, could not act, could not commit, could only, emptily, do, and get through the day. Today, and the next day, and perhaps the next.

She needed to sit and rest, although she could not. She needed, she knew very well, to begin to accept what had happened. She sat in the living room, watching Ryan and Lauren look through the collection of records and tapes Jim had left, torn between memories and hopes with every name they called out, seeing in Ryan's every move, every thought, not the mirror of her own emotions but their negative. Every move he made was towards his new life back in Memphis, and she knew his kindness would pull her after him and away from where she was, but her life had led up to the day she was in and she could not see beyond it.

Ryan's presence was a comfort to her, and then it was a source of grief. He was here, he could put his arms around her, he could be part of her new life, the second half of her life. She loved him fiercely, all the more because Jim had not. This fatherless child, who filled every room he entered, whose voice, whose every gesture, spoke of bewilderment. But a bewilderment at a place where he couldn't drive a car, where the music stations were so weird, where there was no cable, and there was nothing in the house to eat. He mooched around, trying to help her, then trying to keep out of her way, hanging out with Lauren, being her son and, she hated saying to herself, being not Jim's son.

On Robert's suggestion, Ryan looked into flights, and Lauren helped with the house, while he began to deal with the cottage and anything legal. Poker Martin offered to collect the piano and sell it on her behalf, and somehow dispose of the two cars. On Sunday, with Lauren's help, Scarlet took down all the pictures and then, finding the house too bare, put them all back up. She asked Ryan to sort out Jim's clothes into second-hand and too far gone, but he refused, and only after a row did he agree, and emptied Jim's wardrobe into two neat piles. He and Robert took the second-hand clothes to the Oxfam shop in Bath. They said very little on the journey. Each seemed unreasonable to the other, and conversations between them flickered and disappeared like the houses they passed.

At the back of a drawer late that afternoon Scarlet found a wallet of old photographs of Jim and her, and when Ryan went for a run she looked through them with Lauren and Robert. It was a shock to see him so much younger. More of a shock than to see him in the clothing of whatever time it was: the florid shirts, the loud colours, then the neat jackets that looked cheap even when they were expensive, as if worn by a successful bookie. Hairstyles came and went, and so did a moustache that Lauren found 'way gross'. Scarlet, too, sported flamboyant clothes, to which she'd added exotic earrings, and implausible hats. Both of them leaning on the arms of celebrities equally drunk or equally stoned, although the reactions of Robert and Lauren ranged from excitement to flat zeros. But the real shock was to see Jim. Jim alive. Jim smiling, dancing, flirting, gazing adoringly at her. Jim at the piano, playing, taking the applause. Jim overweight on a beach in California, watching the sun go down. Jim in a car with her ready to drive to Chicago. Jim.

"You have to put some of these up," Lauren said. "For when, like, people come back."

She hadn't planned on having any kind of a gathering, but Lauren insisted, and Robert offered to organise the sandwiches, cake, tea and coffee. So together they sat down, and selected twenty pictures, and Lauren wrote down the captions she got Scarlet to suggest, and promised, if someone would take her into town tomorrow, to fix up a display.

They put the pictures neatly in two rows on a work surface in a corner, and Ryan saw them when he came back.

"What the fuck's this?" he shouted.

Scarlet rose out of her chair, but Lauren got to him first and shouted back at him, "What do you think, you moron. It's his funeral. It's his day."

"Fuck that. Fuck him."

327

Lauren went right up close to him, staring up at his angry face well above hers, and said, "We know what you think, so swallow it. You've told me what you think of your dad. I'm damn sure Scarlet knows it. So shut up."

He pushed her aside and ran out of the kitchen, to the front door, and out of the house. She followed him, slamming the door behind her. Scarlet sat back down. Tears started from her eyes, and Robert reached to hold her hands.

"Jesus," she said, "does it never end?"

"One day, maybe."

"You don't sound too sure."

They sat for a minute, trying to collect scattered thoughts, and then Scarlet got up, walked over to the photographs and started to shuffle them together in a pile.

"Don't," said Robert.

"I can't face another row. Not on that day of all days."

"Do you want us to remember Jim? As he was? So alive?"

She turned round, the pictures in her hands, and nodded.

"You want the pictures up? Then put them up. It's your day. Not Ryan's."

She looked at him, exhausted, wounded.

"He'll come round. Not all the way, but enough," he said.

She turned round and started to spread out the pictures, slowly, for a minute, and then she gave a reluctant laugh.

"Look at this one," she said, showing it to Robert, who smiled but looked perplexed. In it, Jim sat by a grand piano wearing a gigantic top hat and a cloak, both items of many colours, and possessed of a truly satisfied but entrancing smile.

"He'd just got the outfit from Dr John. This is in some club in New Orleans, he took them off of himself and gave them to Jim 'cause he'd played so well. Damn, he was on that night." She paused. "They may be in a warehouse somewhere. We had to leave them when we came over here."

"That's what we need," said Robert. "Put it on the top."

They carried on talking quietly, arranging and rearranging the photographs, and drinking occasionally for another half an hour, and then the front door opened and Ryan came in, followed by Lauren. Scarlet got up, and before Ryan could speak, shouted at him, "What's the matter with you? Why did you bother to come all this way?"

"I'm sorry, Mom," he said. "I shouldn'ta done that. But you know how I feel…"

"I know how you feel," she said. "It's time you damn well learned to know how *I* feel."

"I do, Mom,…"

"Then act like it. I loved Jim, I…" She took a deep breath, closed her eyes, and opened them. "I'm not going to explain myself to you. We know you and I can go on for a lifetime at this, but we're not going to do so. Not this week."

She stared at him, and waited, and finally he said. "Yeah, Mom."

She walked past him and out of the room.

On Monday evening Robert returned to London to spend two days in court. Scarlet kissed him goodbye; Lauren and Ryan waved him off, and he drove away through the wet

329

and the gathering dark. When he reached home it was nearly ten. Barbara was watching a film. She paused it to say hello, and kissed him awkwardly as he bent over to kiss her.

"I didn't cook you anything," she said.

"It's OK. I had something before I set off."

She asked how he was, and Lauren, and Scarlet, and seemed satisfied with the simple answers she got, and then let the perfunctory conversation come to a halt. Robert went to the kitchen, got himself a glass of water, and came back.

"How are you?" he asked, sitting down.

"I'm OK." She paused. "I haven't decided… about things."

"I didn't think you would have. Not so soon."

"Look. Don't read too much into this." She was anxious, he could hear it in her voice. "Would you mind sleeping in the spare bed? I've made it up. Just for a bit."

"I mind," he said, quietly. "I mind. I want to sleep with you."

She held up her hand to stop him talking.

"Not now," she said. "I'm not ready to talk now."

"OK, I'll sleep in the spare room. But just so you know, I love—"

She interrupted him. "Don't say that word. Not when you don't mean it."

"OK, I'll sleep on my own, if that's what you want.

"Just for a few nights, till I make my mind up."

They spent the next two days keeping out of each other's way as much as possible, neither of them ready to talk about what might happen next. On Thursday, Robert got up early, packed a dark suit and a couple of changes of clothes, and made himself a strong coffee, ready to drive back down to Bath before Barbara got up. To his surprise, she came into the kitchen, wrapped in her old, grey-blue dressing gown, her eyes puffy from lack of sleep. She sat down at the table and said, "I'll take some of that coffee." He poured her a cup.

"Don't shout at me," she said. "I don't think I could take it."

He sat down and stretched out a hand to her, which she refused.

"I went to the salsa class," she said, "when you were away. I thought the music would cheer me up." She gave a slight smile and shook her head. "I burst into tears. I had to leave."

"I'm sorry."

She clasped her hands together on the table, and said, "Tell me to my face, would you have done it, if she hadn't stopped you?"

There was no other answer. "I would," he said.

"I've lain awake all night," she said, "trying to decide what I'd say if you said that."

"I told you at the time," he said, quietly.

"It's not the same." She drank her coffee. "I want you to leave me," she said.

"I want to stay."

"It's so wrong. I can't… I don't think I can love you…"

"I love you."

"You don't. You care. You like me. I'm one of the people you want to help, like the children. If you loved me you wouldn't…"

"Have been willing to help Jim? That's where you're

wrong. I did what I did because he wanted it, and Scarlet did, because they knew he was going to suffer and all for nothing."

"The man I loved kept people alive…"

"I didn't. I worked in a basement, helping with diagnoses, establishing causes of death. It's good, useful work. But I'm not a heroic surgeon, I'm not a juggler of complex modern medicines. All I really know about is death."

"You used to say your papers saved lives, just those of people you'd never met."

"I know about death when the surgeon walks away, when the juggler has nothing left, and the promises run out. I know what the last samples mean; I teach my students what they mean. And I couldn't sit by anymore."

"For Jim?"

"As it turns out, for Jim."

"Because you loved him?"

He stood up, took a deep breath, and said, "I don't know. Maybe, if we'd had more time. But maybe I did what I did because I finally saw we don't really have a choice."

"But we do. You did."

He pushed his chair away from the table and ran a hand around his neck. "I'm going to retire," he said. "I think I have to, after this."

"Don't do it for my sake."

"I've been thinking about it for some time. This sort of makes my mind up." He looked across the table at her. "It's not for me, as a doctor, to do what I did."

She waited, refusing to speak.

"I have to do what I think is right."

Still she didn't speak.

"I can't be in two places at once."

"You're asking me for forgiveness," she said. "I can't give you that."

Slowly he shook his head. "I used to think love was a simple thing," he said. "I met you, we fell in love, we had the twins. Even when… even when we had Lauren I loved you. And I love the children."

"I want to love you again." She started to cry. "I just don't think I can."

"I'm the same person. I still love you."

"But you're not. How can I love somebody who did… who did what you did?"

"It's not 'can you?' It's 'do you?' "

She got up and walked up to him. He opened his arms to embrace her, she clenched her fists and beat on his chest. "Damn you, Robert, damn you! How could you?"

He wrapped his arms around her and said nothing. For a time, they stood there, until she stopped crying and he released her.

"I don't want to be alone," she said.

"You needn't be."

"I don't think I could start again, looking for somebody else."

"You needn't."

They remained as they were, listening to the sound of their breathing, until Robert said, "I have to go."

She put her arms round him. "When will you be back?"

"In a few days. There are things I need to help sort out."

She nodded. "Take your time," she said.

He arrived at the cottage before ten. Scarlet greeted him with a hurried kiss on the cheeks and, offering him coffee, took him into the kitchen.

"Everything all right?" he asked.

"Probably." She filled the kettle and put it on. Then she shook her head. "I don't know." She looked at him blankly. "I don't know if I can do this."

She slumped down in a chair. "I don't want to cry. I've done nothing but cry these last two days. Since you went away. I'm sure the children are ashamed of me."

"I'm sure they're not. It's started to catch up with you, that's all. They can see that. They understand."

"I want to be strong, for Jim." She looked at him, and then out of the window. The kettle boiled. She got out two mugs, and when the coffee was ready she poured it into the mugs and gave one to Robert.

"I've never done this before," she said. "I've been to funerals. I've even sung at some, but not…"

He cocked his head and looked at her. "Why would you even think you could let him down?"

She smiled and drank some of her coffee.

Lauren came in and greeted her father. At Scarlet's insistence they talked over the arrangements, and Lauren turned to Scarlet. "Are you OK with your song?"

"She's been rehearsing with The Guitarist," Lauren explained, turning to her father. "I think you're going to like it."

Robert looked over at Scarlet and Lauren said, "It's 'Lo siento mi vida'. It's a Linda Ronstadt song."

"You do remember her, don't you?" said Scarlet.

"Oh," said Robert, "I think I was in love with her in the seventies. Me and two million others."

"You were right," said Scarlet. "She sang everything. She was great."

Well before one-thirty, they got in Robert's car. Robert was wearing his suit, Scarlet wore a soft black dress that fitted comfortably around her, an old dark blue coat and a green pashmina, and Lauren sat with her in the back in some dark jeans and a heavy dark red, woollen top that Scarlet had found for her. Ryan squeezed himself into the front, somehow looking the most respectable of all of them in a dark shirt and tie and carefully pressed trousers with a matching jacket. "Hey, I get some things right," he'd muttered to Lauren when he'd come downstairs a few minutes before.

The journey to the crematorium was barely six miles and was supposed to take no more than twenty minutes, but there were roadworks and it was almost half an hour before Robert turned left and pulled into the grounds of the cemetery. Scarlet told him to drive past the building and park round the back."

"It's way grim," said Ryan, looking at the crematorium, and it was. The conical slate feature in the middle of the roof sat on top of a blank, crenelated bay window and added to the impression made by the cramped wings that the Victorians had adapted it from a dungeon.

Robert parked the car alongside three they didn't recognise. They got out into the cold, windy afternoon air and followed the signs round to the entrance, where they were met by an official who showed them into the waiting room.

"Parrish?" he inquired of Robert, who stood aside to let him address Scarlet.

"Of this parish, perhaps," the usher added, with what might have passed for a smile.

"I have simply no idea," said Scarlet, more loudly than she had intended. "But sure, Jim Parrish."

"Quite so, Mrs Parrish. You are, as you know, early, which is most convenient, but we are officiating another service, and I must ask you to wait. Here. If you would be so kind."

Then, after saying that he would take care of any other mourners, and explaining that he could provide neither coffee nor tea because the kettle had been stolen, the usher vanished, leaving them all to wait. Lauren gave Scarlet a hug and she hugged her back, but the nervous, inhibiting feeling of the room enveloped them. It was cold, and there was nothing to read except a few leaflets about the place, which had apparently been built in 1937, and after a time Lauren felt that Scarlet was sinking into herself, and withdrew her arm. Ryan glanced across at her and she looked back, waiting to find out what she should do. She looked at her father, but he too could think of nothing to say, and gradually Lauren found herself lost in uncertainty. It was her first funeral, and she needed to be sure she would not find it too upsetting. It was Scarlet's time, not hers, and yet it was her time, too, and Ryan's in whatever way he would choose to take it, and her father's. Yet, as the cold and the quiet seeped into her, it was hard to feel their different griefs bringing them together.

After a few minutes they heard a car draw up, and footsteps, and the usher returned, followed by Poker

Martin and The Guitarist. Scarlet kissed them both and introduced them to Ryan. Robert came over and shook their hands.

Poker took Robert aside and asked, "How's she bearing up?"

"I've just got back from two days in London. She tells me she's crying a lot."

"It's always unexpected, how it goes," Poker said.

As they walked to the other end of the room Robert said, "You've known them long?"

"I saw him a few times, you know, before his big trip to the States. He was down here quite a bit. There was quite a crowd liked what he did. I never met her, of course, not till he came back."

"You met her right away?"

"I took to her right away. He wasn't well, you could see that, but she was right there for him. She's a fine, strong woman." Robert nodded, and Poker went on, "You never heard them but that one time?"

"Practising, sometimes."

"That's nothing." He took Robert by the arm. "You had to have heard him in full flood. He was terrific. He'd play anything – anything. He could have been great." He stopped. "He *was* great. I mean, he could have been famous."

"Why d'you think he wasn't?"

"You have to be good at that too. Good at selling yourself, good with the suits, good with fame. It's tough, you can't keep your friends. Same with Scarlet. It's musicians they were, through and through. Didn't have room for anything else."

"Maybe he could've been. Why not."

"I was thinking you might have the answer to that one. He'd do a lot of things because he knew he could. Play anywhere, play with anyone. Drunken dives, drugged-up drummers. But he wouldn't do anything he wasn't sure he could do. He'd do crazy stunts, but he'd never take a real risk."

Robert turned his head away, looked at the stone slabs on the floor, turned back to Poker Martin and said, "There's a lot of people like that."

"And most of them never had a chance. But Jim…"

Robert saw the usher come back in, and looked at his watch. "Two-thirty," he said.

"Time?"

Robert nodded, and, as they headed back to join the others, Poker said, "You'll be saying a few words, of course. I'll introduce you." Before he could reply, Poker went up to The Guitarist for a quick word, and then to put an arm round Scarlet. Lauren caught Robert's eye, and he went over to her and gave her a warm smile. She squeezed his arm, and turned back to see if Scarlet was all right. At the door they were joined by Jake, the drummer from The Pupas, who was explaining in too much detail how difficult it'd been for him to get the afternoon off while simultaneously apologising for nearly being late. Scarlet hushed him up and passed him over to Poker.

They made their way into the main room, which had a roughly octagonal shape, with cold flagstones, narrow windows and bare walls that made it seem an insincere copy of a church. A raised platform at the end to their right bore the coffin. The room was big enough to hold sixty people on its straggling rows of pews, and the seven of them sat together in two small rows at the front. Poker Martin, then Scarlet, with Lauren on one side of her and Ryan on the other, and behind them Robert, Jake, and The Guitarist. Recorded, anonymous organ music was playing softly.

The usher stepped forward to a lectern in the middle of the platform. The music stopped. He greeted them as friends of Jim Parrish, deceased, made a few remarks about the building and the purpose for which they were gathered here today, and then said he understood that they wished Mr Martin to conduct the ceremony.

Poker took his place, and looked at them.

"I've never been to a funeral with Jim before," he said. "This is a first. I don't want to be remembering him this way, and I'm not thinking I will. He was too alive for this. Too alive not to have faults; he could be a difficult man. Oh, but when he played. They were wondrous things he could summon up out of a piano, when the music was on him. And he was rewarded. Not with fame. Not with a big deal he'd never have wanted anyway. There's deep reasons we're not in some big church with his fans spread about row after row outside. But no, he was rewarded with Scarlet. As fine a woman as there is, and a voice to match his playing, and a true heart. A woman able to love him, and, Scarlet, you loved him right, no one could've done better. And he knew that. He said so to us when you weren't around. He said it to you, I'm sure, and he meant it. You were his true love."

He stopped, and looked at her with a warmth she had not expected, and she dropped her gaze.

"You asked me the other day," he went on, and now she looked back at him, "to bring something by him. Something specific, did I have a recording? And in fact, I do. And here it is."

He took a CD out of his pocket, gave it to the official, and muttered, "It's just one track."

The official took it away, and Poker said, "This is Jim, playing Bach's E flat minor prelude from Book One." He nodded to the official, and soon the room filled up with one single musical moment spread over what could be forever, one unfolding, delicate, unalterable, coherent idea. A paradox about time, and about life.

Poker waited when the music had finished, and then said, "I know that Scarlet is not wanting to say anything, but I'm happy that Jim's brother Robert does have a few words for us. Robert," and he stepped aside to let Robert come to the lectern.

He looked at the six of them. Not many really, at the end of a life.

"I've known my brother all my life," he began, and then, feeling that his words were too faint, said again, "I've known my brother all my life and I've hardly known him at all. If he had died suddenly a year ago and I'd found out by letter, the painful truth is that I might not have missed him." He sought out Scarlet, who was sitting, head bent, and waited for her to look up, which she did not. "But I was given a second chance to get to know him, and for six months I shared his life." His voice dropped. "I never thought I would ever say what I am about to say. But in the end, I loved Jim, and now I miss him."

Only now did Scarlet look up and look at him. It made a difference, he no longer felt so uncertain.

"I'm glad, too," he went on, "to have met his friends Poker Martin and The Guitarist, and Jake." More confidently now, he continued. "And I'm glad to have met Ryan. Ryan, your choices are yours to make, but I had a chance to catch up with Jim at the end, and I'm glad I took it."

He looked at Lauren, and his voice slowed a little, and softened. "I want also to thank deeply my daughter, Lauren, who was so caring to Jim and to Scarlet and, although I don't think you planned it, to me."

He turned to Scarlet, and for a moment struggled for words. "Scarlet, what can I say to you? Not everyone can love, not everyone finds it. But you loved Jim, and you will live in your music, and I truly hope and believe you will love again."

And then he stopped and looked at them all. "I just want to say that I came as a stranger and today I'm here among friends. For that, I thank you."

He went back to his seat. Poker squeezed his arm as he walked past, and whispered, "That was grand." Then Poker looked at The Guitarist, and at Scarlet, and said, "When you two are ready."

As Scarlet stood up, Lauren squeezed her arm, and Scarlet bent over to give her a brief kiss. Ryan held her hand in both of his and whispered "Good luck". The Guitarist joined her and together they walked to the front. He produced an acoustic guitar from its case, and quickly checked that it was in tune. Scarlet stood next to him, looking down at her feet. A light from a window high up

341

caught on her piano-shaped brooch. The Guitarist looked at her and played the opening chords of the song. Scarlet raised her head, adjusted the green pashmina around her shoulders, and in a sorrowful, reflective voice she began, and the song of lost love filled the room with the shining of the moon, the sleepless nights, the pain of the singer knowing that she and her lover would now forever be apart. The Guitarist filled the silences between the lines with arpeggios that danced and faded like the love itself, that could not last, and the song seized upon its terrible truth. Scarlet sang that she would make it through, and as she sang the final words The Guitarist stepped back and she stood alone, desolate, but unbowed.

She walked slowly back to her seat, the clicking of her heels on the flagstones echoing discordantly, and sat down. Ryan hugged her; Lauren squeezed her arm and kissed her. In the silence the usher stepped forward, and without speaking indicated that the final part of the ceremony would begin. He glanced at Poker, who quickly shook his head. There would be no anonymous music. There was the slight sound of an electric motor, small red curtains in the wall at the head of the coffin drew apart, and with a low rumble the coffin rolled slowly forwards. Scarlet bit her lip and squeezed her hands together tightly, Ryan and Lauren supported her, and together they watched the coffin disappear. The curtains closed, and Jim was gone.

Scarlet got up and walked to the door, Ryan holding her arm and Lauren a step behind, and when everyone was outside they stood clustered round Scarlet, talking quietly. She listened to the usual words of kindness as if they came from a long way away, wrapped in a new loneliness that felt somehow peaceful and yet unreal. Lauren, realising that in the last few minutes she had been half holding her breath, said nothing. Ryan stepped aside, and walked to the edge of the car park. He closed his eyes and breathed in deeply several times, tensing every muscle in his hands, his arms, and his face, and only when he felt ready did he re-join the others.

When he did, Scarlet took his hand and suggested they get out of the wind, and they all moved towards the cars. Ryan and Lauren went with Scarlet in Robert's car as before, Poker took The Guitarist and Jake, who had come out by taxi, and they drove back to the cottage.

The mood in the cars was sombre, but back at the cottage it gradually shifted. Whisky was poured, the display of photographs in the living room drew more memories from Scarlet, Poker weighed in with other stories he'd heard about Jim and her on his trips, and, reluctantly at first but then with more interest, Ryan began to ask about his father. Robert and Lauren mostly listened, and found themselves not only unable to tell truth, pardonable exaggeration, and possible wholesale falsehood apart but also more and more of the opinion that for these brief minutes, it didn't matter. Jim and Scarlet had lived a life like this, if not, they supposed, one exactly like this. Forensics could rest.

Poker left just before six to get back to his pub. He would drop The Guitarist and Jake off at the station and come back on Sunday to collect the piano. There were kisses, hugs, handshakes, and waves; promises were made, everyone was admonished to take care, and Poker drove off.

The four who remained trooped back into the house. Scarlet slumped down on the sofa, blew air out of her cheeks, and said, "God, I don't think I want to go through that again."

"You sang beautifully," said Ryan, sitting down beside her and giving her a hug.

"And Jim played well, too, didn't he," Lauren added.

Scarlet turned to look at her. "Yes, he did," she said. "He ruled it, for me."

They fell silent, and gradually began to notice the scattered cups and glasses and plates, the remains of the food, the empty and half-empty bottles, the mess of napkins, cutlery and crumbs.

"We'll tidy up," said Lauren, and she and Ryan began to sort out the living room and the still more upended kitchen.

Scarlet got up and crossed over to Robert by the window. She took him by the arm and said, "Thank you for what you said. It was lovely."

"I meant it," he said. "Every word."

"Go on," she said, "I bet you don't remember every word."

"Maybe not every word. But every thought."

"Exactly. You were shaping it as you went along, just like a singer."

"You really did sing beautifully."

"You see, you're a musician too. No better thing to be, in my book."

Ryan came in. "You guys know where the black plastic bags are?"

Scarlet looked over her shoulder at him and said,

"Look for them, kiddo, we're having a quiet moment in here."

Ryan retreated. Scarlet turned back to Robert and said, "I go back Monday. You know that, don't you?"

Robert nodded. "I can stay until then. Take you to the airport. Heathrow? You flying with Ryan?"

"No, he's flying back Saturday. He was lucky it all fitted in."

"How do you think he's taken it?"

A flicker of anger crossed her face. She looked around for her handbag and her mobile.

"Jim rang him, you know," she said, "two days before he died. Ryan didn't pick up, so Jim left a message in his voicemail. He sent it to me. You know what it said?"

She took out her mobile and played it back. "Hey, Ryan, this is your dad. I guess it didn't work out between us. But you're a good kid, you'll do well. And maybe you'll have better luck as a father. I hope so." There was a pause, and then: "Be strong."

"Twenty years," Scarlet said, shaking her head, "and all he got is this bullshit."

"I don't know what to say."

"What can you say?" she replied. She breathed deeply, gathering her thoughts, and said, "I wasn't going to tell you."

"I'm glad you did."

They stayed in silence for a while, and then Robert asked her how she was. She didn't want to answer, and so instead she said, "How about Barbara?"

Robert stepped away, and looked out of the window.

"She's taking her time. She needs to, actually. She should."

345

"I—" said Scarlet, but before she could continue Robert put up his hands and said, "Don't. It'll be whatever it is. We're OK, you and me. There's nothing you need to say."

She could settle for that, she thought.

Friday was a nondescript day, oddly full of chores. On Saturday morning Ryan lugged his suitcase downstairs, shook hands with Robert, embraced Lauren, and let Scarlet drive him to Bristol airport for the first of his connecting flights. Once they'd gone, Lauren and Robert went for a walk. It was cold and windy, and after a few minutes Robert turned round and said, "Get in the car and I'll take you somewhere."

"Won't Scarlet wonder where we are?"

"It's not far."

He drove them for a few miles, picking out the signs he remembered until he came to the almost deserted car park. They got out, and he set off up the hill.

"Where are we going?" Lauren asked, now out of sorts.

"You'll see."

He led her to where the paths split left and right, and waving at the expanse to their right said, "Iron Age fort, a big one."

"Yeah, right."

He took the left path, Lauren trudging behind him, until the hillside fell away to their left.

"Now do you see it?" he said.

"Shit. What is it?"

"It's a white horse."

"Is it, like, Iron Age or something?"

"Only eighteenth century, apparently. Scarlet and Jim used to come out here and commune with it."

Lauren looked at him, and then down at the horse. "Bet they came in better weather."

"We could turn round, if you've seen it," Robert said, but something of the strangeness of it seemed to catch her.

"No," she said. "Let's go to the end."

She went to the head of the horse and stood looking silently at it and the view beyond. He stayed where he was, the wind burning cold on his cheeks, looking towards where Jim had lived on his return, and beyond towards Bath. After all, the Iron Age gods had spoken, but now, low clouds summoned up an emptiness in his mind, shapes he couldn't quite see, that unsettled him like an unwelcome friend. He stayed with it for a long moment, and then went to join Lauren.

"Look," he said, "there's something I have to tell you." She turned towards him. "Jim…" he said, "Jim asked me to end his life. He had the drugs."

"You can't do stuff like that, right?"

"No, it's illegal."

Hesitantly, he described what had taken place, and Lauren listened. When he finished, she said, "But you didn't give him the actual injection?"

"No," he said, "but I was ready to."

"Because it was the kindest thing to do?"

"Yes."

He waited. Lauren stared out over the valley below, the wind blowing her hair untidily across her face. Then she turned and kissed him on the cheek.

They walked slowly back to the car.

"Will you carry on seeing Scarlet?" he asked.

"I hope so. I like her."

"She likes you. And what about Ryan?"

"Maybe. No, probably not. We'll WhatsApp a bit." She looked at her father.

"Maybe we'll FaceTime," he said. "You know, social media for grown-ups. People with actual things to say."

She took him by the arm. "I should push you down that slope."

"Yes," he said, "probably you should."

In the afternoon, they took the garden equipment and all the pictures except one into Bath and sold them for ninety pounds, which Scarlet gave to Lauren for helping so much, saying "Hey, kid, it's not money where I'm going. You have it." Lauren took it with embarrassment. Scarlet insisted Robert take the engraving of the man in the alley. "I think it's Jim in the picture, I always have," she said.

On Sunday, Poker came with a large van and a couple of men who shook hands with Scarlet, swapped stories about Jim, and slowly and carefully loaded the piano onto the van and drove away. In the evening, Robert drove the three of them to an upmarket Indian restaurant in Bath where he and Lauren celebrated Scarlet's last full day in England and all her time in England, and then he drove them back to the cottage and himself back to his hotel.

Early on Monday morning, Robert drove out to the cottage. Scarlet was waiting, all packed, as was Lauren. He put the hi-fi in the car, to be taken to Lauren's current flat, and they walked around the house to see that nothing was forgotten. Scarlet said how like the place was to the first time she and Jim had seen it, two and a half years ago. The furniture that had mostly been there when they'd moved in, the front room empty, the kitchen bare, the gardens front and back decaying into winter, the bedrooms anonymous and cold. They'd only moved in for the duration – the house had served its purpose, and now it could keep its memories; she would go back to the world she knew.

Lauren lingered, sitting in a chair facing the sofa, until her father called to her that they had to go. The most recent memories were gradually giving way to earlier ones, but she still struggled to recover the smiling, warm-hearted Jim from his final moments. The first day in her life she wanted to call back, and change. She got up, ran her fingers slowly along the back of the sofa, and joined her father in the hall.

Scarlet closed the front door behind them. "You OK?" she asked Robert as they got into the car.

"I was thinking, I didn't know what to expect when you rang, all those months ago," he said. She looked across at him, and to reassure her he said, "No regrets."

He'd thought once or twice over the past six months, as he did now, of what he might have said had the unexpected caller not been Scarlet but some final reckoner. Not a blonde in a red top and jeans, and not a cloaked, crepuscular figure, but an unmistakable signal that his own life was about to end. Perhaps, that his was a life mostly lived, with enough to be pleased about, hoping to sound honest and not smug, although he would like more time. Yes, it'd been spent finding careful final answers, not to some ultimate question but at least to some of its endless stream of examples. But what if he was to be allowed for once to see himself properly with his own eyes? What judgement would he have to reach then? Surely not that everything was in its place? He shut the car door as if shutting something out, and drove off.

"No," he said more confidently, "I'm glad you called."

The journey to Heathrow was quiet and they got there early. Robert parked the car in one of the Terminal 5 car parks, and they made their way to Departures.

"Don't stay," said Scarlet. "We've said goodbye half a dozen times already."

"Then this is the last time," said Robert.

"Keep in touch," Scarlet said to him, and, turning to Lauren, said, "Come and see me. And Ryan."

"I will," said Lauren. "I'd really like to."

"Then you will," said Scarlet. "That'll be great. You could really learn to sing."

"Yeah," said Lauren, "that'd be cool." But she smiled when she said it.

Scarlet turned back to Robert. "Thank you," she said. "I couldn't have done it without you. Really, I couldn't."

They hugged. A long hug that came to include Lauren. Then Scarlet pushed them away and fished into her bag for a carefully wrapped parcel, which she gave to Robert.

"It's some CDs of Jim and me. All sorts of things really. I got Poker to make them. They're for you. Both of you."

Almost before they could thank her she said, "I've got to go. Keep in touch." And she turned towards the queue for boarding card and passport checks.

"We will, we will," Robert and Lauren said, and as she inched her way to the desks they called out after her, "Keep in touch."

"I will. I love you," she mouthed to them, and then, with a wave, she was gone. She had promised herself not to cry in front of them, and she hadn't. Probably she would in the taxi when she got back home. But what she chiefly felt was emptiness, and a vague sense of things starting again. Not like spring, but as if they had been paused, put on hold, and were now slowly resuming. Or were closing in from the great distance to which they had been banished. She was living in a new world and an old world. Studio sessions, and checking into cheap hotels, saying to herself she was young enough to start again and old enough to know how.

Robert and Lauren drove slowly back to London, listening to Jim and Scarlet playing and singing. They talked about the songs, but not much else, and let the music play. For as long as it lasted, that was good enough. Good enough for Robert, and for Lauren too.

Acknowledgements

I thank the following friends for all their various forms of helpful advice and useful criticism of the book as it developed: Bruno Belhoste and Karine Chemla, David Berry, Mike Laurence, Jonny Lifschutz, Theo Lloyd, Cara Marks, David Mond, Duncan and Caroline Pratt, and Les Ruda. In particular, I thank David Lawton and Amanda Beresford, Bill Shaw and Carolyn Clark, and Monique Charlesworth for their encouragement, careful reading and detailed advice on the final draft.

I also thank Eleni Kyriacou, Martin Ouvry, and Sharon Zink among the good people at Jericho Writers, Rufus Purdy of Write Here, Sarah May, who taught the Faber novel writing course I was in, and my fellow students, especially Edwina Biucchi and Deepthy Iyer.

I apologise to those discerning readers who notice that I've changed the geography around Bath a bit, and altered what I wanted to write in a few places to avoid paying the heavy charges one can incur for quoting even a single line of a song.

Above all, I thank my daughters Martha and Eleanor for their belief in me and the book, and especially my wife Sue for her endless encouragement, precise and helpful criticism, and her love and support.